NO *Small* WONDER

Mary Flynn

Author site: *www.MaryFlynnWrites.com*

Cover art by Michael Butler
Michael by Design, Graphic Design Services,
www.TorqueCreativeLLC.com
ISBN 979-8-9895569-0-8

DEDICATION

*To all the dedicated Sisters of St. Joseph
at St. John the Evangelist Catholic School
in Park Slope, Brooklyn.*

“*De profundis clamo ad te dominum*”

“From the depths, I cry to thee, Lord”

— Psalm 130

Other books by Mary Flynn

— Fiction —

Margaret Ferry
The Flower Cottage
Wishbones and Other Short Stories

— Poetry —

As One Delighted

— Non-fiction —

Disney's "Secret Sauce"

The Little-Known Factor Behind...
The Business World's Most Legendary Leadership

— Children's —

Reggie & Rocky
The Ring-tailed Raccoons

Reggie & Rocky
The Naughty Raccoons

— Middle Grade —

Mrs. Peppel's Pillows

Other Published Works

The Saturday Evening Post Anthology of
Great American Short Fiction

Writer's Digest

Short Short Story Competition Collection

Rhymed Poetry Competition

Acknowledgement

A very special thank you for all those who have influenced my Catholic faith through the years, starting with my beautiful mother. Sincere thanks, as well, to the wonderful friends and family who always provide support and encouragement—among many others Fred Gray for being such an incredible friend and thought partner, my dear friend, Jean Apuzzo, who was the first to read the finished manuscript and offer such a positive response, and my dearest cousin Theresa Kunkel, who I always count on to keep after me to finish the thing. I was blessed to have an excellent editor/proofreader, Ann Frailey, along with my very much appreciated Program Manager at Salem Radio, Pete Paquette, for being so generous with the gift of time. And, of course, my fabulous graphic arts designer, Mike Butler at Torque Creative, who is everything when it comes to the process of putting a book together so beautifully.

Before

Chapter

Long Island, 1953

"WHAT HAVE I done?" Ellen looked out from the porch of her Long Island rental bungalow, staring at the woods and wondering how on earth she had agreed to stay for two weeks. Two weeks. She watched the trees stir. No other movement, no other sound, except the cheep and chitter of the birds in the dense surrounding woods. Without that she would probably be able to hear the blood moving through her veins. "My God."

"Just give it a try," Kate had said. "You'll see how fast the place can grow on you." Now, her dear, optimistic friend had gone back to Brooklyn to start her new job, and here was Ellen, a good two hours from the city … or any place like it. It would grow on her, all right, like mold on a wet carpet.

A wide-eyed gray kitten peeked from behind the white wooden rail at the far end of the porch. Ellen had seen it before, but it wouldn't allow her to get close, poor thing. "Did someone talk you into coming here too?" She'd have to be sure to put some milk out again.

"Wondrous things can happen in Spiritu," Father Elway had promised that first evening she arrived for the abbey's inaugural community event as a favor to Kate. But was it wondrous that a clipped-wing cardinal had flown up out of the boxwood hedge while she was visiting the prayer garden, nearly knocking her to the ground? She should have known better than to go anywhere near something called a prayer garden. Father Elway hadn't seemed at all surprised about the silly bird. "Looks like our little friend has managed to return. I do hope you're all right, Miss Castle."

It was Kate who had discovered this remote Long Island hamlet earlier that summer through a tiny, classified ad in the paper, promptly ditching their plans to go to a fun resort in the Berkshires. Spiritu. Who'd ever heard of the place? Ellen had wanted no part of it. Now, here she was, unable to believe she had let Kate Gannon talk her into using the last two weeks the bungalow was available before the official end of the summer rental season. That Edmond Hillary fellow had just reached the top of Mount Everest. Too bad she didn't go with him—he could have left her up there. That would have been a quicker death than this.

She turned to go inside and gave a nod to the geraniums in the window box. She had to concede, the place was well maintained. No wonder the bungalow rentals were so desirable. Good revenue for the abbey. But for her, just the worst timing.

On the way in, she caught sight of the kitchen clock—9:50. Her heart sank. She would have sworn it was nearly lunch time. She looked closer, praying that the hands had stopped, and saw the black taper sweeping slow and steady like a stiletto. This was going to be another long day, just like the one before.

She would have to find a way to tell them she couldn't stay—tell them something terrible had happened. Make something up—someone back home had come down with … what? … make it good, deathbed stuff. Her brownstone in Brooklyn had caught fire. No, wait—her bungalow had caught fire. Hmm. She'd have to think about that. She made a cheese sandwich and took it out onto the porch along with a small dish of milk for the kitten, just as the familiar wood-bodied station wagon turned into the lane.

A moment later, the all-around, as she had learned it was called, pulled alongside the grass. A tall, lean man dressed in black stepped out with a hurried gait. Father Garrett. "Good morning, Miss Castle." He greeted her with a pleasant enough smile. "Just thought I'd stop by with the morning paper."

"Thank you, Father. Good to see you again. Would you like a cup of coffee?" Ellen wasn't thrilled passing the time of day with a priest, but since she was planning to leave, what would it hurt to be gracious?

"Oh, I can't stay, thank you. I was just wondering how

you've been sleeping. I know Miss Gannon … Kate … had a challenging time at first, getting used to our nights out here. The quiet. It's not for everyone. I think she imagined woodland creatures surrounding the bungalow and eating their way in. But it all worked out. She probably told you."

The nights, Ellen thought. What about the days? She didn't have the heart to tell him that it didn't matter because she was planning to be on the next train back to Brooklyn. Besides, she was typically not afraid of things. It was just a matter of being bored stiff. In fairness, there was a bus she could catch about a ten-minute walk from the bungalow. It could take her to town for a change of pace. Hicksville. The perfect name. She'd been there once, weeks earlier, when she'd taken the train out from Brooklyn to visit Kate. The town was quaint and historic, with nice little shops and eateries, but she was just not up for any of it. She had to admit the people here at the abbey were welcoming and friendly enough, but what did any of this matter right now with her entire life turned upside down.

"Yes, Kate told me how terrified she was that first night, but it all worked out. She loved it here. As for me, I've slept pretty well, Father. The accommodations are very nice." She meant that. The cottage was neat and cozy, with comfortable chairs covered in floral chintz, thick rugs throughout, a pristine kitchen with yellow gingham curtains, and a bedroom with maple furniture. There was a yard, front and back, along with a porch shaded by a huge maple. Mrs. Wick, the abbey housekeeper, had brought over a generous picnic basket of cheeses, bread, eggs, milk, and sweets, along with a pound package of coffee.

"Good to hear," he said. "We'll probably be putting in television sets next season. We wanted to be sure it wasn't just a fad and, also, that Noley's Hardware Store in Hicksville would carry the replacement tubes when one of them blows out." He raised his hand. "Oh, one more thing." He was still standing at the foot of the porch steps, the morning light catching the slight creases in his face. "Hope you don't mind, Miss Castle." He looked away and then back, lowering his voice as if there actually might be someone around who could hear him. "Kate happened to mention that you have had some recent … difficulties. Please know that you are welcome to come and talk with any of us at the abbey—myself, Father Elway, any of the priests. We've been told that we are very good listeners."

Her back stiffened. Just how much of her "difficulties" had her good friend shared with them? Ellen Castle had no intention of discussing anything with them or anyone else. "That's kind of you, Father." She turned and picked up her sandwich plate. "Well, I guess I'd better get a move on, if I'm going to catch the bus into town." She was catching the bus, all right, to get the train back home.

"Have a good day, Miss Castle. Father Elway and I will be away overnight at a meeting up at Fordham, but we'll look forward to seeing you when we get back."

When he had driven away, she went inside to pack. She was done with the place. She dumped the rest of her sandwich into the trash. Who said she needed a good listener? And a priest at that. Kate had no right to say anything. Besides, she knew what Father Garrett really meant—prayer. Well, no thanks. When had any of her prayers been answered when she'd needed them the most.

She caught sight of her reflection in the kitchen window and cringed at the hardness of her face, the fixed downward slope of her mouth. Had she even brushed her hair that morning? Forty-three going on eighty. What must Father Garrett have thought?

She couldn't remember the last time she had felt truly joyful. How had this happened? She put the dish in the sink and a moment later covered her face with her hands, smothering the sobs. No, she didn't need a good listener or a prayer or a shoulder to cry on. What good would any of that do? She looked at her tear-streaked reflection in the window, the face of a woman out of options and out of hope.

Chapter

Ellen stopped at the newsstand for the morning paper. In her hurry to leave, she had forgotten to take the one Father Garrett had brought her. Maybe that would have been a good thing—how many more stories about Josef Stalin's death did she need to read? Still, she'd want something to occupy her mind for the nearly two-hour trip back to the city. She'd already squeezed every last word out of the latest McCall's and Saturday Evening Post issues the abbey had kindly provided.

She made her way to one of the trackside benches, setting her valise on the plank floor and her purse beside her on the seat. The morning rush hour had ended. There was little going on—the buzz of a fly, the light chatter of a woman and a boy waiting as she was; a large, colorful poster of the latest Broadway musical coming soon, "Oklahoma"; two cabbies, now with time to kill, having a conversation, their voices carrying from the quiet side street behind her where the taxis staged for their fares. She wished her state of mind was such that she could appreciate the country charm as much as Kate had—the small red station house where she had bought her train ticket, its window boxes packed with geraniums, the overhang of maples with snatches of bright yellow and scarlet flowers here and there among the bushes that partly lined the perimeter of the Hicksville railroad station. She felt so disconnected from things, from the world itself.

According to the schedule, the train was due to arrive in five minutes. It was still early enough for the sun to feel good on her face without the scorch. Summer was coming to an end, and she tried for a moment not to envision the bleak months ahead when nearly everything in her daily life would be unrecognizable. How on earth had she gotten to this point, headed back home to the brownstone that wouldn't even belong to her in a few weeks? Her business gone, along with her car and her dear, sweet boxer, Tony, now with a family in Connecticut.

Something flashed very close to her head. She bolted to the side, nearly toppling off the bench. Her valise tipped over and her newspaper and magazine fell to the ground. A red streak. Something swooping past. A bird. It flew to the other side of the tracks and perched on the eave above the door of the station house. A clipped-wing bird. For heaven's sake, that cardinal from the abbey garden. Was that possible?

She picked up her newspaper and collected herself as the short blast of an air whistle signaled the train coming around the curve. Squealing on the rails, the great locomotive led the seven commuter cars to a long slow stop. The conductor stepped off. Ellen stood to gather her things, keeping a cautious eye on the bird. More than ever, she was glad to be leaving this place. Odd, yes. Wondrous, no.

She tucked the newspaper and magazine under her arm and picked up her valise. Whoa … wait … where was her purse? She put the valise down and turned in panic, looking under the bench and on the grassy area behind it. Her purse was gone. She hurried, frantic, over to the newsstand to see if she had left it there. Surely, the man would have called after her, wouldn't he? Who else could it have belonged to? In a minute, the train would pull out and she would be unable to board. Worse, she would be stuck far from home with no money or checkbook.

"Can you please help me?" she asked the man behind the low stacked shelves of magazines and morning papers. "My purse is missing. By chance, did I leave it here?"

The man looked about, shaking his head, and gesturing to the space. "There's no purse. You can come back here and look. Everybody knows me. I would never keep someone's purse."

"I've got to call the police." She was frantic.

"Look, there's a phone in the station house. I'm sure they'll let you use it. It'll be better than going all the way down to the end of the platform for the pay phone." He reached into the cigar box under the top shelf and took out a dime. "Here," he said, "in case you have to pay for the call."

His gesture surprised her. "Thank you."

"If you want, you can leave your suitcase. I'll keep an eye on it. Legit, I promise. They all know me here."

She nodded her approval. Then, as the 10:45 westbound began moving out of the station, she hurried to the staircase leading to the bridge that would take her to the other side of the tracks. Inside the station house, she was relieved to find that there was now a police officer chatting over a cup of coffee with the station master.

"Are you sure you had it?" he asked, after following her back to the bench where she had sat. He glanced up and down the empty platform. "Not many people here this time of day. There were only three or four when your train came in. I keep an eye out."

"How else could I have bought my train ticket? And the newspaper."

He was a solid, serious-looking man of about fifty, she guessed, with a deep compelling voice that might make a good radio hero. Or maybe the villain. "I'll do a walkabout," he said. "Maybe you dropped it before you even got to the bench."

She knew that wasn't so but thanked him anyway. A short time later, he returned, shaking his head. "I'm sorry to say it, Miss, but your purse is nowhere to be found."

Ellen sat on the bench, thoughts of every kind racing through her head, none of them good. How was this possible?

"Can I take you back to your house?" The name tag above

his pocket said "Polly."

"No … no, thank you, Officer Polly. I'm not … I don't … I mean I was staying … I am staying at the abbey. One of the rentals."

"But you were leaving."

"Yes and no." She wasn't sure how to answer. How much could she tell him without it getting complicated? "Would it be possible for you to drive me back to my bungalow? Do you know where the abbey is?"

"I know it very well," he said, and after he wrote some notes on a small spiral pad, they headed out of the station.

She felt nervous, her tone sober. "I've never been in a police car."

"That's a good thing," he said.

She thought he might crack a smile, which would at least have put her at ease a little, but he didn't. She was also surprised that he knew exactly where Hummingbird Lane was.

"Number Seven," was all she said, the only words between them on the way. It was warmer now, sweat trickling down the center of her back, as much from anxiety as heat. She thought of getting her handkerchief but remembered it was in her purse.

When they arrived at the bungalow, Ellen reached above the door for the key, aware that Officer Polly kept a close eye on her. She removed the key and was about to put it in the lock when he took the key from her.

"I'll do that," he said, opening the door. And there, sitting on top of the short bookcase just inside the entry, was her black leather purse.

She gasped.

"I take it that's the purse you're talking about?"

"Yes, but … how on earth …?" She reached for it, but he gripped her wrist

"I'll take that," he said. "Step outside, please."

"Wait. That's my purse. This is my bungalow."

"Step outside, please," he repeated, and she stepped out as the officer looked through her purse.

He fingered through a small black billfold containing money. "You said your name is Ellen Castle, but I don't see any ID. No driver's license. No Social Security card."

"That's easy to explain. I live in Brooklyn. I decided to go back home … just to … to make sure everything is okay."

"Did you need to take a valise for that? And what about your license or some other ID?"

"I recently sold my car, so I don't carry my license with me anymore, and I typically don't carry my Social Security card either."

His face didn't change expression. "You seem like an intelligent woman, Miss Castle. Do you always travel far from home with no way of identifying yourself? Do you think that's wise?"

"No, I guess it isn't. But I hardly ever leave Brooklyn, and everyone there knows me."

"Everyone in Brooklyn knows you."

"I mean … not all of Brooklyn …"

He pulled out her checkbook. "Who is Elena Castellanos?"

"That's me. My real name … I mean my full name."

He raised an eyebrow.

"I use Ellen Castle because it's easier for people."

He put the checkbook back in the purse and clicked it shut. "Here's the way I see it, Miss Castle." He rubbed his hand across his chin. "Your story makes no sense. None of it. None at all."

"But it's the truth."

"Then explain to me how the purse you said was stolen at the train station was sitting right there."

She looked away. "That's the part I can't explain."

"No ID. You've got an alias on your checkbook … if it's really your checkbook. And that's going to be enough for me to take you in."

"Wait? What? You're arresting me? Are you kidding?" The loudness of her voice echoed in the surrounding silence. "There's been a crime … or something. I can't explain any of it, but whatever it is, it happened. I'm the victim, not the culprit." Her face was on fire. She could feel the tears building along with her frustration.

He remained cool and unmoving. "The only thing we can explain here, Miss Castle, or whoever you really are, is you trying to pass yourself off as someone you're not, to enter a bungalow belonging to someone else, and claiming a purse that you cannot prove is yours, a purse you insisted you had with you at the railroad station."

The crisp white cotton shirt she had started out with was now plastered to her back. Exasperated, she gestured to the purse. "May I at least have my handkerchief."

"Since you can't prove it's yours, I can't let you have it." He reached into his back pocket and removed a clean folded handkerchief. "You can use mine, if you like. I promise it has not been used."

"No, thank you." She hesitated as he continued to hold the folded white square out in front of her. With a quick dip of her head in reluctant thanks, she took it from him and pressed it against her forehead. "This is my bungalow. I swear. I've been here since … since a few days ago. I came with a friend."

"Where is your friend now?"

"She had to leave."

"Hmm." He locked the bungalow door and put the key back on top. "We'd better go." He led Ellen to the police car and held open the passenger door. She sat in silence for a moment as he opened her suitcase on the back seat and went through her things, after which he got into the car and slammed the door. "Nothing."

"This is crazy," she said, before throwing her arm out toward the windshield. "It's that bird. I know it. That … that cardinal … the one with the clipped wing. I know he's got something to do with this. I know it. When he's around, things happen."

"A bird." Officer Polly looked over at her.

"You might think a bird with a piece of his wing missing would have trouble flying but not this one. No. He's like … like a rocket." She swung her arm up. "He flew past my head right before I noticed my purse missing. I almost fell off the bench. Just like a few days ago when he nearly knocked me to the ground in the abbey garden." She was animated now, her anger and frustration growing. She tried pulling the door lock up to get out of the car, but he took hold of her wrist.

"Maybe I should have put you in the back seat, where there's a grill between us."

She sat up taller and looked straight at him. "You think I'm dangerous? Screwy maybe? I have to tell you, policeman or not, you are a stubborn, unreasonable, and ridiculous man. Here I am a victim, and you treat me like I'm the criminal. Well, we'll see about this. I'm going to report you as soon as … as …."

"You're comfortably in your cell?" He started the car.

"No. Wait. Wait." She tapped his arm. "I know how to prove who I am. I know. Take me to the abbey. Why didn't I think of it before? They know me. Father Elway. Mrs. Wick. They know me. Father Garrett was just here this morning. They know I'm not a thief."

When the abbey door opened, it was not Mrs. Wick who opened it.

"Hello, Thomas," Officer Polly said. "How are you?"

Who was this Thomas person? She had never seen him before. A good-looking man, younger than the others, maybe in his thirties, she guessed, black hair, neatly trimmed, dressed as a priest in the same black shirt and trousers but without the collar.

"I'm doing fine, Frank. How's everything in Dick Tracy world?"

A chuckle. Really? He couldn't crack a smile for her, not once.

They stepped in, and the officer shook the man's hand. "I need your help."

Ellen was nervous and impatient. She stepped forward. "Yes, we really do need your help. I'm Ellen Castle. I'm staying at Number Seven Hummingbird Lane. I've got to see Father Elway or Father Garrett. They can tell this officer who I am. Even Mrs. Wick. She knows me."

"Glad to meet you." He reached out and shook her hand. "I'm Thomas Ryman, but please, just call me Thomas. I'm a seminarian." He led them to the living area and gestured for them to sit.

She gave a quick look about, remembering the large, dark-timbered room with its tall, mullioned windows, the huge crucifix occupying the wall above the great stone hearth. She had just attended a community event there with Kate.

Crimson ornamental rugs, amber lamplight, comfortable sofas, and side chairs. Little had she known what madness awaited.

"I am sorry to have to tell you, Miss Castle, that not only is this Mrs. Wick's day off, but Father Elway and Father Garrett are away, as well. They're at a meeting up at Fordham, and won't be back until tomorrow."

Ellen brought her hands to her mouth, exasperated. "Oh, no. That's right. I forgot. Father Garrett told me."

"How convenient," the officer said. "The only people who might know who you are happen to be away."

Ellen was amazed at how quickly she was able to despise someone.

The seminarian countered the officer's remark by smiling at Ellen. "Let me see how I can help you sort this out, Miss Castle."

"What about your book," Officer Polly said, "your registration list. That's the quickest way to tell who's supposed to be at that address."

"Oh, I can tell you that," Thomas said. "Kate Gannon. Father Elway was just speaking about her."

"Not Ellen Castle," the officer said.

"No, but wait." Ellen stood to better defend herself. "Officer Polly, she's the friend I told you about. Kate Gannon. We live next door to each other in Brooklyn. I came out with her for the weekend. Then she left to start a new job in the city, and I stayed behind to finish her last two weeks. She had been here for the summer."

"Do you have any proof of that, Thomas?"

"I understand that Miss Gannon spent most of the summer with us, Frank. But that's all I know."

"Wait," Ellen said. "Let me call Kate. No, even better, you call Kate. She'll tell you who I am."

Thomas looked to the officer for approval "It might solve everything, Frank."

Polly gave a quick nod, and after Thomas located Kate's number in the registration book, made the call as Ellen stood by fidgeting. On about the tenth ring, the seminarian shrugged and hung up the phone."

Ellen dropped back into the chair. "I can't believe this."

"Can you tell me what's going on?" the young man asked.

Ellen cringed as Officer Polly's explanation made her out to be a felon, until he mentioned the bird.

Thomas broke into laughter. "Oh, goodness. Not Solomon again."

"See? See? I told you," she yelled.

Officer Polly gestured for her to sit still. "You know about this bird?" he asked Thomas. "He has a name?"

"Oh, yes. And not just a name. A reputation. Notorious, by the way. And quite wondrous, actually, although I've never known him to carry off a purse. Seems a bit of a large lift … no pun intended … even for him."

Wondrous! Here we go again, Ellen thought. "That bird is a menace. And now look at what's happening." She was out of patience, and by the look on his face, Officer Polly was not amused by the bird talk either.

"Is there any way we can get in touch with them?" Ellen asked. "Mrs. Wick or the priests? They're the only ones who can vouch for me."

"Mm. Sorry to say, we can't. Mrs. Wick is at the beach with her sister, and there's no way the priests can be pulled out of their meeting. It's more than a meeting, really. There are priests there from all over the state."

Typical, Ellen thought. What good can a priest do when you really need him, when it really counts? When was she going to learn? "Do you understand that this police officer is about to put me in jail?"

The young seminarian's easy demeanor did not waver. "Oh, I don't think that will be necessary." He looked at Officer Polly. "Frank, there's no reason Miss Castle can't use one of our rooms in the guest house behind the prayer garden."

Ellen looked at Officer Polly, hopeful. "That would work," she said.

"Just how would that work, Thomas? She'd be gone as soon as you turned your back."

"Now wait a minute." Ellen again got to her feet. "Police or not, you have no right to paint me as some convict ready to make my escape. You're insulting and pig-headed. How would I even get away with no money and no means of transportation?" She stuck her hands out in front of him. "Well, here then, cuff me. Go ahead. Prove how big you are."

The officer's look darkened, but before he could respond, Thomas stepped in. "Okay, then, let's all calm down." He gestured politely for Ellen to sit. "Frank, I will take full responsibility for Miss Castle. She'll remain here for the day, spend the night, and tomorrow when Mrs. Wick and the priests return, everything will be resolved, one way or the other."

Officer Polly sat with his elbows resting on his knees and looked from the young seminarian to Ellen and back again. "I'm going to have to hold you to it, Thomas, if things go sideways here."

"Oh, really," Ellen piped up. "You think I'll go over the wall or something in the middle of the night?" She looked at the priest. "Is there a wall?"

"Actually, there is," he said. "It's not visible because of all the trees and the vines. You're not thinking about …?"

"No, no. And besides, he'd have you in handcuffs before your morning prayers."

Officer Polly got to his feet, unphased. "Well, I guess it's settled." He turned and looked directly at Ellen. "For now." He put his small spiral note pad and pencil into his shirt pocket. "I'll be back tomorrow, Thomas, to follow up on this. In the meantime, I suggest you try to get in touch with this Kate Gannon person again, and let her know we had to enter her bungalow. I may even have her purse." He shook the seminarian's hand and left.

Though relieved, Ellen kept her eye on the door as if

expecting the officer to pop back in.

"I think you can relax, Miss Castle. I'm sure everything will turn out okay." Thomas gestured for Ellen to follow him, and as they made their way to the far side of the main room, she noticed that he walked with a slight limp. "You must be hungry," he said. "It's nearly lunch time. Let's see what Mrs. Wick has left for us."

Chapter

Three

BEYOND THE LARGE, main reception room, Ellen and Thomas continued down a corridor where the low timbered ceiling and stone floor were lit by two long rows of black wrought iron wall lamps, necessary due to the absence of windows. She was still surprised by how kind he was to her even without really knowing if what Officer Polly said was true. Halfway along, Thomas stopped. "If we were to keep going, we'd come to our beautiful chapel. But for now, we're going down here instead." They descended a short, half-spiral stone staircase opening onto a kitchen that nearly took Ellen's breath away.

Once, years before, when she had flirted briefly with the idea of planning a trip to Europe, Ellen spent hours in the Brooklyn Public Library lost in the pages of books and magazines that depicted the allure of those picturesque French and Scottish towns with their old-world architecture. Like the abbey itself, with its craggy gray stone walls, staves, and long sloping timbers, the kitchen brought those photos to life. It would take little imagination to believe she had been transported to another country in another century.

The focus of the room was an enormous stone hearth with wrought iron rods, hooked at the end for holding heavy kettles. A long dark, rustic wooden table was set in the middle of the room, a bench on either side, and on the walls, open plank shelves for dishes and glassware. Two of the walls were fitted with wrought iron hooks from which hung cooking utensils of every kind, and in the corner to one side of the hearth stood a nest of large pots, above which hung a tall wooden crucifix.

"What an amazing place," Ellen said, turning slowly to take in every inch. "Is this where Mrs. Wick prepares all the meals? Do you all eat here?"

"Sometimes. There's another kitchen upstairs, right off the main room we just came from. That's the one Mrs. Wick typically uses. The priests may grab a bite to eat there, or have a meal in here, or even in our main dining room upstairs. And, as their schedule permits during the day, out in the gazebo. It's a beautiful spot and since it has a fireplace, it's useful all year round. But the priests all fast three days a week. Still, there's always some food prepared." Thomas folded his arms and leaned against the table. "As you can guess, we're an unusual culture, much less regimented than a typical abbey or monastery, whichever you choose to call it. After morning

Mass, each of us keeps his own schedule because of the work we do."

"You all work? I thought you spent your days praying." She was curious about this man who appeared so at ease with a stranger steeped, at least for the moment, in highly questionable circumstances.

"There are many monasteries where that is true. And even where the priests never speak, but our order is devoted to sociability and humanitarianism. We do pray often each day, of course, but our mission is to seek connections with people—God's creations, after all."

He opened the large ice box and removed a few of the sandwiches wrapped in wax paper that Mrs. Wick had prepared from the roast beef dinner the night before. Ellen noticed a momentary tremor in his hands as he placed the sandwiches on a small tray and set it, with apparent caution, on the table.

"So, what kind of work do you do here?"

"I help with office work. And counseling." He looked to the side, then back. "I have a few slight limitations that prevent me from doing certain manual labor."

"You're an excellent negotiator. I know that much. You kept me from going to jail." They laughed.

"Officer Polly is a good man," he said, "even if a bit intense at times."

"Just doing his job, I suppose. Thank you for helping to rescue me."

Ellen took one of the sandwiches from the plate Thomas offered, as he took one for himself.

"But for now," he said, amiably, "it's all about roast beef on rye."

"Mm ... I didn't realize how hungry I was," she said. "I guess a life of crime makes you hungry, although I shouldn't be joking about it. I'm still in trouble."

"I'm pretty sure you have nothing to worry about, especially with Father Elway returning tomorrow." He bowed his head in silence momentarily, then slid a canning jar closer to Ellen. "Pickle? Mrs. Wick does them the best from our own garden cucumbers."

Ellen helped herself to one of the dill spears, and for a short while, they ate in silence. He was pleasant company. She liked his manner and couldn't help considering what a loss for some nice, young woman to not have this otherwise eligible bachelor in the dating mix. She wouldn't ever have imagined enjoying a casual sandwich with a seminarian in the kitchen of an old-world monastery and marveled at the idea of it. "I'm curious," she said. "Do people actually come to the abbey for counseling?"

"Different kinds, yes. Spiritual counseling. That's what Father Elway and Father Garrett handle. They meet with individuals in the community for that, usually on a monthly basis. They'll also meet with a young man in the process of discerning a calling to the priesthood." He turned to gesture beyond the window. "On the other side of the woods, we have a small lodge."

"A lodge? Here?"

"Not your average vacation or ski lodge; nothing like that, but big enough for our purposes, at least for now."

"Very interesting. Not something I'd expected." Ellen set down her sandwich, took a sip of the lemonade he'd set out for her, and gave him her full attention, transfixed by the prospect of what might come next.

"That's where I do my counseling of sorts," he said. "In the course of the year, we take in army men who are in the last stage of their recovery from injuries and shell shock they suffered in the war. We had a number of them from the big war, but they've been gone for a few years. They always keep in touch about how they're doing. The ones that come to us now are from Korea. They've already undergone their long rehabilitation elsewhere. By the time they get to us, they're preparing to transition back home to ordinary life. We have priests here who are wonderful counselors. You've met a few of them—Father Garrett, Father Elway, Father Pelletier. They're amazing with these men, so respectful and understanding of their situations and what they've experienced."

"I had no idea."

"There's also a doctor who comes out once a week from Oyster Bay Regional to check on them, and they get a physical before leaving us. The military funds it; they've seen the success. Several of the men have even chosen to go back to active duty."

"I never knew there was such a place, especially at an abbey. I just pictured monks in long, hooded robes praying in silence all day."

"Make no mistake, Miss Castle, prayer is fundamental for us here. We celebrate Mass twice a day. Father Elway and Father Garrett hear confessions three days a week—happens to be the days they're fasting. Also, by appointment, if there's a local resident in need. But there's a lot more going on here than one might think, Miss Castle."

She reached out her hand as if to touch his sleeve. "Please call me Ellen. I mean, if that's okay. If you're allowed."

"I certainly can, Ellen. Thank you."

"I'm sorry … you were saying."

"Only that, by now, you may be able to see that the abbey is a place of welcome. There's a very special calming energy about it, the perfect environment for these men to start doing a day's work, re-adjusting, and so on. We cater only to the Army. And we're not equipped to take in the women. There's a place for them in Ohio, just as there are different places, as well, for servicemen and women from the Navy, Marines, Air Force, and so on. But the same idea, only I'd like to think ours is a little special." He ran his hand across the edge of the table. "The last few men from Korea just left within the past few weeks. They've gone back home healthy and well-adjusted. We'll be getting another small group within the next week or two."

Ellen sat motionless. "I'm so surprised. I never would

have imagined this."

"Most of the people who visit here never have either, but that's okay. These men need their privacy. But I'd be happy to show you the lodge before the vets arrive, if we get the chance."

"I'd like that, Thomas. Thank you."

He motioned past the hearth. "We also have a small farm on the property. Strawberries. Peaches. Seasonal, of course. We've got well over four hundred acres, and it's a good thing because more and more people are moving out to the Island from the city. We'll need to maintain our seclusion and way of life."

"With the size of the land here, I doubt that it would be a problem. I'm just so surprised that I'd never heard anything about Spiritu or the abbey."

He smiled. "True. Many haven't. They'd also be surprised by all that goes on here in our little part of the world. But, believe it or not, people still find us. They want to visit, to hold events here, especially at Christmas. We cannot accommodate that." He took a sip of lemonade, then pointed off. "We have a wood shop, and a tool shop where we handle the repairs and so on needed for the lodge, the bungalow rentals, and the guest house, along with the things we build to sell. We have a small bakery. Two of the priests bake bread that they sell at the Nassau Farmer's Market every week. Very popular items, along with the tea biscuits, pies, and such that Mrs. Wick contributes. We are blessed."

As they continued with their lunch, Ellen felt a joyous rush, totally unexpected, given her experience with that crazy bird at the train station and Officer Polly, the other crazy bird.

"Now, I'm the one who's curious," Thomas said. "What actually happened today?"

Ellen set her glass on the table. "It was almost as Officer Polly explained, except without all the crime talk. I really was waiting for the train, and I really did have my purse with me, believe it or not. How would I have been able to pay for my train ticket and newspaper otherwise? Just as the train arrived, Solomon swooped past, upsetting everything, and the next thing I knew, my purse was gone. But then, later, when Officer Polly and I opened the door to the bungalow, there it was sitting right on top of the bookcase inside the door." She shook her head and took a deep breath. "How is that even possible?"

"I have to admit that's pretty puzzling, even for Solomon. I'm also curious about something else, Miss Castle … Ellen." He leaned in. "Were you not enjoying your stay? You had your suitcase with you. Were you leaving permanently?"

The look on his face was so earnest that she didn't have the heart to tell him the truth. "I needed to get back to the city. Work … you know."

"I understand."

They finished their lunch in silence before heading over to the guest house, another quaint stone building with a long sloping roof and arched windows, all of it mimicking the charm of the main building. After entering, Thomas stopped at the first heavy plank door marked with a small porcelain plate bearing the word "Sunflower" painted in yellow. He took a key from his pocket, put it in the lock and opened the door to a room furnished with a single bed, dark wood dresser, and a cream and blue colored plaid armchair. It was a modest square whose warmth was reflected in the deep Tuscan gold walls and the view of the orchard that appeared to fill the entire room, a welcoming space that delighted Ellen.

"I'm happy to say that this is not one of our fast days. Father Xavier, our main pastry chef, will be cooking for us tonight. Dinner at 6:00. Chicken pot pie. You're welcome to join us in the dining room, or I can have a meal sent over, if you prefer. But please know that you are most welcome to sit with us at dinner. We don't get too many guests here. Some of the priests are quiet, but all are kind and friendly." He turned to leave. "Oh, and I'll have your suitcase sent right over."

"Yes, please, on both counts. And thanks again, Thomas, for saving me from the long arm of the law." They laughed as he handed her the room key and turned, taking hold of the door jamb on the way out to steady himself.

Ellen quickly reached toward him. "Thomas …"

"I'm fine. Not to worry. Every now and then … you know."

When he was gone, she wondered about him, about his "limitations," as he called it. He was an otherwise fit and decent-looking man, and pretty steady on his feet, despite his limp. She felt bad for him. Polio? Is that why he was choosing the priesthood—to find shelter from a world that he believed offered him few options? She remembered the old woman in her Brooklyn neighborhood who had contracted polio as a child and never dated or married. Ellen wanted to be hopeful that there might someday be a cure. Many didn't believe there ever would be.

She slipped out of her sandals, appreciating the thickness of the rug, then walked across the room where rows of apple trees filled her view. She pushed open the window to let in the flow of warm sweet air. Eyes closed, she drew a long, deep breath, and smiled before a knock on the door brought her back. She slipped into her sandals before answering.

A pleasant looking man of about sixty—dressed as a priest—smiled. "Miss Castle? I'm Father Pelletier. Welcome. This, I believe, is your suitcase." He was tall with gray at the temples of his light brown hair. Like Father Garrett, he appeared lean and fit, and she was tempted to ask what his role was at the abbey.

"Thank you, Father."

He gestured to the small wooden stool by the window. "Is that okay?"

"Yes. That's fine."

He walked over and set the suitcase in place. "Peaceful, isn't it?" he said, glancing at the window. "It may take a little time to get used to, but the longer you're here, the more you know how much you'd miss it."

"Oh, I'm only here for the night. I wasn't supposed to be here at all. There was just a big mix-up. I'll be leaving in the morning."

He headed for the door, still smiling. "You have no idea how many times we've heard that."

"But…"

When he was gone, she stood wide-eyed, staring at the door.

After putting her feet up and relaxing for a while, Ellen changed her blouse and removed a few toiletries from her suitcase, no longer so neatly packed thanks to Officer Polly pawing through everything. She freshened up, now and then turning her attention back to the orchard where she could see a few priests on ladders picking the apples. All was quiet. No one spoke. A scene of calm beauty, which, after all the strangeness and tensions of the day, she found comforting. Still, the more she thought about it, the more uncomfortable she felt about joining the priests for dinner. With Mrs. Wick gone, she would be putting herself in the awkward situation of being the only female.

She found Thomas in the library, and after taking him up on his offer to have supper in her room, asked for permission to stroll about. It had crossed her mind to steal away to her bungalow—she wasn't guilty of anything, after all. They were bound to realize that once they'd made contact with Kate or when the priests and Mrs. Wick returned. But what good would it do—Officer Polly had her purse, and she would never betray Thomas or get him in trouble. Besides, Father Xavier's chicken pot pie was too tempting.

"Of course," Thomas said, cheerful. "You'll enjoy a walkabout. The orchard's a beautiful place." Thomas gave her a satisfied smile, clearly pleased by her desire to see more of the abbey grounds. She liked his cordial manner. "I know I don't have to caution you about entering the woods," he added.

"Believe me, Thomas, I wouldn't dream of entering the woods." She lingered. "I have to ask—the priest who delivered my suitcase … Father Pelletier … he made an interesting comment when I said I would be leaving tomorrow. Something about how he'd heard that many times before, as though he didn't believe I was leaving."

"Ah. Father Pelletier. What a delightful spirit in that man."

"He mustn't have realized I'm a visitor, an outsider."

"Do you really believe that's what you are?"

"Of course, I do. I really have no place here. You took me in as a kindness." She chuckled. "You rescued me."

"That's right," he said, a joyous expression on his face. Then, he glanced up with his finger in the air a moment before the mantle clock chimed. "Yes, there it is. Always right on time and a reminder that you'll want to get your stroll in before dinner."

She looked at him then at the clock, bewildered by his prescience. Bewildered. Again.

Chapter

Four

FATHER ELWAY WALKED the length of his study, hands clasped behind his back, the afternoon light streaming in color through the tall stained-glass mullioned windows. "Well, what's the verdict, John?"

Father Garrett tapped the pencil against his chin. "All 'n all, we're okay, Leo."

"Any shortfall?"

"Like an Olympic gymnast, it appears that we've once again landed on our feet. We've stuck the landing, as they say. And that's taking into account that everything's gone up but the rent we charge. We still had to do the routine maintenance on the lodge and all the bungalows, plus a bit of storm damage from last year's hurricane. And don't forget the expansion of the reception area."

"But even with the rentals closed until next spring, John, the new, expanded community events we're planning should help bring in donations throughout the year, especially during the holidays. That's been the plan, hasn't it?" He took a seat near Father Garrett, the wall of bookshelves behind them, and looked directly at his closest associate and friend. "And what about the event we just had, our first? Everyone seemed to like it. They all made donations, although, I really don't want this to be about money."

"People were generous, yes, and thank God. Most importantly, and this should please all of us, they expressed surprise at how much they loved being able to come to the abbey for the first time for such a special occasion. Mrs. Esposito especially seemed to enjoy it. She loves the sacred beauty, as she put it. A lovely woman. She lives in one of the new developments going up in Plainview."

"That's a promising thing to hear."

"Very promising, I'd say. And we've noticed more of the locals coming to morning Mass. There may come a time when we'll have to expand the chapel. Wouldn't that be a happy challenge, Leo?"

"Well, another season, and we're doing okay. I'd say we couldn't ask for more, but you know I have been asking for more and for a very long time."

"Keep asking, Leo, because we are nowhere near even thinking about the expansion of the abbey lodge, let alone building a retreat center. That's miracle territory."

"That's fine. Like you, I have no problem asking for miracles."

They were sitting in silence when Mrs. Wick came

through the doorway with a tea tray. "Oh, I know that sound," she said, setting the tray on one corner of Father Elway's large mahogany desk. "Much too early for weighty pondering."

"Ah, the tea biscuits." Father Elway lifted his face, taking in the sweetness. "You always have a good remedy, Mrs. Wick. And how was your beach day with Grace?"

"A fine day, thank you." Sober-faced, she set out the small white linen napkins. "Why do I think that it's going to take a bit more than tea biscuits. It's barely noon, and already the air is heavy with thought. Am I right, Father Garrett?"

"Tea biscuits and prayer, Mrs. Wick." Father Garrett smiled, placing one of the powdery teacakes onto his small plate. "Oh, and maybe a miracle here and there."

She poured each a cup of tea, then left the room, nearly bumping into Ellen.

"Oh, I'm so sorry, Mrs. Wick."

She was an impish, sturdy little woman of some years, with a hint of an English accent and just enough curl in her hair to frame a face that could still boast porcelain skin that many a younger woman would die for.

"No bother, dearie. I know you're eager to have Father Elway help fix things with Officer Polly. Maybe this wouldn't be such a bad moment to interrupt. They can use a break."

Ellen glanced past the wide cased opening. One deep corner of the library doubled as Father Elway's study. Mrs. Wick had told her that Father preferred it that way instead of a private office—he didn't like being separated from …

things. Ellen remembered the room from the night of the community event, still impressed by the dark wood wall-to-wall bookshelves, the stained-glass windows, winged back chairs, and oriental rugs that fit so beautifully with the vintage ambience. "Thank you, Mrs. Wick. Officer Polly will probably be here soon."

"Not to worry," Mrs. Wick said, her tone comforting. "I'll do my best to take care of Officer Polly." She winked. "Sometimes biscuits speak louder than words."

Even with all the confusion and inexplicable goings-on, Ellen had to admit she was again feeling more relaxed, something else for which she had no explanation, especially since there was a police officer intent on seeing her in a jail cell.

The doorbell chimed. "I'll bet this is your friend now." The feisty, silver-haired matriarch stiffened her short, commanding figure, then headed to the door, leaving Ellen at the library entrance.

"Oh, good morning, Miss Castle." Father Elway called to her. "Come in."

"I hope I'm not intruding."

"Not at all. Father Garrett and I have just wrapped things up." He gestured for her to sit. "Have some tea and one of Mrs. Wick's biscuits." He laughed. "Father Garrett believes eating one of these is a spiritual experience."

"Let her see for herself," Father Garrett said.

"I'm sure that's true, but Mrs. Wick fixed a wonderful

breakfast for me. She's a very kind person." Ellen looked over her shoulder. "I believe Officer Polly just arrived to arrest me."

Father Elway rose from his chair. "Yes, we heard all about it," he said with good humor. "So glad you stayed here at the abbey last night. Come and join us."

Ellen could hear the officer's deep, stern voice, and soon he was standing behind her in the doorway. She walked farther into the room and took a seat near the priests.

"Good morning, Father Elway, Father Garrett. Sorry to have to break in, but I've got a little business to finish regarding this woman, one Ellen Castle alias Elena Castellanos, who claims to be staying here at one of the rentals." He was carrying Ellen's purse, which he placed on a side table. "I'll leave this with you, and I'll trust that you'll be discreet until we learn the truth."

Ellen rolled her eyes.

"Ah, yes," Father Garrett said. "We're big fans of discretion."

With as little motion as possible, Ellen glanced at the priest, surprised by his dry humor.

Father Elway greeted Officer Polly with a handshake, as Father Garrett rose and meandered to the bookshelves. "Good to see you, Frank. It's been a while. Have a cup of tea and one of Mrs. Wick's biscuits."

"I can't right now, Leo. Mrs. Wick already offered. I've got a report to fill out to wrap things up."

Ellen turned toward the officer. "I thought I heard Mrs.

Wick explaining things to you."

The officer continued to speak directly to Father Elway. "Mrs. Wick's explanation didn't cover a few vital missing pieces."

"Well then, let's get it cleared up, Frank," said Father Garrett with a wry smile, gesturing to the chair next to Ellen.

Officer Polly sat and removed the small spiral notepad and pencil from the pocket of his tan uniform shirt. "It seems that although this woman has been verified as staying here, she is believed to have falsified facts during our conversation, which we can deal with in a minute. First, I'm going to need the truth." He turned directly to Ellen. "Why did you lie about the purse?"

"I didn't. I…"

Father Elway put up his hand. "Do we know that a crime was committed, Frank?"

Officer Polly turned his head alternately from side to side as he enumerated. "False complaint. Questionable ID. A wild goose chase, at best."

"And how many geese does it take to make a crime?" Father Garrett, took a sip of tea.

"Now, Father, with all due respect, you've got your work here, and I've got mine."

"Forgive us, Frank," said Father Elway. "Of course, you're right."

Officer Polly went on. "You have to admit that the circumstances, the complaint, are all strange. I can't just ignore bits and pieces that don't make sense."

Father Garrett had removed a book from the shelf and was thumbing through the pages. "Strange doesn't have to mean wrong or bad, does it, Frank? Otherwise, how would anyone explain aardvarks?"

"With all due respect, John, I'm not here about aardvarks, unless you know of one that tried to steal a purse. I've got a report to finish on this woman, and there's got to be some logic here somewhere."

Father Elway rubbed his chin. "Oh, yes, logic. Always a tricky one, isn't it? But, well, it is very simple, Frank. Ellen was meant to stay."

Ellen gave the priest a quizzical look but remained silent.

Officer Polly glanced around the room and, after a moment, stood and put his notepad and pencil back into his pocket. "I can see that I'll have to sort out the confusion on my own." He turned to Ellen. "And don't think you're off the hook, Miss whatever your real name is." He waved his hand in the air. "A missing purse that was never really missing? A low-flying bird? This isn't over."

Father Elway walked around and patted him on the shoulder. "Frank, I have a feeling it's all going to work out somehow. In the meantime, please give my warmest regards to Catherine and the boys." When the officer was gone, Father Elway returned to his seat and his tea. "Don't let his gruff demeanor fool you, Ellen; Frank Polly is a good man."

"Yes, he is," Father Garrett said. "It's just that he's got a list of official duties stacked like firewood in his head, and if one were to get loose, he probably believes they would all come tumbling down around him. We'll remember to say a prayer for him tonight."

Officer Polly made his way to the patrol car, dissatisfied with his unfinished business. Father Elway had him over a barrel, all right—it was hard to argue with a priest, especially one who'd been a good friend over the years. He paused to look about at the near woods, always a beautiful setting. Years back, he and Catherine had enjoyed coming to Sunday Mass here, now and then having tea and scones afterwards with a few of the priests. Once the boys came along, it was easier to go to St. Ignatius in Hicksville, especially with the nearby ice cream parlor serving as a useful bribe to keep the kids quiet during Mass.

Something shot past, brushing Polly's shoulder. He backed away, ducking, then rose gradually, looking about. He turned and, again, something darted past. Red. "That bird? That crazy bird?" It came back around, and he waved it away, crouching at the side of the patrol car. After a moment, he reached up and gave the driver's door a tug to yank it open. Then, rising clumsily, he jumped into the car, nearly slamming the door on his foot as the bird came shooting past once more. "What the blazes?" He tossed his cap onto the seat beside him and waited until it appeared the bird was gone. He thought about going back inside to tell Father Elway what had happened but wasn't comfortable making a target of himself again by getting out of the car. He would make a note of it, though, and reached into his shirt pocket for the small, spiral notepad. It wasn't there.

Exasperated, Polly opened the car door and craned his neck to look about for the bird before stepping out. Once outside, he searched the ground around the vehicle. The notepad was nowhere in sight. He got back in the car and noticed the small pencil on the floor, but still no sign of the note pad. He started the car and pulled forward, thinking that in the fray, it may have ended up under the vehicle, but after one last glance around, he shook his head and got back in behind the wheel.

He took a few minutes to collect himself before calling the station house to see if anything needed his attention and was relieved to learn that there was only a harmless fender bender on Wantagh Parkway that Officer Stover was taking care of. After a sip of coffee from his metal thermos, Polly headed back to the police station, feeling thwarted not only by the unfinished business but by his inability to make sense of it.

He pulled into a parking space outside the small red-brick building that had been his home-away-from-home for the last twenty-two years and went directly to his desk. "Hot out there, Henry. An end-of-summer boiler."

"Get ready, Frank," the other officer replied. "You can bet

it'll be another crazy pool day up at Levittown Parkway."

The station house felt muggy. Officer Polly tugged at the rim of his shirt collar, then placed his hat on top of the file cabinet next to the wooden coat rack, his head damp and warm with sweat. After turning on the oscillating fan, he reached for a legal pad and eased into his creaky wooden chair to fill out his report, incomplete as it was. "Great good glory," he whispered, jumping back at the sight of his small spiral notepad sitting in the center of his desk.

A moment later, he called out. "Henry, who was at my desk?"

"Like who? Who would be at your desk? Everyone's out. Nobody here but me."

"I was just wondering, you know, if anyone came into the station?"

"Nobody." Henry chuckled. "And it's a good thing with me trying to chase a bird out of here."

"Wait. What do you mean?" Polly got to his feet and went around to Henry's desk. "What bird? What kind of a bird?"

"A cardinal. Beautiful thing. I had propped the door open to see if I could get some air circulating, and here he comes like he belonged here. I chased him around, trying to get him towards the door. Then I felt bad when I saw there was something wrong with his wing."

Polly stood perfectly still and said nothing.

"Frank? You okay?"

Chapter

"You believe me, don't you, Father?"

Father Elway patted Ellen's arm. "I have no reason not to."

She felt better hearing that. "If you don't mind my asking, how was your meeting at Fordham?"

"Wonderful and rewarding in more ways than one." he said, rising from his chair. "Would you believe, Ellen, that we finished our meeting just in time to get to the radio and hear Mickey Mantle hit an inside-the-park home run in the seventh inning at Yankee Stadium?"

"Wow. That's a thrill."

"Quite a feat for a twenty-one-year-old." Father Garrett said, rubbing his hands together, gleeful. "They beat the White Sox. Ha!"

"Do you think they'll clinch the pennant?"

"They're bound to." He raised an eyebrow. "And then Father Elway and I will have a real dilemma because they'll probably play Brooklyn, and we love those bums." He gave her a side glance. "I guess it's easy to know who you'd root for."

"The bums, all the way." And they all laughed.

Ellen rose from her chair. "Well, I think I'd better not overstay my rescue," she said.

"Ha. Good one," Father Elway said, rising along with her. "But first, why not walk with me. I left my breviary in the prayer garden."

Ellen thought of excusing herself but instead left the library with Father Elway and crossed the large reception room to the door leading to the garden. Before stepping out, she hesitated. "No crazy bird again, I hope."

"One can never be too sure," he said, amused.

She liked his ways. She took him for a man of confidence and good humor, a neat man, maybe early sixties, his manner one of ease and kindness, wise in his dealings with people. She also observed that while Father Garrett appeared to move about more or less in a rush of lanky energy, his words were calming and sincere, and in serious matters, as was clear in his handling of Officer Polly, sometimes ironic, even witty.

She needed to keep in mind that none of them had anything to do with her loss of faith. Nor had anyone made her uncomfortable by pressing her about … things … or asking her to pray with them. The priests had defended her at once to the officer when there was no logical reason why they should. It was the same with Thomas, although she was still trying to make sense of those random comments about how she was meant to be there, and how she was no outsider. And even the comment Father Pelletier had made about her not leaving, when he delivered her suitcase.

"I enjoyed my stroll yesterday," she said, looking at Father square on to see if he appeared to approve.

"Wonderful."

"I really didn't go very far."

"I know."

His answer gave her momentary pause. "Thomas said it was okay for me to go past the garden. The orchard is beautiful. I sat in the gazebo for a while."

"A lovely spot to rest and think."

"Beyond that, I could see the planting field. And the woods. There's so much here. I'd had no idea. Thomas told me about the lodge and all the things you do. I think it's pretty amazing."

"We are blessed." They stopped at the low stone wall that surrounded the grotto where the large wooden cross stood. "Here. Let's sit. Were you curious about anything in particular?"

"Just the sight of priests picking apples."

Father Elway smiled. He looked up and pointed to one of the rooftop peaks. "I don't believe that weathervane has moved in two days. Is it this muggy in Brooklyn? Haven't been there in years. Has it changed much?"

Was this his way of getting her to begin talking about herself? "It's about the same, Father."

"You must miss it. You were eager to return home."

Ah. She was right. Now, what? She couldn't bring herself to lie to him. After a brief silence, she pointed to a tall, slender tree with clusters of dark pink flowers and bark the color of cinnamon. "Father Elway, is that a type of wisteria? It's beautiful. Different. I've never seen one just like it, definitely not in Brooklyn."

"Crepe myrtle—rare in the north," he said, giving her a meek and knowing glance. The slight crinkle around his eyes gave him an impish look, part of his charm, she thought. She recalled that he was almost playful with Officer Polly. And come to think of it, they were all this way—Father Garrett, and Mrs. Wick, and Thomas, as well. Still, she was not yet ready to discuss Brooklyn.

They heard the abbey door close and turned to see Father Garrett coming along the path toward them.

"There you are," he said. "I was wondering, Miss Castle, if you'd like a ride back to your bungalow."

Odd that it hadn't even occurred to her. This was supposed to have been just an overnight stay at the abbey to avoid jail. What was it now, she wondered, gripped by an unexpected sense of disappointment at the prospect of going back to her rental instead of staying at the abbey for a while longer? How strange.

"I was hoping Miss Castle would like to stay for lunch," Father Elway said, turning to her. "What do you say?"

She was surprised and pleased that he seemed to know

what she was feeling. She found comfort in that … almost like … she couldn't put her finger on it. Maybe an ever-so-slight sense of belonging. "I think I've imposed enough."

"We think not," said Father Garrett, clasping his hands together. "I'll tell Mrs. Wick you'll be staying."

When he turned to go back inside, Ellen called after him. "Father Garrett, do you still have this morning's 'Newsday?' I was thinking, maybe I'd go into Hicksville later. I think I'd like to see that new movie with Gregory Peck and this new actress, Audrey Hepburn. They say it's wonderful."

He smiled. "Yes, 'Roman Holiday' I think it is. I've read the same thing. I'll be right back with the paper."

For a long moment, she and Father Elway sat in silence, the garden peaceful, the late summer air thick with the sweetness of apples.

"I'm curious, Ellen." The priest gently ruffled the well-worn pages of his prayer book. "What was it that made your stay here unpleasant for you? It might be something we need to improve upon."

At first, she bristled. She looked down, smoothing the lap of her pale blue trousers with her hand. "It wasn't this place, Father, although I think I had convinced myself that it was. It's … complicated … and if it's okay would you mind if we don't talk about it right now?" She looked off. "It's been a hard time for me these past months."

He looked at her. "I've sensed as much." He touched her arm. "If you should find yourself with even the slightest desire to talk about it, you can be sure it will be the right time."

They looked over to see Thomas coming through the gate at the far end of the prayer garden. "We have that meeting, Father Elway. Hello, Ellen. I hope you had a good night here."

"Yes, Thomas. Thank you."

"See what good company you are, Ellen Castle. I completely lost track of time." As he rose to leave, he held out his breviary to her. "Would you please hang onto this for me? Every time I take it with me to a meeting, I end up leaving it behind."

She took the prayer book. "Of course. I'll give it to Father Garrett."

When they had gone, Ellen remained there waiting for Father Garrett to return with the newspaper, unsure if the breviary would be considered too private for her to look through. It was a worn and weighty volume, its page ends darkened with long use, the black leather cover lighter in color at the spine from handling. She riffed the pages as Father had but didn't open it.

There were still times when she wished she could believe as she once did, as her faithful mother had. Even if she could, what would she pray for? Would her business come back to her? Her home? Tony? Would the trusted partner who cheated her out of her business, her livelihood, her savings, and her home, leaving her with thousands in debt, suddenly restore her funds? She turned to look up at the cross. "At this point," she said, more a challenge than a question, her heart burdened with resentment and doubt, "just what would an answered prayer look like?"

As she stood to go inside, a small piece of paper fell to the ground. She picked it up, worried that Father Elway might have used it to mark a particular page. It appeared that the handwriting was rushed, but it stopped her all the same. Be still and know that I am God.

Chapter

Six

"So, what do you think, Stu?"

The balding fifty-year-old turned in his chair and looked out the third-floor office window at the people and traffic below. "It's a big move, Lenny. Look out there. Court Street. A thing of beauty. People who don't know any better might say it's a busy mess. So be it, but we know this busy mess. We've thrived in this busy mess." He turned back and faced his partner of twenty years. "Things work for us in Brooklyn. Why go elsewhere?"

"New territory. New opportunity. Pelham. Long Island. Westchester County. Nassau County. People are moving there, Stu. People we know are moving there. The North Shore. The South Shore. The center of the Island. Take your pick." He laughed. "We can make a new busy mess."

"I'm not saying it wouldn't work. But we'll be starting from scratch, Lenny, and at this point, I'm not sure we want that kind of undertaking. There's a lot of risk."

"Hey, there was a risk coming up in the elevator this morning. Look at the woman over in Mays Department store yesterday—she almost died when the elevator dropped four floors. Her life must have flashed before her eyes as she flew past haberdashery and women's lingerie."

Wasserman didn't smile. He rose and walked around from behind his desk. "I'd have to think, Lenny." He started pacing.

"It doesn't have to be this hard." Lenny twisted around in his chair to face Wasserman. "Right now, you're making me dizzy. And by the way, when did you not manage any risk we ever faced? You're not getting old on me, are you?"

"Esther keeps talking about Florida."

"I thought it was Arizona."

"Florida. Arizona. Back and forth. She makes me crazy." He waved his hand. "I can't keep up."

Lenny reached over and removed a cigar from the cherry wood humidor on Wasserman's desk. "Take her to Cuba. You're running low."

"We'd need contacts," Wasserman said, not listening. "We'd need someone we can trust. Someone to give us … you know … decent advice that's in our best interest. That's not easy to find. But it's the most important thing if we want to keep doing things the right way."

"Hey, we put together high-rise apartment complexes with no advice from anybody. What are you talking about?"

Wasserman stopped pacing. "But in these new areas,

you'd be talking developments—single-family homes, dozens and dozens of them, something we never did before on that scale."

Lenny threw his hands out. "And? So?"

"We're not kids anymore, Lenny. We have a lot more to lose now. We could end up with bubkes. Don't you get that?"

"So, it's 'No?'"

Wasserman walked back around to the over-sized brown leather chair behind his desk and sat. "No, it's not 'No.' I didn't say it was 'No.'" He took a cigar, snipped the end with his wedge cutter, and lit it with a long, slow draw, sending up a curl of gray smoke. "I'll take Esther to Cuba for a week. You go and look into things." He pulled his large shoulders up in a shrug. "When I get back, we'll see."

Lenny jumped to his feet and clapped his hands. "You're gonna love it, Stu." He headed for the door. "You're gonna love it."

"Now, remember." Wasserman wagged his finger. "Don't talk so much on the street. If people get the idea Court Realty is moving out, God forbid, they'll think we're going under."

"You don't have to worry. There's only one person I'm gonna talk to."

Wasserman squinted. "Have we done business with him? He better be good."

"First of all, he is not even in our line of work. Second, he is not even a he."

"Don't start making me nuts with some wild-goose chase."

"No wild-goose chase, Stu. This lady has the one piece of information that's going to get the whole thing rolling."

"Well, does she have a name?"

He smiled and threw a salute as he headed out the door. "Kate Gannon. Have fun in Cuba."

"Wait! What does she know about real estate?"

Lenny shouted from the other side of the door. "Absolutely nothing."

Chapter

Seven

ELLEN WALKED ALONG the tree-lined avenue in Hicksville, her heart heavy with the movie's unexpected ending, a particular sadness she knew well—two people deeply in love when love wasn't enough. Oh, Patrick.

She passed The Sweet Shoppe and Englert's Bakery without a thought of stopping. Oblivious to passersby, she sat for a while on one of the sidewalk benches before moving on to the corner of Marie Street to catch the bus. Earlier in the day she had felt uplifted by her visit at the abbey. Odd how the only thing that seemed to be working for her right now was the kindness of the people there, and Father Elway's gracious insistence that she return whenever she pleased.

"Lady, are you coming?" the driver called to her. "Sorry for the delay."

She made her way up the steps and dropped in her dime. "Hey, I know you," he said.

Startled, she looked up at the dark-haired man behind the wheel.

"You're friends with Kate. Remember me? A month or so ago. I'm Sal."

"Oh … yes. Hi." She did remember. Kate had even talked about him and how his friendliness had been a high-point at the beginning of her stay there.

"Hey, I don't like that sad look." He held up his left hand. "You know when you see my ring finger, my only intention is a sincere compliment—you're too pretty to be unhappy."

She took the nearest window seat. "Sorry. I just saw a sad movie."

"Oh, don't tell me. 'Roman Holiday.'"

"Yes. Silly, right? It's just a movie."

"Yeah, but movies grab us. I remember the first time I saw that 'Maltese Falcon.' When did that come out, ten, eleven years ago? I still daydream sometimes about being a private investigator. Dumb, right?" Sal rotated the big wheel and moved out, looking into the rear-view mirror before throwing a quick glance in Ellen's direction. "And that movie you just saw—you know how many miserable women come on this bus after seeing that movie? Why would those stupid people make a love story that makes women miserable? That's what I want to know. They should at least warn you that you're not going to be happy about it. I hope my wife doesn't see it."

She had to smile—of course, she remembered him. The big, friendly Brooklyn guy who gave up the constant buzz of city life for the more pastoral Long Island lifestyle. How could you not feel better with a seat on Sal's bus and the friendly chatter that came with it? Twenty minutes later, with the last of sundown closing out the day, Ellen stepped off. "Goodnight, Sal. Thanks a lot."

"Be good," he said. "I'll see you next time around. And I'll be looking for that smile."

She headed to her bungalow with a lighter step and the words that kept finding their way into her thoughts, Be still and know that I am God.

The next morning, with the sun up and the early warmth of the day coming on a waft of pine and wood must, Ellen took her cup of coffee onto the front porch, having finally decided between her temptation to linger for another day or two and her need to return to Brooklyn. Leaves glistened from the overnight shower, the occasional whiff of lilacs, and cut grass, a momentary distraction from the uneasiness of her decision.

Normally, she would have missed being away from her beautiful brownstone. That's when it was still her home before the rooms were in varying states of undoing with packing boxes scattered about. She mustn't dwell on it or on the wonderful neighborhood she would soon leave behind—the luncheonette and the bakery, the corner park and the streets lined with sycamores. Father Elway and the others had all been so good to her. The last thing she wanted to do was have them think she was dismissing their kindness. But there was much to do at home before the move, sorting through closets, drawers, and cupboards, keeping this, getting rid of that. She had made up her mind. She would telephone the abbey and let them know she was leaving today.

An elderly couple, no doubt on one of their final strolls before departing, called out as they passed, "See you next summer." She waved back, thinking about the little gray kitten that had peeked through the porch rail. She hadn't seen it. Maybe it belonged to one of the renters, and now it, too, was on its way back home. She put her cup down, walked to the far end of the porch, and looked around the side of the bungalow. No kitten, but there was something there that was most unexpected. Ellen turned and hurried across to the porch steps to investigate. Around the far side of the bungalow, obscured by a thickness of viburnum, she found exactly what she had thought it to be—a shiny, dark blue, lady's two-wheeler bicycle.

For a long moment, she stood looking at it. She hadn't been aware that there was a bike that came with the rental. Kate had never mentioned it. Maybe Kate never knew about it. But Ellen found herself taken with the alluring two-wheeler. She hadn't been on a bike in years. She looked at her watch. It was almost ten. If she dared to go for a ride, she'd still have plenty of time to get to Hicksville for the 1:15. Was she being silly? Maybe it was okay to enjoy a bit of silliness, rare as it was.

She tugged the bike from the tangle of vines, then checked the tires and chain. Everything seemed fine as she wheeled it around the front of the bungalow and leaned it against the rail post. With the quick step of a child's delight, she went in to get a cloth to wipe off the seat and handlebars, then changed from sandals to Keds. She wouldn't go far, just in and out of the nearby lanes.

Unsteady at first, she made her way in a slow, smooth rhythm, glad there was no one around to see her close her eyes in a moment of mild euphoria. It had been years, and now, in of all places, to find such a treasure.

With the rush of warm air against her face, she found herself enjoying her surroundings in lanes she had not seen before—bungalows nestled in the overhang of elms and maples along with the occasional dogwood and magnolia, flowering bushes of every color and fragrance, butterflies, and fresh-cut grass. It had been many months since she'd experienced such a rush of excitement, a feeling most welcome and unexpected.

Hummingbird Lane became Mockingbird Lane, then a turn onto Swallow, then Warbler, Woodcock, and Plover, not that she was paying attention to the names or how many turns she'd made, left then right then left again, on and on in the woodsy quiet of a late summer morning. "Okay, Father Elway—wondrous. Finally. Ha!"

She remembered that there was a hotdog stand up on Old Country Road. She had gone there with Kate. And since she hadn't yet had anything to eat, why not go there now? It wouldn't be the first time in her life that she'd had a hotdog for breakfast. She laughed remembering those mornings at Coney Island, unable to pass up Nathan's before heading down to the beach. Besides, she had read an article in The Saturday Evening Post about how important it was for people to exercise as they got older. Well, here she was.

One of the lanes led almost directly to Old Country Road, but which one? At the next lane, she back-pedaled to brake and looked in both directions. It only took a moment for Ellen to realize that she didn't know where she was. Not only did she not know which of the lanes led to Old Country Road, but she had no idea which one led back to her bungalow.

She looked about. Would there even be someone to ask? The renters had begun packing up for the season, many already gone. She felt a twinge of anxiety. The couple that had passed her porch might still be around, but where exactly would she find them? Or anyone? In a pinch, she could go to the abbey, but how would she find her way? It was evident that she had a bit of a problem—how long could she go up and down the lanes, beautiful as they were, without being able to get back and still head into Hicksville on time for the train?

Chapter

Eight

ELLEN TURNED AROUND to re-trace her route, grateful that she would be able to cover more ground on a bike than on foot, but after a few turns, she was no closer to finding Old Country Road, the abbey, or home. She rode up to a nearby bungalow, made her way to the sheltered walkway, and knocked on the door. There was no answer. She approached another and saw that the shutters were already closed, then she headed back into the lane, continuing along with growing anxiety.

As she made her way around Sparrow and onto Starling, she heard an odd scratching noise behind her, like pebbles skipping on pavement, and turned to see an elderly man on a bike fall onto the grassy shoulder.

She turned the bike around, hurrying to offer help. "Are you okay?" She laid her bike on the pavement and carefully moved the man's bike to enable him to get up, if he could.

"I … I think I'm fine." He chuckled, breathless. "Not sure,

but I think I am. Sometimes it takes us old birds a little longer to figure that out."

"Do you think you can get up? Let me help."

Ellen reached over and took his arm to steady him as he got to his feet. He appeared to be in his early seventies, a shock of white hair that had likely been neatly combed before the accident now fallen onto his brow. When he stood, he was taller than Ellen and had the posture of a man who might have been athletic in his youth.

"Thank you," he said, with a playful grin. "Thank you," he repeated, brushing off his trousers. "I don't know what got the better of me, but I sure tumbled into a roadside pile, didn't I?"

Ellen laughed. "Yes, but are you okay? I'm not sure how we can get help. I could try if I knew my way around."

"Oh, nothing to worry about. Look. I'm already upright, like a phoenix rising from the ashes. No blood, nothing broken." He pushed his hair back and leaned in. "We always seem to think we know where we're headed," he said in a loud whisper, "but then, ha!"

"Your arms," she said. "Those scratches won't be much fun. If I knew how to get to the abbey, I could get help. Or your bungalow. Is it nearby? Is anyone there I could tell? Your wife?"

He took a few steps back and forth before his leg buckled. Ellen grabbed his arm to keep him from dropping to the ground. "I've got to get you some help." She could see that the front wheel of his bike was twisted.

He touched the bike with the toe of his shoe. "There's finally something in worse shape than I am."

She looked about. "Unless you sit on the grass, there's really no place for you to rest while I get someone. But the grass is still pretty damp, and I wouldn't feel comfortable leaving you standing here by yourself."

"My windbreaker is on the back of my bike," he said. "Maybe we can use it."

She reached down and removed the windbreaker from a small cloth pouch behind the bike seat. She folded it into a square to create as much of a seat as she could, then placed it on the grass. "Here, let me help you down."

He didn't resist as she helped him sit on the windbreaker.

"I feel like a silly fool," he said, laughing. "I was sure I was just meant to be out for a little bike ride."

"Well, then, we're both silly fools because I'm out here just as you are, and I don't even know where I am anymore. And I'm supposed to catch a train in a few hours."

"Oh, that's not good news. But we're in luck," he said, pointing toward the end of the lane, "because the abbey is left, right, left, and you'll be on the right road. It's simple. Left, right, left."

"Okay. But what about your bungalow? Is it closer?"

"The abbey is our best bet. And thank you. Left, right, left."

As she pedaled away, she turned to see him sitting there.

He waved. Such a nice man, and such a positive attitude. Thank goodness he wasn't badly hurt, she thought, but after that tumble, he'll likely feel worse by the hour, and she still wasn't comfortable leaving him behind, even for a short while. It suddenly occurred to her that she hadn't even asked his name. How could she not think of that?

Less than ten minutes later, Mrs. Wick pulled open the abbey's heavy plank door. "Oh, now, good morning to you, Dear Ellie. You couldn't have come at a more perfect time. I was just about to pick late strawberries. They're the sweetest of the season, you know. Why not come along. Our little field is right out the back past the prayer garden."

"There's a bit of an emergency, Mrs. Wick. I'll need some help. A man fell off his bike in one of the lanes, and I believe he might need medical attention."

"Oh, dear. Let me get Father Garrett. He'll…"

"I'm right here." Father Garrett came out of the library. "What's happened?"

"I was taking a little bike ride, and I saw a man fall over with his bike. He's got some scrapes and doesn't seem able to walk very well. The bike's front wheel is bent."

Father Garrett headed out the front door, with Ellen behind. "We'll take the all-around. Where is he? Did you get his name?"

Ellen rushed behind. "He's on Starling. And I was in such a rush to help, I didn't even think to ask his name. He doesn't seem to be badly injured, but he does need help."

"So, you were out for a bike ride. A lovely morning for it. Where did you manage to get a bike?"

"It was there. At the bungalow. I found it around the side. I had never noticed it before, and Kate never mentioned it."

"Interesting," said Father Garrett. "There hasn't been a bike at Number 7 for a few years. Wonder how it got there."

"It's like new … oh, wait, look, there. There it is. Starling." They had gone by way of Warbler, then Sparrow before turning onto Starling.

Father Garrett slowed the car, watching carefully as he turned, to see the man they were looking for. "Where did you say he was?"

Ellen turned to look behind them to the other end of the lane. "We just came from Sparrow. I paid close attention when I left him. He should be right up ahead on the left."

"I don't see anyone. You said he was sitting on the grass?"

"Yes, there was no place else for him to wait. I even folded his windbreaker for him to sit on. The grass was still wet."

Starling Lane was not very long. None of the lanes were. Father Garrett proceeded slowly as they both looked side-to-side.

"He must have moved. Maybe the ground was still too wet or the heat was getting to him. But how would he have been able to walk? His leg gave way the first time he tried."

Father Garrett pulled over to the shoulder and stopped. "Did he say where he lived?"

"I asked him, but he said I'd be better off going to the abbey for help."

The priest turned the car around. "Let's go down the other nearby lanes. Poor man might be limping along. And where's his bike?"

"Maybe someone came by and gave him a ride." As they searched in vain, her thoughts went to Officer Polly not making sense of her missing purse. Was this shaping up to be yet another impossible tale?

Lane after lane, they made their way, slow and watchful. All was quiet, except for the occasional bird chatter and fly-buzz. To Father Garrett's amusement, Ellen screeched when a bee flew in but quickly flew out the back window. Then, he stopped the car. "Well," he said, "what can we make of this?"

"I don't know, Father."

"Let's pray that Our Lord will guide the gentleman safely to where he needs to be."

This was the first time any of them had said a prayer in her company. She liked the way it sounded, although she didn't put much stock in it. The poor man might be lying in a place where they simply missed him, an unlikely possibility, since they'd made as thorough a scan of the lanes as they could. Surely, he wouldn't have wandered into the woods. He seemed to have his wits about him.

"In any event," Father Garrett said as they headed back to the abbey, "we're glad you came by, even if not for the most pleasant of reasons. Mrs. Wick had been trying to reach you by telephone to invite you to our little harvest dinner tomorrow evening. We have it this time every year. Father Elway wants you to know that you are most welcome. Mrs. Wick's sister, Grace, will even be there, along with one or two of the nuns from St. John the Evangelist."

How on earth had she gotten so entwined with these abbey people? She didn't know what to say. Clearly, she was not going to make it to Hicksville, as planned. Even if she left her bike at the abbey, there was no longer time to pack, and the only trains she'd get now would be filled with the rush-hour crowds. If she agreed to attend the harvest dinner tomorrow evening, she wouldn't go home tomorrow either. And it was no small thing that she'd telephoned Kate and told her she'd be home today. Kate would be on the lookout for her. Ellen hoped to be able to reach her again by phone when she got back to her bungalow—Kate would be worried sick if Ellen didn't show up. She took a deep breath. What the heck.

"Sounds lovely, Father. I'd like that, thank you."

Chapter

"Sounds like you've decided to have a good time."

No matter how many times she and Kate had aggravated each other through the years over this or that, she loved her dear friend and knew it went both ways. She was glad to hear her voice. "In a manner of speaking, I guess you could say so, but it's not without some kind of extenuating circumstance."

Kate laughed. "How long did it take you to come up with that one? But, hey, listen, I've got to bypass the small talk. A man called for you today. He said it's important, that he heard you might be away on vacation or something but that he could probably reach you through me. You have to admit, Ellie, that when you move, you'll be leaving quite a wonderful little busy-body neighborhood behind."

"Well, it's not by choice."

Kate didn't respond.

Ellen rummaged through the drawer of the phone table in the bungalow for a piece of paper and a pen. "What's this man's name and did he say why he wanted to reach me?"

"You're worried, right? I can hear it. Don't be. I think he wants to talk to you about something to do with business. Maybe a job. He didn't sound at all threatening. And, by the way, there is no reason in the world why anyone would be a threat to you. So, don't think like that."

Now, it was Ellen who didn't respond.

"He said his name is Lenny Feinman. Do you know him?"

"Lenny Feinman? Yes. I do. He and his partner own one of the most successful real estate development companies in Brooklyn."

"Wow. Maybe it really is about a job. He'd be getting the best. Here's his number. Ready?"

The next morning, Ellen was still mulling over the idea that Lenny Feinman wanted to talk with her. She tried not to feel anxious about it, but after all that had happened over the past months, she had a bad taste in her mouth, none of it having to do with Lenny Feinman. She would call him after breakfast.

She had returned the bike to its place around the side of the bungalow, pondering the odd turn of events. What had happened to that injured gentleman? Why did everyone seem surprised that there was a bike at the bungalow? She still hadn't forgotten about the bird, the purse, and Officer Polly. If only she could get back to some kind of normalcy, although even back home in Brooklyn, normalcy had taken a sharp turn.

In the meantime, here was Spiritu, quirky and remote, a hamlet that very few people had heard of, a monastery, of all things, with apple orchards, strawberry picking, and bike rides on country lanes, a place of occasional wondrous happenings along with an abundance of peace, quiet, and tranquility, and right smack in the middle of it all, the oddest kind of things that she had never experienced before and that couldn't be explained. She would stay for the harvest dinner that evening, but the very next day … no matter what … she was going to be on a train back to the city.

At 9:30, she called Lenny Feinman.

"Ellen Castle, good morning. It's so good you called me back. Thank you. I know we never met, but we've heard of each other, right? You were very good at what you did, and Stu Wasserman and I, we've been in business since what, the flood?" He laughed.

"Yes, of course. Everyone knows of you and Stu. I'm curious as to why you're calling me, though." She was glad he sounded friendly. He put her at ease.

"I would like to meet with you on a business matter that I cannot discuss over the phone. I don't know where you are; I just know you're not in Brooklyn. More importantly, I also know that you enjoyed a wonderful reputation in the industry, and unless you're in … who knows where … Canada, I will come to you. Just tell me where we can meet."

Ellen felt her heart skip. She wanted to believe this was good news, but what did he want that he couldn't even mention on the phone. She couldn't have him come to her house; it was in such disarray. Boxes everywhere. She had even taken all the pictures off the wall. She didn't want to meet him at a Brooklyn restaurant where people might recognize him or her or both. Kate was right—lots of loveable busybodies. "Lenny, I'm so sorry, but this isn't a good time."

"I can call you later, if that works better."

"No, I mean not a good time in general."

"I say that in general, there's no better time."

"Lenny, a lot has changed since I had to close the business. Things are topsy-turvy, and I'm not in a position to entertain…"

"You're in the best position for what I want to talk to you about. Let me meet you for lunch."

"I just can't Lenny. I hope you understand."

The excitement in Lenny Feinman's voice only heightened. Ellen had always heard that he was the real energy at Court Realty. Now, she knew why. "Hey, everybody knows none of that was your fault," he said. "The only bad decision you ever made was trusting the wrong person. That's why we want you, because Stu and I know you're the person we can trust. That makes you the perfect fit for our business, and for what we have in mind."

Ellen was at once flattered and uneasy—just how much was everyone saying about her? Had she become the local story, a topic for gossip? Was that her legacy?

"Tell you what," he went on. "Let me share, confidentially, of course … what can you call it? A headline. Just listen: 'Court Realty Going Big-Time on the Island.' Tell me you're not interested."

"You're leaving Brooklyn?" Ellen couldn't imagine it. Court Realty was the backbone of the real estate business in much of the borough. Always smart and honest, a powerful force in the industry.

"See, that's exactly what Stu was afraid people would think. But, no, no, we are not leaving Brooklyn. We're expanding. Okay, so change the headline: 'Court Realty Expands Big-Time on the Island.' Good, right? We want you to be part of it, Ellen Castle."

What an offer this would have been a year ago. "Believe me, Lenny, your goal sounds intriguing, and I'm very grateful that you would think of me, but I've got to focus on other things right now. You shared confidentially with me; let me do the same—my life is completely upside down. I've sold my brownstone and my car. To be perfectly honest, I had to."

"I'm sorry to hear it's that bad."

"I'm moving to a one-bedroom apartment in Astoria. I even had to find a new home for my beautiful boxer, Tony, and trade in some of my war bonds. You can see that everything has changed. Everything. Please understand, Lenny. And please tell Stu how grateful I am for the offer. I feel honored."

Ellen was impressed by his kindness. He said he was

not giving up, and after he wished her well, they ended the call. She sat for a long while in the bungalow, thinking about what had been and what was to come. She wished she could believe. It certainly would make Father Elway and the others happy, but that fantasy ended long ago for her.

The morning had gradually warmed to the familiar late August stifle. The airy breeze that had puffed the curtains after daybreak had heated the walls by noon. Now, with the drone of the oscillating floor fan overtaking the quiet, Ellen slipped into a rare morning nap, the telephone still beside her on the chair.

Chapter

ELLEN'S MOTHER HAD never failed to remind her how important it was to be thankful even for the smallest of gifts. "Sometimes, you may not realize it's a gift. It might be just a word, or a gesture, or a kindness that could be overlooked so easily if you're busy paying attention to the wrong things, to the meaningless worldly things that can take hold of us." Ellen had lost her mother when they were both too young. She had never stopped missing her. Her mother would know that the people at the abbey were surely a gift.

Father Garrett was to pick her up in the all-around at 7:00. She had felt like dressing up and was glad she had packed something with a bit of glitter. She could have worn it for the event at the abbey that she attended with Kate, but she was not at all in a glittery mood that weekend. Why now, she wondered? With a small gold clip, she gathered up a curl of dark hair as an accent, turning it nicely into a French twist. Then, she gave one final check of her nylons, running her hands up each calf to be sure the seams at the back were straight—she hadn't worn nylons in weeks. One final glance in the mirror satisfied her that the face looking back at her was not the picture of gloom she had seen these many weeks. Her eyes were brighter, her mouth relaxed as if ready to smile.

When they arrived at the abbey, Thomas greeted her at the door and welcomed her into the large reception room, so different late in the day with its warm lamplight that deepened the richness of the dark timbers as well as the burgundy and amber furnishings. This was the first time she had seen all the priests along with the nuns. She had no precedent for such an occasion. Half expecting a quiet, prayerful setting, she was again taken with the gaiety of the room, with Mrs. Wick and her sister, Grace, acting as ambassadors in the midst of the affable clergy dressed in long black cassocks. Well, it was the fifties after all, she thought.

Two of the nuns sat on the sofa, chatting with a priest, but soon came forward to engage everyone. Ellen recognized the habits as Sisters of Saint Joseph from her school days at St. Sabina in Bridgeport, Connecticut. Grace, who appeared older than her sister, greeted Ellen just as warmly as Mrs. Wick always did. The entire room was steeped in a festive ambience.

Mozart played in the background from Father Elway's Victrola, which he kept on a small mahogany table behind his desk in the library. Thomas would later show Ellen the abbot's extensive collection of 78s, containing everything from Prokofiev and Rosemary Clooney, to Gene Autry and Enrico Caruso. The collection also contained a number of Hank Williams's songs, which Father rarely played since the sad and untimely death of the singer only a few months earlier.

Before they all went into the dining room, Mrs. Wick made introductions. Ellen sought out Father Xavier to let him know how much she had enjoyed his chicken pot pie.

"The best I've ever had," she said. "And that should mean a lot since Howard Johnson has always made a good one."

"I'm very glad to hear that. And you must be telling the truth because you know we have this thing called confession." They laughed as Ellen grew more comfortable amid the friendliness and the charm of rustic elegance in this most unexpected of settings.

Father Elway crossed the room to greet her. "By chance, were you still expecting a bunch of hooded monks moving about in silence with their hands clasped in front of them?"

"No." She laughed. "Well, maybe. But I think I'm finally beginning to understand what this historic stone and wood treasure is all about. Well, at least in part. There are many surprises here." She took the glass of red wine that he handed her. "Thank you … especially for the kind invitation."

"Father Garrett told me about your little bicycle adventure."

"Odd as can be, but you may be pleased to know, Father, that before that poor man fell over on his bike, I was finally experiencing a wondrous moment."

"Ah," he said, offering his arm. "Let's go in." And with that, Father Elway led Ellen and the group to the large dining room for the catered feast that began with a prayer of grace. The gaiety continued around the table over a hearty roast beef dinner as Ellen reminisced about her parochial school days with Sister Evangeline. It wasn't necessary to reveal to the nun that she had long since lost her faith, but the conversation was pleasant, and the evening itself was a much more sociable event than she had expected. She was glad she didn't pass it up.

Father Elway stood and clinked his glass with his spoon. "I want to say a special word of thanks … more than a word, but I'll spare you the blabber. First, of course, let's give thanks for this wonderful meal, which our Mrs. Wick did not prepare but could have; it was that good. Praise God, we are blessed." Cheers and applause filled the room. "You have all once again demonstrated your great Godly devotion on so many levels. You have all once again joined in blessed community for our mission and our meaning. I thank you. I thank God for you. I thank God for all. May the Holy Spirit continue to enflame your hearts with passion for the good and holy." He raised his glass of wine, and all followed. Ellen would have imagined feeling out of place, but she didn't. Instead, she felt surprisingly at home raising her glass, as well. She felt more at home than she had in a very long time—a joyful occasion with caring people. She would raise her glass to that any day of the week, and a very fleeting thought reminded her that if it weren't for that odd gentleman on the bike, she would have been back in Brooklyn missing it all.

As she was saying her goodnights, ready for the short ride back to her bungalow with Father Garrett, Father Elway came up to her. "I pray more of this for you, Ellen. More of the delight that is evident on your face. Can you come by tomorrow? There's a little something on my mind."

She didn't resist. "I do have to get back to the city, but …"

"Good," he said, taking her hand. "I'll see you in the morning."

Just after dawn, Ellen sat on the front porch enjoying the fragrant woodsy dampness of the cool morning air. The last day or so had been interesting. She had allowed herself to enjoy the leisurely hours, reading with rare abandon through more of her favorite magazines that the abbey had replenished—Redbook, McCalls, Time, Ladies Home Journal. She was surprised to find herself sitting still even for the Ipana toothpaste and Bromo Seltzer ads, along with the weighty articles covering everything from the Coronation of Queen Elizabeth the Second, and the first open-heart surgery, to the execution of the Communists, Julius and Ethel Rosenberg. She was beginning to believe that there was something to be said for having little else to do, major responsibilities gone, no plans, lists, timelines, budgets. Yes, there was actually something to be said for losing everything.

She was also having a glimpse of something else—the early hours at the bungalow had become lovely, a good time for allowing sweet memories. She thought about her beautiful mother. She thought about Tony. She still felt bad about being unable to explain to him why he must go to a new family. He'd kept looking back as they led him off on his brand-new brown leather leash, young Rosie and James hopping with excitement and talking endlessly to him about all the games they would play. She hoped that by now he was happily settled in with his new playmates. She missed him so much. And, as always, there was Patrick—beloved, unforgettable, everlasting Patrick.

She had taken the bike out twice again and learned to navigate the lanes. She could now easily find her way up to Old Country Road and back. There was packing to do at home in Brooklyn, but for some reason, she was no longer uneasy about it. Things would get done; much already had been. There was more time than she would admit back when Spiritu was an unwelcome distraction forced upon her by Kate. Truth was, her feelings had tempered. As for packing up the house, the family down the street had already taken the dining room set. She was pleased that the Queen Anne cherry table, chairs, and breakfront that had been her mother's, would now enjoy many more years of use.

She had not forgotten about the man on the bike, nor the crazy bird, nor the infamous Officer Polly and the mysterious purse incident. She had also not forgotten Father Elway's words to the officer that day when everything had gone haywire, "Ellen was meant to stay." If that were true, then, why? He would have to know that she wasn't about to buy into any of that religious hocus-pocus. In any case, the affable priest had something on his mind, and although she wasn't completely comfortable with the prospect, at ten, purely out of respect, she rode the bike to the abbey.

Chapter

KATE GANNON SAT in her living room, looking over the list of things to be done before her wedding day, and things were pretty much under control. As usual, Matt had been a big help. Now and then, she had to pause to consider the blessing he had become in her life and how she never would have imagined only months earlier that she would find the love of her life in a tiny hamlet far from her Brooklyn home. Father Elway had told her that wondrous things happened in Spiritu. It had taken her a while to see what he'd meant, especially with everything that had happened with the flower cottage.

She put the list down, thinking of Ellen. Was there anything wondrous that was possible for her dear friend? Kate felt guilty about having talked her into staying at a place she really had no interest in. Ellen had been through so much, none of it of her own doing, and now Kate prayed that Ellen would find at least a modicum of enjoyment away from her topsy-turvy world. She did pick up a hint of that the last time they spoke by phone.

Ellen had proven herself the dearest of friends when Kate struggled to get through the worst time of her life, losing her professorship at Milston College. Ellen had kept her own struggles to herself, not wanting to add more burdens onto what Kate was going through.

Something outside caught her eye. Through the window she saw a woman stepping from a two-tone blue DeSoto and making her way toward Ellen's front door. Kate knew she had seen the woman before; she recognized the car but couldn't place her. Since Ellen wasn't there, she decided to go out to see if she could help.

The woman had already gone up the steps and rung the bell.

"Hi," Kate called out. "I'm the next-door neighbor. Miss Castle isn't home. Can I help?" When the woman turned, Kate knew immediately who she was—Tony's new owner. "Oh, I know you. We met the day you picked up Ellen's boxer."

The woman came back down the steps of the Brownstone, a woeful look on her face. "Yes, hello. I remember you too." She turned and gestured toward the house. "Do you know when Ellen will be back. I have a slight problem."

"With Tony? Is everything okay?"

"Well, nothing that's his fault," the woman said. "We discovered that my son is allergic to dogs. So, we can't keep Tony. The children are heartbroken."

Kate knew it had broken Ellen's heart to find a new home for Tony. Was this good news or bad? Ellen would get Tony back, but he would still need a new home. "I'm sorry to hear this. Ellen was so happy that Tony would be with you and your family. I can only imagine how disappointed your son is."

"We all are. Tony is a wonderful dog. He's in the car," the woman said. "I wouldn't dream of finding another home for him without checking back with Ellen. Do you know how I can reach her?"

"She's away on Long Island and a little hard to reach. But I will keep trying, and I'll explain everything. In the meantime, you can leave Tony with me. He knows me; we've been friends for a long time."

"So, what do you say, Ellen Castle?"

Father Elway had a look of such happy expectancy that Ellen didn't know how to answer. The last thing she wanted to do was appear disrespectful by dismissing his offer out-of-hand, but it seemed …

"You probably think it's ridiculous. I understand." He stood. "Why don't you think it over and let me know later on today."

On her way to the front door, she took a detour and walked across the large reception room to find Mrs. Wick in the kitchen. When Ellen opened the door, she saw Mrs.

Wick's yellow-aproned figure at the vintage wooden table, snipping string beans. Thomas sat across from her, holding a screwdriver and a hand-mixer."

"Are you staying for lunch?" Mrs. Wick asked, gleeful as usual.

"Perfect timing," said Thomas. "Maybe you can help make the sandwiches."

"I'm actually here on a business matter, and I'm so glad you're both here." Ellen set her cloth purse on the side bar. "I need your advice."

Mrs. Wick stopped what she was doing. "Father has talked to you, hasn't he?"

"You know about it?"

Mrs. Wick gestured toward Thomas. "We both do."

Ellen sat on the bench next to the seminarian. "I'm so surprised. I don't know what to make of it."

"Do it," said Mrs. Wick, back to snipping string beans.

"Great idea," said Thomas, tightening a screw in the hand-mixer.

"Just like that?"

"Just like that," said Father Garrett, standing in the doorway. He had just come back from the cold shed, where they stored the week's apple harvest. He took a seat on the stool near the sink. "Father Elway was right when he said we can really use the help. You're a businesswoman, perfect for the job." He picked a few grapes from the yellow bowl on the counter. "Go to Brooklyn, do what you need to do, then come back here. We'll send Thomas with you to help, if you like."

Thomas put down the screwdriver and turned directly to Ellen. "Once things get going here with the veterans, I won't be able to divide my attention. You can easily do the office work I've been doing. You're a natural."

Father Elway had explained to her that there would now be four more Korean War vets coming instead of the additional two they had been planning for. She could understand how impossible it would be for Thomas, even with Father Garrett's help, to work with all of the veterans and continue his office work for the abbey. Ellen would still pack up her house, but instead of moving to an apartment, she would move into the residential part of the abbey upstairs where Mrs. Wick's lodging was located. "Think of it as a useful transition," Father Elway had said with that fetching smile of his. "It benefits us in a way that also benefits you with a salaried role and lodging in a place with people you've come to know."

Father Garrett headed for the door, patting Ellen's shoulder on the way out. "I came to tell you to call Kate."

Chapter

Twelve

ON THE WAY back to her bungalow, Ellen thought over the whole crazy idea. Was it really so crazy? Or was it just so unexpected and so benevolent or … God help us … wondrous that she couldn't fathom how it came about, even though it really sounded logical. Why not do it? She had grown comfortable with them, secure in their acceptance of her for who she was, someone who no longer believed as they did. No pressure. She could live among them, temporarily, of course. That was the deal. She would be fine doing the work Father Elway and Father Garrett needed.

Father Elway had explained that her living quarters would be an ample, two-room suite, with her own bath, just like Mrs. Wick's, and that, however temporary, she could furnish it to her own liking, bringing with her whatever items she wished. Kate's fiancé, Matt Reagan, a general contractor, who still did construction work for the abbey when needed, would help with his pick-up truck and a trailer if need-be.

There were two important factors: she was not asked to make a long-term commitment; she would have to decide quickly. The veterans were due to arrive, possibly in the next day or so.

Okay. Okay. She'd do it. What was there to lose? She hadn't yet signed the lease for the new apartment. Over the years, she had placed many tenants in that apartment building, for which the landlord was happy to show her appreciation. She walked into her bungalow and immediately called Kate. "You are not going to believe this."

"You sound so … happy," Kate said. "What's going on?"

"Kate, you won't believe what happened. I'm actually going to be living, at least for the short term, at the abbey."

"Are you kidding?"

"No. Sounds ridiculous, doesn't it? But Father Elway needs office help, and I'm available. Why not? I won't be in the bungalow, though. That's closing down at the end of the week with all the others. I'll be living at the abbey, upstairs where Mrs. Wick lives."

"How did this happen?"

"Some change of plans that took the priests by surprise. They suddenly realized they're going to need extra help, and they're going to need it fast. So, they asked me to work with them … you know … temporarily, as I said. It's going to be a bit crazier for me, if that's possible, because I've got to be all packed up this week."

"Oh … uh … wow. That's … incredible news."

"What's going on? You sound strange. Are you okay?" There was a momentary silence. "Kate?"

"Tony is back."

"Oh, God. Is he okay? Did something happen?"

"Not anything you would think. Tony is fine. The family is fine, except that the boy is allergic to dogs. No one had a clue about it. They're truly sorry and heartsick. But they had no choice. They brought Tony back today. He's here with me."

Ellen's thoughts fired off in ten directions. Her beautiful Tony. She couldn't wait to see him. But she would only have to part with him all over again, find him another good home. It had taken weeks last time. This time around she didn't have weeks. Kate wouldn't be able to keep him for as long as it took; she had her own time challenges with her new job and the wedding right around the corner. "Well, it did seem too good to be true, didn't it? Such a lovely family. I'll just have to start from scratch to find him another home."

"I know it's all going to work out. Don't worry. I'll help any way I can, Ellie, you know that."

"The way it looks now, I'll be home tomorrow. I'll tell Father Elway I can't accept the job. I'll find another home for my buddy. It'll take a little time, but it's okay. Thank you, Kate, for being there for me and for Tony."

"I wish there was something I could do. I'm in the city all day. There wouldn't be anyone here for him. Otherwise, I'd keep him for as long as it took."

"I know you would. Honestly. I know." She sighed. "I'll see you tomorrow."

Ellen hung up the phone and sank into the chair, a dizzying jumble of thoughts banging around in her head. "God," she said quietly, as she looked up at the ceiling, "if there is a God, do you see why I cannot, no matter what, cannot trust you, cannot ever trust you? Can you see that?" She pounded on the arm of the chair and yelled. "Can you see that?"

She got to her feet and paced the floor. "Do you understand? Do you see how impossible it is to even begin to believe in a God who just lets people stew in their misery? One thing after another and another. Loss upon loss." She reached over, and in a fury, swept the small stack of magazines across the room. "My mother always said you were a God of mercy. Ha! That's a laugh. I see no mercy in you, and you are not my God. You never will be."

She went to the kitchen sink, poured water into a glass, and took a sip, her hand trembling. Father Elway needed her answer as soon as possible, but some flash of reason allowed her to realize that she couldn't call him in this state. She went back into the living room, picked up all the magazines, and put the stack on the table, feeling guilty about her flash of temper. She stood looking through the screen door, tears welling up, then went out onto the porch. Why not just leave? That's it. Leave everything. Get on that train to Brooklyn and never come back. She'd rent a car, take Tony, and drive until the wheels fell off. Start fresh. She may have lost everything, but she wasn't broke. The remainder of the money from her bonds and the sale of her brownstone was enough to make a new start somewhere, modest as it may be, preferably far away. Yes, the farther the better. But for now, she needed to talk to Father Elway.

She went around the side of the bungalow and took out the bike, then pedaled as fast as she could in and out of the lanes before slowing down with a huff. She wasn't twenty anymore. The streak of tears had dried on her face, and while an odd sense of loss nagged at her, the rush of air as she moved along was comfortably warm, allowing her to settle into a slow, mindless rhythm, drifting lane after lane—Warbler, then Starling, then … She squeezed the brakes so hard she nearly unseated herself, stunned. Up ahead on the right, just where she had last seen him, exactly where she had left him sitting there on the folded windbreaker mat—the man with the white hair.

She slid from the seat as if in slow motion, then approached him with caution, staring as she went. How was this possible? "What happened to you?" she asked, more demanding than sympathetic. "How did you get here?"

"You know all that. Oh, but I'm much better now," he said, giving her a quizzical look. "I simply waited. You said you'd be back. Thank you."

"I was back. Days ago. You were gone. We drove through

every lane. Round and round. How can you be here now in the same spot, exactly where and how I left you?"

"You said you were only going to the abbey. I knew you wouldn't forget about me. You just strike me as that kind of person." He ran his hand through his hair. "Timing is everything, isn't it? If we just wait …." His voice trailed off as he attempted to stand. Reluctantly, Ellen put her hand under his elbow for support. "I'm actually okay now." He took a few steps back and forth as Ellen stood watching in disbelief.

"I don't know what this is all about, what you're up to, what kind of a crazy game you're playing, but Father Garrett and I drove these lanes. All of them." She made a sweeping motion with her arm. "In one lane and out the other, round and round. I may not have known exactly how to find my way, but Father Garrett knows every twig and pebble on every one of these lanes. You were nowhere to be seen. No sign of you or your stupid, crippled up bike or that dumb windbreaker we used for a mat. You were gone." She kicked at the damaged bike with her toe. "You and your silly bike."

He brushed at his khaki trousers. "I see the grass has finally dried. Things just have a way of working out … even when we tumble and fall, tumble and fall." He gave her a side glance and a wink. "It all works out. No matter what."

"I don't see how anything has worked out. You disappeared, wasting my time as well as Father's. And you still have no usable bike." She got back on hers. "Well, mine is still working, and I'm fresh out of good deeds for the day, you crazy man."

"I understand," he said, picking his bike up off the ground. "But look, mine works too. As long as I hold up the front, I can walk along, rolling it on its back wheel." He circled around, then went on straight ahead toward Warbler, calling back to her. "See, I said things work out, one way or another. Things go wrong and things go right. All in good time. Trust that they will. No matter what."

For a long moment after he was out of sight, Ellen remained, straddling the bike, imagining that this time she must surely be going mad. Was this how it worked? Things that can't possibly happen, happen? Or we only think they do? Things like a crazy bird, although, in truth, everyone at the abbey knows about that bird. But what about this? She imagined that Father Garrett must have had a hard time believing that there had actually been a man in the grass in the first place. What would he think now if she tried to explain this? She couldn't possibly tell him. She shook her head in frustration. Oh, how she needed to leave this crazy place. And she still had to let Father Elway know she couldn't take the job. What on earth was going on? The one question she didn't dare ask – "What next?"

Chapter
Thirteen

Thomas opened the door wide as Major O., as he was called, and three younger men in uniform stepped out of the dark olive army sedan and made their way up the stone walk leading to the lodge.

"Major O., Good to see you, Sir."

The Major shook the seminarian's hand. "Good to see you too, Thomas." He turned to introduce the others as they came forward. "I'd like you to meet Corporal Joseph Hopper, Sergeant Edward Banacki, and Corporal Eugene Tarantino.

As Father Augustine and Father Pelletier greeted the men and tended to their duffle bags, Thomas led the way to one of the round tables in the fireside room, a large yet welcoming place, lit with wrought iron chandeliers below a dark beamed ceiling. Father Xavier had set out sandwiches, along with a choice of cold beer or soda on a crisp white tablecloth.

"We're all so glad you're here," Thomas said. He was always told ahead of time about the individual backgrounds of the veterans who came to the abbey. Corporal Hopper, aged 21, Chagrin Falls, Ohio, middle child of five, son of the local clock-store owner. His was a prosthetic lower left leg, the result of a land mine near the Yalu River. Sergeant Banacki, 31, oldest boy in a West Virginia coal-mining family. His was a steel plate in his head and deafness in his right ear caused by a mortar attack as he fought alongside a New Zealand artillery crew near Kumsong. And Corporal Tarantino, 22, Teaneck, New Jersey, only child of a single mom whose husband had died of tuberculosis when Eugene was a child. He bore no signs of physical injury; the trauma he had suffered was the result of being the only survivor of a bomb that killed everyone else in his platoon.

Major O., 44, career army, with a patch over the right eye he had lost at Sainte-Mere-Eglise nine years earlier during the D-Day invasion of Normandy. Although the injury took him permanently off the front lines, he distinguished himself in various strategic command positions over the years that followed. And having experienced first-hand what the returning wounded were going through, he chose his current administrative role as he approached his twenty-year retirement date option. The big question for him now: Should he retire or continue in what he considered to be the most gratifying role of his career?

Over lunch, the group shared stories about home and rehab, and the promise of returning to everyday life.

"You'll find your stay here the perfect place to transition," said the Major before wagging a thumb in Thomas's direction. "And I think, by now, you can see you'll be in good hands."

With enthusiastic nods from the young men, Thomas explained. "The abbey has proven to be a highly useful and enjoyable last stop on the journey back home. This can actually be a fun and rewarding time." He gestured to the surroundings. "It's a large property where much goes on. You might choose to work alongside the priests to help with the maintenance and repairs needed for our rentals and our main building, even things to be built or mended here at the lodge. Maybe you'll help with whatever farm work we have going on right now, little as it is, but there's still apple picking, and we are anticipating a fine pumpkin crop this year." They laughed. "Or you might like helping out with the baked goods at the Nassau Farmer's Market. You'll find out what a crazy, fun place that is, with great food, by the way. You may try your hand in the kitchen. Father Xavier and Mrs. Wick are excellent cooks. You can help them and they can help you if you like. Who knows, you might decide to become a line cook or a chef. Whatever it is, it'll be great therapy, and you may find it very useful when it comes to employment opportunities unless, of course, you're planning to make use of the GI Bill to go to college." He picked up a sheet of paper. "I've given each of you a schedule that will help you get organized. You'll find it in your room. It's going to be important for you to begin getting comfortable again with a daily routine."

Thomas turned as Mrs. Wick came through the door with a platter of freshly baked cookies. "Here's Mrs. Wick now. She's definitely someone you'll want to get to know," he said with a chuckle.

"I hope you like cookies," she said, delighted. "Oatmeal raisin and shortbread." She turned to the Major. "And here's a special goody bag for you to take with you, Major O.. I'm happy to see you again."

"Ditto." The Major took the bag, patting her shoulder. Then he turned to Thomas. "No offense, my friend, but I've always said that Mrs. Wick is the highlight of my trip here. None better."

Her presence brought a cheer from the group as they helped themselves to the platter.

"Mrs. Wick uses her kitchen as a cover." Thomas said with good humor. "She actually runs things around here. She's also responsible for the basket of goodies you'll find up in your rooms. Speaking of which." He nodded toward Father Augustine and Father Pelletier, who had joined the group. "Please allow these fine men of the cloth to show you to your rooms. They've already put your bags there. And if there is anything at all that you need, just dial zero on the telephone in your room. Oh, one more thing—you'll each make a trip to our local town here, Hicksville." He saw their smirks. "I know. Funny name, but a great little place, quaint and historic. Movie theater, bake shop, ice cream parlor. A tavern. It'll give you the chance … your first, I believe … to go off on your own, take the bus, and so on. You'll have our full support for this, as well as everything else you do here. For now, just relax and settle in. Supper down here at 6:00."

Corporal Tarantino extended his hand. "I can't tell you what this means to me." He looked at the others. "To us. Thank you, Thomas. And Major. And you, too, Mrs. Wick."

"Yes, thank you so much," said Corporal Hopper, shaking Thomas's hand, before saluting the Major. Sergeant Banacki followed suit.

"We're all looking forward to finally getting back home," the Sergeant said. "Thanks so much for helping us do that. We appreciate it."

Major O. tucked his wheel cap under his arm. "I'll be back in about a week or so, fellas, with three more. I'm pretty sure you know one of them—Corporal Selby. Rick."

"Oh, that's great," said Tarantino. "He's a good guy. We all did rehab together with him." He put his head down. "Both legs."

"Yes, both legs," said the Major, "but he's as ready as you are. You're all going to make it."

Mrs. Wick offered a cheerful goodbye, then turned to the three veterans. "I'll be seeing a lot more of you. Be sure to tell me and Father Xavier some of your favorite things to eat."

As the men departed, the Major turned to Thomas. "Okay if I stop in to say Hi to Father Elway and Father Garrett?"

"They'd be disappointed if you didn't."

They shook hands. "Thanks again for all your help, Tom. See you in a few days."

Ellen felt exhausted as she pedaled up to the abbey. Things were taking a toll. Nonsense things. Crazy upside-down things. As she walked the bike up the abbey's circular gravel drive, she noticed a dark olive sedan driving away and wondered if that was the military car that had brought the veterans. It was Father Garrett who answered the door.

"Good to see you today, Ellen. Come in, come in."

Ellen knew his exuberance had to do, at least in part, with his belief that she would be working with him and Father Elway, especially now that the veterans had just arrived with more on the way. She dreaded telling them her news.

Ellen motioned toward the driveway. "I believe I just saw a military car."

"That's right," he said, clasping his hands. "Our veterans are here. Saints be praised, you couldn't be joining us soon enough."

"Is Father Elway here? I need to speak with you both."

The lanky priest led the way to the library, where Father Elway worked at his desk.

He stood as soon as they entered. "Ah, here you are on a day of days—the men have arrived, we've just gotten to see an old friend, and now you, as if on the wings of angels. Please have a seat."

"I'm sorry that I can't stay, Father. Please forgive me."

The two priests looked at each other, then back at Ellen. "Now, you must sit, please, and tell us what's happened. We can tell something is wrong."

She remained standing, feeling reluctant, even a little foolish to have to explain that the reason she couldn't take this job that was clearly so important to them was because of a dog. "Something has happened at home. Something that … that I have to attend to, and it's going to take a while to do it." She dropped her head. "I'm truly sorry."

"Won't you please let us help you," Father Elway said.

"Father Elway, Father Garrett, I've come to trust you both enough to believe you would help me if you could. Thank you for that. It means more to me than you know. But this is something that … I can't get into."

They watched her in silence, as she looked from one to the other. "Honestly, I know you would help if you could, but this is something … you know … out of your line of work, you might say."

They kept silent.

"It's about my dog." She had a feeling they'd stare her down until she came out with it.

"Tony?" Father Elway blurted out. "Has something happened to your buddy?"

Ellen looked at them in shock. "You know Tony? Tony, my dog? You know about him?"

"Only what Kate mentioned," said Father Garrett. "We felt

very sad that you had to find a new home for your beloved friend."

"Yes, thank you," she said, a bit mindlessly. How on earth? "The problem now is that the family had to return him. The young boy is allergic to dogs. It took me weeks to find a good home for him, and now I have to go through the whole process all over again."

"No, you don't," said Father Elway, full of delight. "Bring him here."

"What?"

"Yes," said Father Garrett. "You have to admit we've got the best home for Tony right here. We've needed a good mascot for some time. We used to have a collie. Oh, she was a good one. 'Fiona.' We were at such a loss when she passed away. She was fourteen."

"Fourteen years," said Father Elway, "And a friend to all. She romped around the property, sleeping in the sun, lying right over there by that big old desk. You can still see some scratch marks."

Father Garrett laughed. "Getting in Mrs. Wick's hair, stealing biscuits every chance she had."

Ellen was too stunned to comment.

"Well, what about it?"

"What do you say?"

Overwhelmed, Ellen reached out her arms for a joyous, if tearful, hug. "I've never hugged a priest. Now, I'm hugging two. I hope I'm allowed. I don't know what to say."

"Well," said Father Elway, "I believe that's because everything has already been said."

Chapter

Fourteen

As soon as Kate opened the front door of her Brooklyn brownstone, Tony came tearing across the living room for his happy reunion.

"Oh, good boy. Good boy. Yes. Yes. You're a good boy." Ellen rubbed his head, and when he plopped down at her feet, she scratched his belly, his tail wagging back and forth on the floor in pure delight. The eighty-pound canine jumped to his feet again and circled her, nudging her legs, and licking her fingers. A powerful dog, he jumped to nuzzle her chin, nearly knocking her off her feet. "Okay. Okay. Good boy," she said. "Oh, how I've missed you."

When she and Kate finally sat down in the living room, each with a cold bottle of Coke, Tony sat staring up at her, his blunt, square muzzle resting on her knee. "I can't believe this," she said, rubbing Tony's head. "It's all been such a crazy time. And I haven't even told you what happened when I spoke to Father Elway and Father Garrett."

"Nothing bad, I hope."

"You know, I have to admit, nothing is ever bad when I speak with them."

"Hmm. Sounds like you've had a bit of a change of heart."

"Only in some ways, yes. Strange things happen out there. All kinds of things. I swear, Kate, some of them have left me scratching my head, wondering if I'm losing my marbles. But here's the good news—Father Elway wants me to bring Tony to the abbey. To stay."

Kate put her Coke down on the side table. "You're kidding!"

"You have no idea how glad I am that it's true. And once they explained, it made total sense. It just never crossed my mind that an abbey would welcome a dog as a pet. He could be their mascot, they said. Crazy, isn't it? But they had a collie for fourteen years."

Kate leaned forward, pushing back a soft curl of brown hair. "How amazing, and I would never have thought of it as a possibility either. Oh, thank God." She looked at Tony. "You'll have a brand-new home. The best. Yes. Yes, you will," she repeated as the brawny mastiff sauntered over.

"How are your wedding plans coming along?"

Kate sat back and let out a long sigh. "Hectic, but still on track. Time is going by fast. I'm sure I'll be ready, but I still get butterflies when I think how it all happened with Matt. The new job. All of it. Gives one hope, don't you think?"

"If you mean men, well, don't look at me. I think my time

has come and gone."

"How can you say that? You're still a young woman. Look at yourself in the mirror. When you're happy, you glow. Find more ways to be happy."

Ellen turned the soda bottle in her hand. "Truth is, craziness and all, I've had more moments of happiness lately than I'd had in these last many months as the bottom started dropping out of my life."

"Sounds like a minor miracle to me."

Ellen looked away. "I knew you were going to say that, but you know I don't believe in miracles."

"Just because you don't believe in miracles doesn't mean they don't happen." She moved to the edge of her chair. "And not all of them are big and showy. Everyday life can be filled with minor miracles if we only pay attention." She leaned forward. "I want you to ask Thomas to show you the jacket."

No matter what the situation involving Kate, there was always the possibility of surprise, of expecting the totally unexpected. Sometimes, it was okay, sometimes not. "What kind of a jacket?"

"Just tell Thomas that Kate said to show you the jacket."

Ellen spent the next three days filling a few boxes to take with her to the abbey and packing up the rest to donate to St. Vincent de Paul. She had seen her new living quarters next to Mrs. Wick's and was pleased that it was actually an ample-sized suite. She knew she could take her bedroom set along with one of the loveseats, her favorite winged-back chair, and a couple of side tables, as well as incidentals. Kate's fiancé, Matt Reagan, rented a trailer from a company named U-Haul, and, along with a friend, delivered Ellen's things to the abbey. On his next trip, he delivered Tony to his new home.

In the midst of it all, Ellen had moments when she was taken with her own happiness and had to stop and wonder about such a curious turn of events, temporary as it all might be.

Chapter

Fifteen

It was during her first week living at the abbey that Ellen encountered one of the veterans. She had come upon him unexpectedly in the gazebo where she had gone to read, and he had gone to enjoy his lunch.

"Oh, I'm so sorry," she said, backing out the screen door after entering without realizing it was occupied.

"It's okay. It's fine," said Corporal Hopper, getting to his feet, awkward and off-balance.

The season had finally come around to the last of the steamy hot days. The young man, dressed in a white T-shirt and khaki Bermuda shorts, was the first person she'd ever seen with an artificial leg.

She held up the used Erle Stanley Gardner novel she'd bought for fifteen cents at the Nassau Farmer's Market. "I didn't mean to intrude. I was going to read a bit. I'll just go over to the patio on the other side of the chapel."

"Oh, no, Ma'am. That won't do. I'd be pleased if you joined

me." He waited for her to take a seat at the redwood picnic table, then offered her the small plate of cookies Mrs. Wick had provided with his lunch.

Ellen wasn't sure what to do. The lodge was at the far end of the property. She hadn't expected to run into one of the veterans. She didn't even know if she was permitted to engage them. Should she stay or leave? She didn't want to end up accidentally offending the young man in any way. He had such an expectant look, such a welcoming smile. He was bright-eyed and nice-looking, with a glint of blonde in his brown, brush-cut hair. Except for the faint curve of a scar along his left jawline, his skin was smooth as a boy's. He was a boy, after all, a boy whose mother likely had told him not to kick the football into the neighbor's yard, to be careful climbing trees, riding his bike in traffic, driving his father's car. A boy with his leg blown off.

"Thank you," she said. "I'm happy to meet you, Corporal. I'm Ellen Castle."

"Nice to meet you, Miss Castle. And, please, Ma'am, call me Joe."

"Nice to meet you, Joe. You can call me Ellen."

The young man reached down and pulled something on his prosthetic that clicked, enabling him to bend his leg and sit back down. "This is my second one," he said, cheerful. "My first leg … the one they gave me last year when I arrived at the rehab center … that was not as good as this one. Sometimes, I couldn't get it to work." He chuckled. "I'd have to plop into a chair with my left leg sticking straight out." He patted the metal appendage. "This one's more advanced. They tell me I'll probably get a new one every couple of years as they come up with better and better ways to make these things work."

To show that she was comfortable with the situation, Ellen helped herself to one of the cookies. "How do you like it here? The food's wonderful, isn't it?" She sat opposite him.

"Oh, yes, Ma'am. Good as my mom's, and that's saying a lot." He looked about. "This is a special place. I never figured on anything like this as my last stop before home. A monastery. Imagine. And I'm not even Catholic. Too bad they can't accommodate all of us, just five or six out of almost twenty-five who'll be transitioning. And there'll be more coming back home after that. They've signed an armistice, but there's still fighting going on. That means more of this." He gestured to his leg. "Korea was brutal, but then what war isn't? So, I've got to say – Eddie, Gene, and me – we're blessed, all right. Rick also. He'll be here with the other two or three next week. Boy, oh, boy. Blessed, for sure." He leaned in, more serious now. "You're the first true civilian I've met since all this happened. I mean, the others here are civilians, too, but they're part of the process. If you don't mind my saying, you seem like a nice, regular person to kind of practice on. You know what I mean?"

"Yes, I do, Joe. And thank you. That's a great compliment."

"People are going to react the minute they see us. They don't know what they're supposed to do or say. Many of us are okay by now, but people aren't. The military does a lot to prepare us to go home, but I don't think the folks at home are prepared. It's all new to them, like you, for example. No offense, but I saw your face when you opened that screen door. It's natural to be uncomfortable. We've got a bit of a rough ride ahead of us, but we're all more okay than you would think."

Ellen was captivated by this young soldier's exuberance. How does someone who went through war and shellshock, injury, scars, loss of a leg, loss of fellow soldiers, friends who might have died right before his eyes in horrific ways … how can he look, sound, and behave so normal? No, better than that—so outgoing and positive.

"What do you do, if you don't mind me asking? Have you been here long?"

"No, not very long, but I have to agree this is a special place. I'm living here temporarily to help the priests while Thomas is working with all of you." She paused, "By the way, how did you get over here from the lodge? You surely didn't walk. Did you?"

"Yes, Ma'am. All the way from the other side of the property. I do have to use a cane if I have to walk far. You've been over there, right?"

"No, not yet."

"Oh, it's a ways away, all right. I had to just poke along. Might have bitten off more than I could chew. Took me forty minutes. I was pretty worried after twenty minutes or so.

Grass, mulch, woodsy kind of ground. I wanted to try it out, but it's a pretty bumpy walk."

"Seems to me you're pretty brave."

"I need the practice, and I had good company. They have this really friendly dog. A boxer."

"Tony."

"Oh, great name."

"I still think you're a brave young man, Joe Hopper. You all are. I can't imagine where any of us would be without men like you who fight for us."

"Just promise to remember all the ones that didn't come back from the fight, including all the women. Don't forget the women, mostly nurses, of course. But many of them died, too. People don't realize."

Later in the day, Ellen brought some papers into the library for Father Elway to sign. Her work centered around keeping things organized and timely since the priests spent a portion of their day in prayer and counseling. She and the abbot had found a comfortable routine that worked for both of them and Father Garrett, who reviewed all the bills that came in for Ellen to sort through. There was also a smattering of random donations, many of which became part of the funds that the abbey used to support various charitable causes. It had become clear to Ellen that it was more important for them to help others than to satisfy their own particular wishes and needs.

Having believed that Spiritu was as unknown to others as it had been to her, Ellen was surprised by the number of inquiries as to whether the abbey was available for spiritual conferences and retreats. It was Father Elway's practice to respond with a personal, polite refusal, a task that now fell to Ellen to create for Father's signature. She was also surprised to learn that every month, either Father Elway or Father Garrett traveled to a different church, many times out of state, to speak at a Sunday Mass about the work and needs of the abbey and to remind people that there was much work to be done to help our military returning from Korea.

"I met one of the veterans today, Father," she said. "Joe Hopper, Corporal Hopper. What a wonderful young man. It was by accident in the gazebo, and I wasn't sure if it's okay. Is it?"

Father Elway, straight-backed as usual in his large, worn, leather chair, looked up from his papers, fixing his eyes on her. "Can't think of a better tonic."

Something in his lingering gaze made her wonder if he was including her in that prescription.

"He's an amazing young man," she said. "To be honest, I wasn't sure if I was allowed to talk with him."

"Oh, yes. The more, the better. Makes everybody more comfortable."

She set a small stack of papers in front of him, noticing that two or three daily newspapers had been read and folded aside, as they were every day, most times still showing glimpses of headlines about President Eisenhower and the war. "He's very appreciative," she said. "He just feels bad for the ones that the abbey lodge can't accommodate."

"Pierces my heart. We went through the same thing some years ago, with the big war. All those men." He removed his reading glasses and dropped them onto the desk. "A disappointing state of affairs." He sighed, sitting back in his chair. "I suspect you have some acquaintance with great disappointment of your own. So, you know."

She chose to ignore the personal reference. "But what a wonderful thing you're doing for those who do come. And there will be more."

"For years now, it's been a dream of mine, a constant prayer, and Father Garrett's, to have a place large enough to really do some work, to even hold retreats. You've seen the mail."

Doesn't God even answer the prayers of his worthiest of servants? "Isn't there any way to raise the money?"

"Not the kind we'd need for such a project. As Father Garrett puts it, we're in miracle territory here. But just imagine." He put his glasses back on and returned to his paperwork. "Ah, well."

Working with him for some small part of most days, she had begun to notice the things one sees when more time is spent in someone's company—his ups and downs, the veins in his hands, the silvery strands threading his light brown hair, more than she had first noticed, his meticulous black vestments, the way he thumped his finger against his nose when trying to remember something. She enjoyed his company. All of them. She enjoyed being around all of them. Feisty Mrs. Wick, friendly Thomas, even the gentle, sometimes wry, and endlessly helpful, Father Garrett, whom she regretted being critical of at the start.

"Seems a pity," she said. "Such an enormous property, and no way to make the most of it."

"Yes, enormous, and grateful for that as the Island grows and this whole area continues to populate as it has in the last five years. City folk. Lots of city folk."

She pointed in the general direction of the gazebo. "I'm curious, Father. What's at the other end, if you go beyond the abbey lodge? What does this property border?"

"If you've been on the bus to Hicksville, you've passed it. Old Country Road."

"Old Country Road? Are you serious?"

"Oh, yes." He smiled. "No one realizes all that wooded frontage is ours. We'd like to keep it that way."

Mrs. Wick came in with a tea tray. "Father Garrett is on his way from the chapel. Will you take a cup, Ellen?"

"She has to," Father Elway jumped in.

"I guess I'll have to." She laughed. "He's my boss now."

Chapter

Sixteen

THE CHAPEL WAS located at the far end of the main abbey building, an extension of the corridor that led to the kitchen staircase and connected to it by a stone passageway with a row of low, arched openings facing the prayer garden. Each morning, the veterans who wished to attend seven o'clock Mass were shuttled over from the lodge by Thomas in the roll-about, a small four-wheeled vehicle pulling a seated trailer, a quirky rig put together by Father Pelletier for navigating the rough, less cultivated areas of the property. Ellen had seen them before daybreak from the second-floor window of her sitting room, catching sight of the headlights moving like giant lightning bugs at the far end of the woods.

An early riser who once had much to do before rushing off to her ten-hour workload, Ellen now enjoyed the quiet settling in of the day, a day she could look forward to even more since Tony's return. "Good boy," she said, leaning over to stroke his smooth, brown head. He, too, had settled in, taking his daily treks through the woods and finding the priests, wherever they were, whatever they were working on, whether in the wood shop, the tool house, or in one of the large garden sheds, often returning to make his way into Mrs. Wick's kitchen for a snack or a few laps of cold water she'd set out for him in a decorative blue ceramic bowl. Now and then, he joined Father Garrett in the all-around for a trip to the Nassau Farmer's Market, later on finishing his adventures with a nap at the side of Father Elway's desk. "Good boy."

The lovable hound had even found his way to the lodge, where the veterans enjoyed him as a welcome presence, creating a connection with home, something they had long been missing. Oddly, Ellen had found her own connection of sorts in the quaint lodging that had become her temporary home, especially now that a few of her own furnishings and pictures had been set in place. The heavily textured walls, deep gold in color, along with the arched door, had the same centuries-old story-book vintage as the rest of the abbey whose architecture she found enchanting.

Occasionally, Father Pelletier brought fresh-cut flowers from the garden for her and Mrs. Wick, and, in the morning, Ellen sipped coffee provided by Father Xavier as she skimmed the large, crisp pages of Good Housekeeping or Life Magazine, a serene entrée to the day ahead, a day like all the others now that she very much looked forward to. Whatever may lie ahead, she had decided to enjoy these moments to the fullest. She had even stopped dreading the face in the mirror, her brown eyes somehow brighter now, perhaps with the glint of hope. Her new hairdo helped—Mrs. Wick had been right about Lorraine, who tamed Ellen's dark waves into a more stylish fifties bob just below her ears.

A little before eight each morning, Mrs. Wick would knock at Ellen's door, her invitation to breakfast. She and Ellen would take their meal in Mrs. Wick's homey kitchen, the others in the large kitchen on the lower level. It was a pleasant ritual, and Ellen couldn't help wondering if Father Elway regretted the arrangement he'd made with her. After all, the work was fairly minimal and routine, the benefits much more on her side, she thought, than on Father's.

She considered it a bonus that she was also getting to know Mrs. Wick better. This quirky little woman seemed an indomitable presence among all of these scholarly, prayerful men and was obviously held in the highest regard by all.

"How did you come to work here?"

"My husband, Raymond, and I had a little Cape Cod not very far from here in Wantagh. This is where we came to Mass every Sunday. Raymond was a civil engineer, and so, we were blessed to have the kind of income that enabled us to buy the house outright. We never had a mortgage, which turned out to be especially important when the stock market crashed in 1929, and Raymond was one of many thousands who lost their jobs. Our savings, plus the occasional contracts the city offered him, helped us through the first couple of years of the depression, although it wasn't anywhere near as bad for us as for most. But …" she breathed a deep sigh, "in June of 1936, his heart just stopped."

"Oh, I'm so sorry, Mrs. Wick."

"I was completely lost. We had no children, and except for Grace—who was also widowed—just a couple of distant cousins in England. One day after Mass, Father Garrett, who was relatively new here at the time—he had been a teacher at Marymount before coming to the abbey—and had done Raymond's funeral Mass. He asked how I was doing. One thing led to another, and here I am."

Ellen had a sudden shiver. One thing led to another, and here she was.

Most afternoons, when her work was done, Ellen took a bike ride up and down the heavily shaded lanes, emptier now that the rentals were closed for the season. Entering Starling, she always held her breath, hoping that the mysterious white-haired man with his crumpled-up bike and his intrusive advice would not somehow appear again. She often felt a twinge of disappointment that this would all come to an end when the veterans left and Thomas returned to his administrative duties. He had mentioned that there would be more wounded coming back from Korea with the end of the war, even though the armistice had not yet stopped the fighting, but they would first go through what was typically a long period of medical and psychological treatment, followed by extensive rehabilitation before moving on to the abbey for their transition home. She would have to move on long before that.

More than once, when Kate had been staying there in Spiritu, Ellen had accused her friend of losing touch with reality. Is that what Ellen was now doing? Should she worry about herself the way she had worried about Kate? After all, what did any of this have to do with her life, her real life? But then, what exactly was her real life these days since every aspect of it had changed? Still, she had to wonder…

Labor Day weekend came around quickly, and on that festive Monday, Ellen joined Mrs. Wick and Grace for a fun afternoon watching the Firemen's Relays up near the pool on Levittown Parkway, a huge annual community tradition—four different fire stations coming to compete in events such as the fastest man up and down the truck ladder or the quickest team to un-roll and re-roll the truck's water hose for what was called a "water down." Some of the priests would attend, but not Father Elway or Father Garrett, who enjoyed hearing all about it over their next dinner. Truth was, the baseball season was winding down, and the race for the postseason was hot and heavy. Ellen's two favorite priests would be glued to the radio. More than once, she had seen them changing stations back and forth between the Yankees' game and the Dodgers' game.

Although the day was hot, summer had lost its exhausting humidity, and a nearby store offering an "air-cooled" respite provided cold drinks, ice cream, and sunglasses, along with shelves of sundries and snacks. More than a dozen firetrucks and engines parked in the large open field where the relays took place, with firefighters in full gear and helmets and the excited crowd responding to every challenge with loud cheering, laughter, and applause. Ellen had never seen anything like it.

"I told you it was fun," Mrs. Wick yelled to her above the crowd. Because of her work at the abbey, the woman knew many of the firefighters who came to Mass with their families.

"And even more fun," Grace chimed in, "when your favorite team wins. Ha."

As Ellen stood in the midst of the great, exuberant rabble, alongside the two women whom she now considered dear friends, something far off to the right caught her eye. Something red. Oh, please, not that crazy bird, she thought. In the glare of the afternoon sun, her sight finally settled on it, a young boy in red shorts. A little boy walking alone toward the street.

Ellen gasped and took off running across the grassy field. Only Grace noticed at first, then Mrs. Wick turned as she heard a young woman in a wheelchair scream, "My boy! Help me! My son!" A few others happened to take notice and began yelling for help as some started running. A young man walking from the store, dropped the cold drinks he carried and ran, yelling at the top of his lungs. "Billy. Stop! Billy, Billy. No. Stop!"

When the boy turned and saw Ellen running towards him with his father and others following behind, he began to run, laughing.

Ellen ran faster, panting heavily. "Oh, God." Within moments, the boy stepped off the curb, with Ellen nearly at his back, yelling and reaching for him as the oncoming vehicle rounded the curve. In a last burst, she grabbed hold of the boy's collar and spun around, tossing him back onto the grass as the car struck with a squeal of breaks.

Chapter

Seventeen

Louise Crowley entered the living room and shook her head. "Dad, you're still here?"

"I'll be going in soon," John Caraballo said. "They'll be okay. They don't need me every single minute, and I wanted to be here when you left to see Miss Castle." He looked down at his grandson. "She has a boo-boo too, you know."

The boy looked up. "Boo-boo."

"Yes," his grandfather said. "Boo-boo." He picked up the three-year-old and rested him on his knee. "You're getting to be a big boy. Too big to be so naughty."

"Pop-Pop is right, Honey. That nice lady also got a boo-boo. All because you were a naughty little boy. Do you understand?"

The boy dropped his head. "I sorry," he said, his voice faint. He looked into his grandfather's eyes and touched his face. "I sorry, Pop-Pop."

"You're going to see the nice lady today, Billy," the

grandfather said. "Will you tell her you're sorry, too."

The boy nodded again, then laughed. "She throw me. Like this." He swung his arm around over his head.

"She tossed you out of the way so the car wouldn't hit you," his mother said. "And then what happened?"

"I got a boo-boo." He pointed to his arm, the blue of his bruises fading. "Here." He touched the scab on his chin. "Here."

"What else happened?" his grandfather asked.

"Daddy ran fast, and Mommy yelled." The boy giggled.

"Yes, and the nice woman was hit by that car. She got a boo-boo, a big one."

"Ohhh." He was wide-eyed now, searching his mother's and grandfather's faces.

"Yes," his mother said, "and she has more boo-boos than you have. Being naughty is not nice. The lady got hurt saving you. Please remember this, Honey. And let's remember to say thank you to God for sending us the kind lady, okay?"

Billy nodded.

"Yes, thank God. And thank that woman," the grandfather said, shaking his head. "An angel, if there ever was one. How many people would do that, running into traffic at the risk of their own life?"

"Thank God it was only as bad as it was," Louise Crowley said. "I'd hate to imagine otherwise."

The grandfather looked wistful. "I was thinking about your mother, God rest her soul. There were days I prayed until I had no breath left in me. But no use. No use at all. When God decides this is your time, that's it. Off you go. But when God decides it's not your time, a volcano could swallow you up, and the angels would come from everywhere and lift you back to safety. It really is something." He hugged the boy. "You won't run off like that again, right?"

The boy dunked his head and covered his eyes with his hands.

"Peter and I are going to see her in about an hour, Dad. I have a feeling she will love to see Billy nearly all well and being a typical little boy. Do you want to come?"

"Not today. We don't want to overwhelm her. Give her some space. She's recovering, too. I'll go in another day or so, maybe tomorrow."

"Good idea," Peter said.

Billy jumped off his grandfather's lap and ran across the living room, grabbing his father around the knees as he entered the room.

"Hey, you rascal, you're pretty spry." He picked the boy up, careful of his sore arm. "Want to go see Mrs. Castle?"

The boy nodded, his finger curled in the corner of his mouth.

"We're taking her a check," Louise said.

Her father shrugged. "How much could make up for what she did? My first grandson. My only grandson."

Louise rolled the wheelchair to where her father sat. "Bye, Dad. Don't brood."

"You worry too much," he said. "I'll be going into work in a little while. Be good."

Kate Gannon adjusted the blinds against the glare of the late afternoon sun, then straightened the white sheers. "Better?"

"Better. But don't you have more important things to do than arranging my curtains? You're getting married next week, for heaven's sake. Matt will end up hating me."

"Matt can't get over what you did, Ellie. So, relax. We just want you to get better."

"I'm fine. Look." Ellen set the cane aside. "The doctor doesn't even want me relying on this." Now that the stiffness was subsiding and the extensive bruising had faded to calmer hues of green and yellow, Ellen was eager to get back to normal. Slow and cautious, she'd been up and about each morning during the last week, insisting on picking up where she'd left off in Thomas's little office off the main reception room, where she feared things were piling up.

"Just don't overdo it. Although I still think this was all one big ploy to get out of being my maid of honor." Kate looked out the window. "By the way, have you met this officer who brings the veterans? I only caught a glimpse of him as he was heading down the driveway to his car, but if I didn't already have the most handsome, wonderful man in the world, I believe I'd have given him a look."

Ellen looked up with a thin smile. "Once upon a time, I had the most handsome, wonderful man in the world. But that was long ago, Kate. All of that's over for me."

"You're crazy, but that'll be a discussion for another day, my friend. Right now, we have other business. Mrs. Wick says the family's coming this morning."

Ellen got up from her chair. "They've been so kind. They've called every day since the accident. They seem like very nice people. I don't know why I feel so nervous."

"I don't know either. You're a hero. You saved their child's life. Thanks to you, he only has a few scratches and bumps." She put her hand under Ellen's elbow. "Okay, now, off we go. You're sure you're okay with the stairs?"

Ellen moved in slow steps. "Stop babying me. I've been up and down these stairs for more than a week."

When they got downstairs, they found that Mrs. Wick had already seated the family in the reception area.

"I wish I could hug you," Louise Crowley said to Ellen, "but as you can see, I'm still tied to this contraption." She was a slight and attractive dark-haired woman with a pleasant demeanor, the blond-haired son, now a vision of sweetness, fair like his father, and not at all the feisty runaway.

Ellen walked over to the woman and leaned in for a hug, encircling Billy, as well. "You have no idea how happy I am to share this hug," Ellen said, stroking the boy's hair.

Peter Crowley dabbed discretely at the corner of his eye. "There isn't a single thing we could say or do that would be adequate for what you did, Ellen Castle."

"Anyone would have done the same," she said as Kate helped her to one of the brocade armchairs. "This is my friend, Kate. You've already met Mrs. Wick." She looked at the boy. "I feel bad that I had to give our little guy here quite a toss. That was awful." She smiled at Billy, who smiled back before burying his face in his mother's chest.

Peter reached over to pat his son's head. "Still hard to believe he just ended up with some scrapes and a bruised arm, which, I imagine, he'll have a lot more of as he grows up." He looked at his wife, "And ice cream goes a long way to fixing everything."

"It always works for me," Kate said.

"We're just so glad that it all turned out okay," Mrs. Wick said, handing out the glasses of lemonade she'd set on a tray. "We hope you'll be up and around soon yourself, Mrs. Crowley."

"Please, call me Louise," she said, then gestured to her leg. "Mine was just a careless stumble when we were in the Catskills a few weekends ago."

"I love the Catskills," Mrs. Wick said.

"Oh, I do too," Kate had taken a seat closer to the family. "Did you see anyone special?"

"Perry Como," Louise faked a swoon. "He was wonderful, and the comedian that opened the show was Myron Cohen. Hilarious."

"Thank you, Mrs. Wick." Peter Crowley took a sip of the

cold refreshment, then turned to Ellen. "So, what's the latest from the doctors, if you don't mind my asking?"

"Good news. The doctors poked and probed, took x-rays and such, but finally agreed it's mostly just bad bruising. There's a little hairline fracture that's already started healing. They insisted on my walking every day this past week. I'll be fine. And the people here at the abbey couldn't have provided better care and support. I'm embarrassed by it, actually. Like the guest who came and never left."

Peter Crowley ran his hand across the top of his head. "It was all pretty amazing—that car coming right at you. But that's how miracles work."

Here we go again with the talk about miracles, Ellen thought. Kate must be in hog heaven. "Believe me, I'm grateful. From what they've told me, when the car jammed on its brakes, it swung around to the left, and the rear of the car actually did me a favor by bumping me about fifteen feet back onto the grass." She laughed. "Rear to rear, you might say."

Peter put his glass down. "A scary moment all around. We got there just in time to pick up Billy as everyone around us jumped in to see what they could do for you and for us. The firemen were there, too, remember. They were great. Billy was terrified. We don't think he'll be quick to go running off after that. Right, kiddo?"

The boy didn't look up.

Louise took her husband's hand. "When Peter went to get

us cold drinks, I was sure I'd be fine with Billy, but this little scamp moves awfully fast, and honestly, in the blink of an eye he was gone." Her eyes welled up.

Kate brought her a tissue. "Thank God, it's all okay now. Everyone is okay."

Louise turned to see Tony coming out of the library, walking toward them, slow, calm, and curious. "Oh, what a beautiful dog."

"This is Tony," Mrs. Wick said. "Quite friendly and safe. He's Ellen's, but now he lives here with us."

Tony went directly to the wheelchair and gently nudged the boy's foot with his broad, square muzzle. Billy turned, then, wide-eyed with delight, scampered down from his mother's lap. The three-year-old looked the boxer in the eyes, laughed, and hugged him around the neck, as Tony licked the boy's ear.

Peter picked his son up and rested him on his knee. "Billy, what do you think? He's a good doggy. A good doggy." He turned to the others. "I've never seen him like this with a strange dog. Well, any dog, for that matter. He's usually scared, but it looks like he's making a new friend."

For another half hour or so, there was more talk and more lemonade, more playful boy and dog, more sharing and laughter. Father Elway and Father Garrett returned from hearing confessions in the chapel and joined in.

"A lovely family," Father Elway said, placing his hand gently on the boy's head. "Please know that you are most welcome to visit again, maybe for Sunday Mass or just to spend a bit of time in our beautiful prayer garden."

"You don't even have to be Catholic," Father Garrett said with a mischievous grin. "And we promise not to twist your arm about it." They all laughed. "All are welcome here."

"But before you go," Ellen said, "I must thank you both. I've been told that you're paying all of my medical expenses. I didn't expect that, and it really isn't necessary."

"Of course, it is," Peter Crowley said. "There's no way we could even think about your paying for anything. You saved our son. And ...." He reached into the pocket of his sport jacket. "There's more." He handed Ellen a folded paper.

She took the paper and opened it before realizing it was a check. "Oh, no. No," she said, looking at the number written there. She reached out to hand it back. "Absolutely not. I cannot possibly accept this kind of ..."

"You must," Louise cut in. "Really, Ellen. You must. Please."

Ellen shook her head. "I can't take this money. Look at this child. His life is all the payment anyone would want."

"That's a very noble thought," Peter said. "But please. And if there's ever anything I ... we ... can do for you. We have no idea what that might be right now, but my Louise here happens to be a very talented artist, and I just tag along as a struggling architect, new to that line of work but hopeful."

Ellen looked from one to the other. "Thank you both very, very much." She dipped her head. "I will never forget you."

"You'll hardly have the chance," Peter said. "My father-in-law is planning on coming by in the next day or so, if that's okay? We hope you'll see him. He's overwhelmed with gratitude."

"Of course, I'll see him. I'll be happy to. Please tell him."

With Father Elway's blessing and Tony sidling along to the front door, the family left.

Chapter

Eighteen

Carrying an opulent bouquet of pink and blue peonies set with baby's breath and tied with a large, white satin bow, John Caraballo stood aside at the front door as three young men in T-shirts and khaki trousers exited the abbey with laughter and only slightly hobbled steps.

"Thanks again, Mrs. Wick. You're wonderful."

"We love the roast beef sandwiches," one of them called back as they headed down the driveway where Father Garrett waited in the all-around.

"Please watch your balance on the gravel," she shouted.

"I promise we'll have more fish than you can handle when we return."

"Boy, that's a beauty," one of them said, pointing to the black Cadillac sedan parked on the other side of the curved drive.

"Maybe you can trade this in for one of those, Father."

They all laughed as they piled into the all-around.

"So sorry, Mr. Caraballo." Mrs. Wick opened the door wide for him to enter. "A bit of odd timing there. Such good boys. Please come in. The flowers are beautiful. Ellen will love them."

"I hope I haven't come at a bad time," he said.

"Not at all." She still had laughter in her voice. "We are mostly a quiet little place, but there's always the possibility that something is happening or about to." She led the way across the main reception area to the office where Ellen worked at her desk. "Ellen, Mr. Caraballo is here."

Ellen rose awkwardly when the two came to the doorway, just as her cane slid sideways to the floor.

"Oh, no, please. Don't get up," the man said, gesturing hastily for her to remain seated. "Please." He laid the flowers down, then picked up her cane and leaned it back against her side of the desk.

"Thank you, Mr. Caraballo." Embarrassed, her face flushed as she sat back down. "The flowers are beautiful. Thank you, again. But there was no need. It's just very nice to meet you. I met your lovely family the other day. They came for a visit." She gestured to a chair opposite. "Please."

"I'll get a vase," Mrs. Wick said, stepping out.

"I'm very happy to meet a real-life hero," the man said.

"There's too much hero talk around here, Mr. Caraballo."

"Please call me John." He reached over and shook her hand. "And before I say anything else, thank you from the bottom of my heart."

Ellen felt the depth of sentiment in his voice—this mature, strong-looking man perhaps more tender than he might at first appear. She closed her eyes and offered a slight bow of her head. "Believe me when I say that I am the thankful one … most thankful …." she said, "that it all turned out to be no more than it was."

"But only because of you." He looked about as if securing his composure. "The boy is my only grandson."

"Such a beautiful boy. Just beautiful. Your whole family, so thoughtful. They called every single day. And they have been much too generous."

"There couldn't be enough."

"I understand. There was no convincing Louise and Peter otherwise."

"It's odd," the man said, gesturing to the surroundings. "This place, I mean. An abbey. Odd that you would be in such a place, and yet, maybe not."

Ellen couldn't control her smirk. "You have no idea, Mr. Caraballo … John."

"I understand you live here."

"And work here. For now, yes. Temporarily. I'm in kind of a transition."

"Looks a little busier than I would have imagined. I saw three young men leaving here, going fishing, I think they said. Are they new priests? Seminarians? I'm curious. They looked like college kids."

"They're soldiers."

"Soldiers?" The word stopped him. He sat back. "But it sounded like they're staying here too. Is that true? Soldiers?"

"Yes. Actually, they're also in transition. You may have noticed that one or two of them are still just a little unsteady on their feet. Prosthetics."

"Who would have guessed?" Caraballo said. "An odd combination—recovering war veterans and a monastery. Your Mrs. Wick called after them as if they were her own."

"In a way they are," Ellen said. "You could say they belong to us all, you included."

"Quite a thing to know."

"One of the great missions of the abbey is to provide a temporary home to military men who were badly affected by the war. Many have suffered shell shock. Nearly all are amputees. They've had treatment and rehabilitation elsewhere, of course, and now they're ready to go home. This is their last stop before they do. A place to reacclimate, to get more of a true feel for being back to normal."

The man said nothing. Ellen could see he was processing what she said as his eyes looked over the room, settling on no one thing, giving her the feeling that she should explain a bit more.

"They don't actually live in this building. This is for the priests, our chapel, and so on." She gave a slight turn, pointing toward the window behind her. "There's a building at the other end of our property for the soldiers, only enough room for six or so. It's called the lodge. It has long been a dream of our abbot, Father Elway, to expand the lodge in order to accommodate many more. Between the big war and now Korea, you can imagine that there continues to be a great need."

"Yes, I can definitely imagine. So many died, so many have come back, still suffering the horrors. What a wonderful thing that this is a place that can help them. I never heard anything about this."

"I hadn't either. One of many surprises about the abbey."

"I'd like to know more."

"Well," she said, hesitating, as Mrs. Wick returned with a vase for the flowers. "I wonder. Is Thomas around?"

"He should be returning from the chapel any minute," Mrs. Wick said, placing the bouquet into the water.

"Do you know what his schedule is?"

"Let me find out," Mrs. Wick again excused herself.

Ellen turned her attention to John Caraballo. "Thomas is our seminarian. He's in charge of the soldiers, and…"

"Did I hear my name?" Thomas took a seat as Ellen introduced the man.

"So nice to meet you, Sir. We were very happy to meet your family the other day, especially that feisty little grandson of yours."

"Thank you, Thomas. That feisty part got him into a lot of trouble and didn't do much for this brave woman."

"Children will be children," Thomas said. Then he looked over at Ellen. "And heroes will be heroes."

"Oh, not again," Ellen groaned. "You all must stop with this hero talk."

John Caraballo kept his gaze on her. "You're blushing again."

Ellen reached over and turned the large vase of flowers. "I don't know when I've seen a bouquet this beautiful. Thank you, again, Mr. … John."

"I understand you're interested in knowing more about our Lodge," Thomas said. "Maybe taking a tour?"

"Only if it wouldn't be an inconvenience. I realize my request is out of the blue. I'd perfectly understand if we couldn't."

"Not at all. In fact, what are you doing for lunch? I'd be happy to have you join me for a bite. Mrs. Wick is serving roast beef sandwiches today."

"As long as it's no trouble," said Caraballo, "how can I pass up an invitation like that? Thank you." He rose from his chair, looking at Ellen. "I hope you'll be able to join us?"

"I'd like to, but I'm nearly caught up, and I'd better keep at it." She offered her hand; his felt strong and somehow comforting. "Very nice to meet you, John. And thank you again for these beautiful flowers. You couldn't have known that peonies are my favorite."

Father Garrett shook his head. "I'm sorry, Leo. I've tried everything. She won't listen to reason."

Father Elway tapped his finger on the desk blotter as the two men sat looking at each other while the Victrola provided a background of Chopin's Nocturnes. "How can she even think of such a thing?"

Ellen ducked her head around the opening to the library. "Am I intruding?"

"Perfect timing," Father Elway said. "Come in."

Ellen moved across the room in the slow, steady gait she'd gotten used to since giving up the cane altogether.

Father Garrett pulled a chair closer to the desk for her. "How are you today?"

"Better than yesterday. Better each day. I just thought I'd stop to say hello. I haven't seen much of you, Father Elway." She sat and gestured toward the music. "That's pretty."

"Who doesn't like Chopin?" the abbot said.

Father Garrett gave her a wary look. "You've been busy. You're not overdoing it, are you?"

Ellen laughed. "You're both too kind to me. I have work to do around here, remember? That was the arrangement."

Father Elway came from behind his desk and took a chair closer to Ellen. "Here's something that was not part of the arrangement." He held out the folded check in front of her. "What on earth is this all about?"

"Well, it does have a name, Father." She gave him a mischievous smile. "More than one, actually—a gift, a donation, a contribution, a thank-you."

"You know we can't take this," Father Garrett said.

"I don't know that, Father." She looked from one to the other. "Why is this a problem?"

"For one thing," Father Elway said, "it's fifteen hundred dollars, nearly enough to buy a new car."

"Exactly. Enough also to buy many things needed around here." She looked directly at Father Garrett. "And not that I don't love the all-around, but maybe it is time for a new car. And besides, what if I were a parishioner at Church who just dropped it into the collection basket? You wouldn't quibble."

"We'd still be unsettled," Father Elway said, "if we knew, as we do in this case, that the money could be put to better use for the giver."

"My brownstone is ready to close. With the money I'll have left over after paying certain expenses, I'll be all right for a while. Honest."

"Please, Ellen," Father Elway said, placing his hand on her arm.

For a long moment, she didn't answer. There was such soulful expectancy on their faces that it made her wonder. She recalled Father's words to her in the garden a few weeks back—If you should find yourself with even the slightest desire to talk about it, you can be sure it will be the right time. She looked from one to the other. "Do you have a few minutes?"

"Of course," Father Garrett said.

Father Elway kept his eyes trained on her.

Ellen drew a deep breath, exhaling with resolve. "My

mother," she began in a slow, low voice, "was a beautiful person. Meek. Kind. She had such faith. She taught me to pray. We prayed together. I remember at Christmas time when I was little and my father had gone to bed, she would sit with me on the floor near the tree and tell me the story of Mary and baby Jesus. She told it with such heartfulness that I thought they were part of our family." She chuckled. "I actually thought they would be at my aunt's or my grandmother's table for the holiday dinner."

"How beautiful," Father Elway said.

"I always prayed. I prayed for her when it was clear that she wasn't feeling so well and kept at it as her health grew worse." She looked down, rubbing her thumb. "I prayed by her bed when I saw her take her last breath. She was not even forty. I was fifteen."

"What a terrible loss," Father Garrett said. "How hard it must have been for you."

"I talked with Father Rosetti at Church. A wonderful man. My mother loved him. I wanted to know how God could take such a person." She pressed her lips together. "What could he tell me? Certainly not an answer that made me still believe that God was kind and loving. Merciful."

"How did your father take this loss?" Father Garrett asked.

"He was as wounded as I was. He buried himself in his work. He did his best." Ellen's eyes slowly swept the room for the memories. "He was a strict father. He could see that's what a motherless daughter would need. Maybe he was right. My aunts helped wherever they could." She stopped. "I'm so sorry. I really shouldn't take your valuable time telling you all this."

Father Elway straightened up. "Oh, please don't think that. What could possibly be a more valuable use of our time?"

She ducked her head in modest acknowledgement. "When I was twenty-three, I fell in love with a young man my father didn't approve of. My father was a strict, traditional Greek, and because of that, I had lived a very sheltered life. The young man was twenty-four, from a wonderful family. I'd never known anyone like him. It was as if he breathed life into me.

"Granted, my experience was very limited. Still, he was handsome, a hard worker. He worked with his father, who was a skilled carpenter. He also had the most wonderful sense of humor. We loved being together. We laughed. We enjoyed life in a way I had never known."

She moved in her chair. "At first, it didn't seem to be a problem. My father was busy with his work, nervous, and worried all the time because we were in the midst of the Depression. He became obsessive about my future, afraid of what might become of me in this world where, in his mind, money dictated everything about your life. He began to see that my relationship with Patrick was a serious threat to my future—he would never accept anyone who was not Greek, in the first place, least of all some foolish Irishman, as my father called him, whom he believed would never be able to provide for me. To him, all an Irishman did all day was hang out in the local saloon."

Father Garrett removed his wire-rimmed glasses and rubbed the bridge of his nose. "All those old fears and prejudices. How destructive they were. Still are."

"In fairness, the Depression had taken its toll. My father saw the desperation of poverty in so many hopeless people. But Patrick and I weren't worried or desperate. We weren't hopeless. In fact, it was the opposite—we saw a bright future for us. Patrick talked about joining the military, as so many young men did back then. And once we were married, we would live on base wherever he was stationed." She looked from one to the other. "My father would have none of it."

"One night, he caught us trying to elope. He was furious. If I ever tried that again, he would disown me. By then, his health was failing. I couldn't abandon him, and, of course, he played on that. He banned me from ever seeing Patrick again. It's hard to believe this is possible now, in 1953, but back then …" Ellen cupped her forehead with her hand, struggling with the memory.

"My aunt was living with us by then. She was the sentinel at the gate with orders to receive all mail and take all phone calls. I was forbidden to go out of the house alone. The doctor said anything that upset my father might kill him. A month later, we moved away, leaving no forwarding address, and six months after that, we moved again. We moved twice more until my father believed the trail was cold." She looked down, her hands clasped and resting in her lap. "So much was taken from me—my mother, my freedom, the man I loved. I never saw Patrick again. And I never prayed again either." She looked up. "I'm sad to say I never did find my mother's merciful God."

"What a terrible time for you, Ellen," Father Elway said, touching her arm.

"But that's been the story of my life, Father. Loss upon loss upon loss, and all these years later, after running a successful business, losing that, too, along with everything I own. For a time, even Tony." She looked from one to the other. "Does God have any limits on what He takes from us? Or on the pain that we suffer?"

Father Elway stood and took a few steps before turning, his hands clasped behind his back. "You know, Ellen … so many times when these things happen … when life is especially hard … it's even harder to accept that He's got something else in mind for us. Something else that can fill us. And who ever knows what, where, or when that might be? It can be a difficult thing to understand, especially when we've lost so much and thrown in the towel on our faith." He sat again. "But if we know that the Lord is on our side, the way he turned out to be with Job, who also lost everything and then had it all restored to him, then we can endure the loss and bear the wait with a surprisingly peaceful heart."

The three sat there, silent. After a few moments, Father Elway stood and walked slowly to his desk, pensive, then returned. "I'm curious. What do you suppose your mother would say about all this?"

"She would be heartbroken. I know. My father's actions alone would have broken her heart."

"What do you think she would have done then?"

Ellen let out a cynical laugh. "Oh, she would have prayed until she was blue in the face. She would have prayed for a miracle that would never come." Ellen wiped a tear from the corner of her eye just as Father Elway handed her a clean, pressed handkerchief, for which she nodded her thanks.

"Amazing, isn't it," he said, "that your mother always kept right on praying, right on believing? Why do you suppose she did that?"

"I don't know, Father," she said with a break in her voice. "I no longer think about it. None of it did her any good."

"Are you sure?"

"She died anyway." Ellen pressed the handkerchief to her face as a few tears trickled down her cheek. "The only thing I can say is that at least she died in peace. She was that kind of person."

Father Elway leaned in. "Exactly. The kind of person who knew that, even in death, all would be well in the Lord. That kind of person, Ellen, is a true believer."

"And," Father Garrett said, "have you considered that she might also have been at peace knowing she had taught you to love God as she did? Maybe she was comforted knowing that she was leaving you in good hands."

Again, there was silence before Father Elway spoke. "Tell us a little about the man you met later on. Kate mentioned that you're divorced."

"Just a story I made up because of my aunt. When she saw that I was getting older without another love in my life, she managed to convince me that men were more attracted to a divorced woman than to an old maid. I can't believe I agreed to something so stupid. I had intended to tell Kate the truth, but so much time passed, and I just never thought about it. It was a very foolish thing that somehow made sense at the time."

"Sometimes when we're desperately lonely or bereft, we do things that we normally wouldn't even consider," Father Elway said.

Father Garrett nodded his agreement. "Was there ever anyone else?"

She shook her head. "After a number of years, I thought I might be ready, but it didn't work out. I was thirty. The men who wanted to date me at that age were a little older themselves, and often that meant they were divorced or still married. A friend once tried to match me up. When I met the man, he seemed nice enough, but my heart wasn't in it. Eventually, I shut down completely. And, just as my father had done, I lost myself in my work. Although during the big war, I stepped away to work at the Brooklyn Navy Yard."

"That must have been interesting work," Father Elway said.

"And important." Father Garrett chimed in. "Our own 'Rosie, the Riveter.'"

"Well, I learned to get along. I ended up getting Tony … man's best friend." She smiled. "Truly. I took him to the office with me most days. Everyone back in my Brooklyn neighborhood loves Tony. The wonderful people at Lenny's Luncheonette would sometimes take turns coming by to walk him. It must sound silly, but I've been lucky to live in a great neighborhood."

Father Elway gestured toward the doorway. "I think our favorite fellow has heard his name."

In his typical slow gait, the brawny canine crossed the room and went from one to the other, first brushing Ellen's leg and nuzzling her elbow, then moving on to Father Garrett for a pat before settling his muscled body at Father Elway's feet. "Good boy."

"How did you get into real estate?" Father Garrett asked as he reached over to stroke Tony's head.

"My father. He had become a successful realtor in Brooklyn. That's where we ended up and stayed. I worked with him. He taught me well. So much so that when he died, I was able to take over the business. I also made a trip back to see if I could find Patrick, but his family had moved away years before."

Ellen's face was flushed. She had hoped never to speak about this. What good would it do, she'd always thought. "Anyway, after my father was gone, his oldest, most loyal friend came to work with me to manage the accounts, to help take care of things for me, as he put it. Why would I not have trusted him? He was closer to my father than anyone else in the world. He was from the old country. I was actually grateful for his interest in the business. His help freed me up to focus on our many clients. But then, little by little, my business dropped off. I couldn't imagine why. I had two wonderful sales agents who were very successful. We had an excellent reputation. There had been plenty of business, plenty of opportunities.

"One day, someone came to me about a debt. A very large amount of money that he said I owed. I had no idea what he was talking about. Two days later, the same thing—another business owner came to collect the money that I supposedly borrowed. I never borrowed from anyone. That's when I found out that this loyal old friend, who, by the way, I learned had just taken a European vacation with no plan to return, had pirated my clients in order to set up his son-in-law in the business, and racked up enormous debts by borrowing in my name." She sat back as her shoulders slumped. "I had to let my people go, close down, and sell what I owned to pay everything off."

Father Garrett took a deep breath. "Well, all I can say,

dear Ellen, is that it is no small wonder that you've struggled in despair. What great and terrible losses—your livelihood, your love, your sense of hope."

"And most terrible of all," Father Elway added, "your faith."

Ellen straightened herself and looked from one to the other. Then she stood and walked slowly to the doorway, where she stopped and turned. "I've never had this conversation with anyone, ever, not even my best friend, Kate. I only told both of you because I wanted you to know that even with all the … the craziness in my life … with all the unexplainable things that have happened here, I have found more joy and peace in this place than anywhere else that I can remember in … years." She pointed to the check on Father Elway's desk. "That money. It is just a way … and a small one, at that … for me to thank you for your great kindness, your great generosity, your complete acceptance of me without even knowing if maybe I really was a felon."

None of them could hold back a chuckle.

Father Elway turned to Father Garrett. "Then," he said with a stiff nod of finality, "we gladly accept your wonderful, generous gift." He paused and tapped his finger against his nose. "I wonder … I know it's a big thing to ask of you, I know it, but would you do us the honor of joining us at morning Mass tomorrow in the chapel." He quickly extended his arm as if to ward off rejection. "You don't have to pray. You don't have to believe. You don't have to do anything but join us in the place where all of us here encounter our greatest joyfulness and peace."

"Yes, Father," she said, without hesitation. "I will." She turned to Father Garrett. "I will."

Chapter

Nineteen

JOHN CARABALLO STOOD before the polished cherry shelf of photos, searching his favorites. There were many, and more than one that could easily bring a smile or a tear. He reached for the sterling silver frame. Christmas 1940. How quickly the time goes, he thought. Marjorie. So beautiful. So fragile.

He put the picture back and touched the one with the wooden double-edged frame. "Daniel. You were just a boy." He took it down, kissed it, and pressed it to his chest as he had a hundred times, then reached for the newest one—little Billy blowing out the candles of his birthday cake. Such a lovable handful, he thought, setting it back in its place. Marjorie would have eaten him up, but she died before Louise even married. And here he was, 51, still wondering how all the years went by so fast.

He turned to his burled walnut desk and sat for a few minutes, running a finger mindlessly along the edge of its fine leather top, wondering. He picked up the weeks-old morning papers, all of them folded to a particular page—The New York Daily News, top of page two—"Woman Risks Life Rescuing Child." The New York Herald Tribune, bottom of the front page—"Woman and Child Nearly Die in Rescue." The New York Journal American, front page—"Heroic Woman Nearly Killed Saving Child."

So many ways to lose a child. The greatest of losses. This woman. He looked closer at the photos, recognizing that she was much better looking in person. A beautiful woman, really. He had no way of knowing if she had children of her own. The articles never said. He did notice when he met her that there was no wedding ring. What was her story? How often do you get to meet such a woman?

There was a tap on the door before a man entered. "John, you'll want to come and see this."

"I'll be right there, Leon," he said, without looking up, his eyes still glossy.

"Okay, but we've got to get moving on them." He closed the door behind him.

John Caraballo blew his nose before heading out into the small, elegant, private gallery where Leon was waiting.

"Take a look. These are fabulous," Leon said, a proud smile on his face. "From the Belgian dealer."

John took a seat at the table where the diamonds were set out on a velvet swatch as deep blue as the walls of the private salon that held a small, handsome collection of original art. He reached for the tweezers and picked up one of the glittering gems. With the other hand, he held his jeweler's loupe close against his left eye for the inspection and, with a deft touch, turned the stone several times. "Hmm. Yes. Wonderful."

After inspecting the others, he set the tweezers and the loupe on the table. "Very nice. Talk to Uri. Let's get these set as quickly as we can." He patted Leon on the shoulder as he headed back to his office. "Make sure he has Maurice set the two-carat for the Park Avenue store." He turned. "Oh, and Leon, tell Ida to start working on the Christmas gift list. You know, the usual … Chivas Regal, show tickets, playoff tickets. Work with Ida. It's a lot. She's getting on in years. Help her out."

"You got it, John."

"Months fly by. It's already September. Make sure we're booked at Tavern on the Green for the week before Christmas. People go on vacation. It's been another good year, and I want everyone there for the bonuses."

"Tavern on the Green. Ida. Everything."

"Get that new kid to help. He needs to learn the people are part of the business."

"Got it."

Back in his office, he was barely seated behind his desk when Ida called. Caraballo listened as she began asking more questions than he would normally have patience for. "That's fine, Ida. Work with Leon." He listened for another moment.

"Ida, listen. Listen, Ida. I want you to work with Leon. Yes, I know it's a lot of money. You say that every year, but it's okay. It's important to reward people. Share the wealth. Work with Leon."

When he'd hung up, he looked again at the newspaper article, the picture of the woman, the young boy. Then he glanced back at the shelf full of pictures. How blessed to have had a child snatched out of harm's way.

Not even in her days as a practicing Catholic, occasionally attending Mass at the majestic St. Patrick's Cathedral in Manhattan with her mother during Christmastime, had Ellen been so captivated by a church. The moment she set foot inside the small stone, cloistered chapel with its dark timbered crossbeams, the sense of sacred intimacy was striking—the large crucifix centered between pastel stained-glass windows that bore the first of the morning light; the centuries-old wooden altar where dozens of votives set in delicate glass and wrought iron formed a semi-circle of ethereal radiance. Without thinking, she made the sign of the cross, then caught herself, glancing quickly to the side to see if anyone had noticed.

With the local visitors seated behind them, Thomas and the priests occupied the first two of the ten pews, their chanting resonant and sublime, Ellen thought. She chose to seat herself at the rear as Father Elway, wearing a green chasuble, reverently swung the ornate silver thurible that emitted the smoky incense. For a moment, she forgot about the prayers that had not been answered, forgot that she no longer believed.

A priest once told her in confession many years earlier that one of the most essential parts of a faithful life was to wait, that when one trusts the Lord, one waits, even in the worst of times. But for how long, she had asked herself? For how many years? As she had done over the days since her strange encounter with the white-haired man on the bike, she recalled what he had said as he went off mumbling: "We wait and wait," he had said. "But it all works out. All in good time." Who was he to say that to her?

Now, having racked up years of loss and disappointments, Ellen tried to hold back her resentment in an attempt to pray, but who would she pray to—the great, merciful God that her loving mother had worshipped? She was troubled, wondering how long she would carry this antagonism, but never more so than when she watched Father Elway consecrate the bread and wine, and felt the sting of regret that she was unable to receive the Eucharist. As everyone in attendance began forming a modest line to the altar rail, Ellen rose, head down, and quietly left the chapel.

As she walked along, passing the low arches that formed the colonnade leading to the main house, the prayer garden caught her eye. The damp morning air had the fulsome scent of cut grass and cedar, of woodsy mulch, and the must of fresh-turned earth. She took a deep, satisfying breath that lifted her from her slump. The fog had not yet fully given way to the morning, and the veiled light revealed only the silhouette of the cross. She continued along, then paused, thinking how much like a veiled image the cross had become in her life, the fullness of its meaning obscured over the years by latent despair. She intended to resist but, finally, turned toward the silhouette and, after walking a little farther, paused again before taking the first opening to cross the wet grass.

Chapter

Twenty

"You're awful serious."

The Major looked at his long-time friend and lifted an eyebrow.

"Well, okay, more serious than usual."

"It's getting to be that time, Jack." The Major moved a small stack of signed papers to the wire outbox in the corner of his Army-issue gray metal desk. "I guess I'm feeling it a little."

"No wonder. Twenty years is no small thing." Jack took a seat in front of Major O.'s desk. "So, which way are you leaning?"

"I'm leaning in so many directions, I feel like one of those Joe Palooka blow-up dolls that's taken a pounding."

Jack leaned in. "Except that you're the one throwing all the punches. The possibilities can't be all bad."

The Major stood and took his cup over to the glass coffee pot sitting on its portable burner. He turned and held up the cup.

"Thanks, but I'm all coffeed out."

"There are days, Jack, that I feel like I'm ready to pack it in and start over … I don't know … maybe I should go for that chicken farm all the guys talked about right after the war, but what do I know about chickens?" He stirred two teaspoons of sugar into the cup. "Then I say, maybe I'd like to teach somewhere. I think I could handle history or math. Maybe even coach, although I'm not going to kid myself—who'd want a forty-four-year-old coach? Forty-five in two months." He stood briefly by the window, then gestured to a couple of men working on one of the Army Jeeps. "I've worked with enough parts to open a repair shop somewhere. Maybe that's it." He returned to his desk and sat. "Or re-up. I may or may not make Colonel in another year or two. Either way is okay with me. If I stay, they might let me pick my assignment—stay right here, doing what I'm doing with these boys."

"What does Ann have to say about it? This may not be the time to ask, but how are things working out between you two?"

The Major set his coffee cup on the desk and sat back. "Things are okay, I guess. I don't know. I … don't know, Jack." Who else but easy-going, devoted Jack Michaels—Colonel Jack Michaels—would he ever consider opening up to, especially after once being holed up for an eternity in a mud-thick winter foxhole, bits of shrapnel pinging off the top of their helmets? It was Jack who had torn the boot off his own foot so he could use his dank, hole-riddled sock to stop the flow of blood pouring from the empty socket that had held his friend's eye until help came.

"Listen, my friend, I know Ann. I know she loves you. And I know you love her. You talked about marrying her. So, what gives?"

"Restless, I guess." He fingered the rim of his cup. "Not with Ann. She's still beautiful to me. Devoted." He looked up. "She says I'm distant. Time of life stuff, maybe. Something in me feels … I don't know … unfinished. Hard to explain."

Jack stood up and circled the chair, silent.

"I know what you're thinking, my friend." The Major spoke without looking up." Don't even say it."

"It's true though, isn't it?"

"That was a very long time ago. A long time."

"There's no statute of limitations on that sort of thing."

"Oh, c'mon, Jack." He waved his hand, dismissively. "You're sounding like a … a stupid Valentine card." The Major picked up his pen and pulled a sheet of paper in front of him. "And I've got work to do."

Jack sat back down. "Every few years, you circle back to it. To her."

"Enough."

"You must know that if you don't work this out once and for all, you and Ann will never stand a chance. You'll never stand a chance with any woman."

Major O. tossed the pen onto the desk. "Well, if you won't

get out of here, I will." He picked up his wheel cap from the top of the metal file cabinet, then stopped. "I appreciate that you're trying to help me, Jack. You're the best friend a guy could have."

"Now, who's sounding like a Valentine."

The Major headed for the front door.

"But Pat, you've got resources at your disposal that they didn't even have twenty years ago."

Major Patrick O'Shaughnessy pushed through the exit of the small field building. "Not interested."

"Liar. They can help you find her. If she's still alive, Elena Castellanos has to be somewhere."

Mrs. Wick found Ellen in the gazebo, where she'd gone to have her lunch. The place had been quiet with some of the priests and a few of the soldiers off to work the market and the rest out and about elsewhere. Ellen was surprised by how much she'd come to enjoy the solitary peace along with the occasional bustle.

She relished the coming and going of the soldiers, seeing them fitting in so well, satisfied doing this and that—sawing wood for repairs or working the beds where the pumpkin seeds had been sown a month earlier. She enjoyed their dropping in at the abbey, usually entering the back door of the kitchen, comfortable with everyone, reading the funny sheets in the daily paper, or sharing the news of the day, as

Mrs. Wick referred to it.

How different her life was in Brooklyn, a mostly busy life, a noisy life, a life of subways and buses and car horns, nights at the movies and trips into Manhattan for Carnegie Hall or Radio City, a day at one of the museums, a special-occasion dinner at Tavern on the Green. Hot Pastrami sandwiches at Katz's Deli. The city was great, but she loved her Brooklyn neighborhood even more, with its aroma of Italian or Polish or German food wafting through the hallway or out an open window where in summer, up and down the street, there was always the sound of a Yankee or Dodger game. She would miss Frankie Falcone waxing his car at the curb outside his brownstone and Mrs. Koch, in her flowered smock, sweeping the airy way or snipping her boxwood hedge until the sweet, milky aroma perfumed the street.

But this place, this wonderful abbey experience, was making it easier for her to detach from her Brooklyn life, something she would have to do once she moved to Queens. It would be altogether different there, a place where she would once again be a stranger, but she couldn't imagine that things would go so well there as they did here. Oddly enough, she hadn't really ever felt like a stranger here. How could she have anticipated the relationships she would have with, of all people, a group of priests? Just the evening before, she and several of them had sat in the living area near the fireplace, where, between dinner and vespers, they enjoyed small talk and laughter, along with the punch that Father Pelletier occasionally concocted with the freshest of garden fruit, and the added delight of a splash of cognac. She couldn't help but wonder what any of these priests knew about heartache and suffering, sheltered as they were in this idyllic, other-worldly hermitage.

Now, in the heat of the early afternoon, with Tony stretched out on the floor beside her, whimpering in his dream of some canine adventure, Ellen put her head back to breathe in the distinctively pungent aroma of viny oil coming from the tomato rows, the silence now and then pierced by the squawk of geese in their flyover above the woods.

"Hello, dearie."

The cheery greeting was quick to bring Ellen back. "Mrs. Wick. Come sit," she said, half dreamy.

"I think I will," the woman said, breathless. "I have a little something to tell you about. Something you need to do." She swatted at a fly that had followed her in through the screen door. "Just a formality."

"Oh, okay." Ellen picked up the Life Magazine that had been resting unread in her lap and placed it on the redwood table. "What is it?"

Mrs. Wick sat upright at the edge of one of the Adirondack chairs next to Ellen. "We received a call from … Officer Polly."

Ellen stiffened. "Oh, please, Mrs. Wick …"

"No, no. It's okay. It really is. Just a formality … about the accident. And I have to say he was surprisingly polite, even apologetic, although I still believe he carries a little spiral pad in the pocket of his pajamas."

Ellen couldn't help smiling. "But you're sure it's okay. Officer Polly has a way about him."

"Mustn't worry. This is just a technical detail. He promised. You just have to sign the paperwork about what happened. A pure formality. The police already made a full report from all the witnesses who were there and saw everything that happened. So, you just have to go to the courthouse in Hicksville to sign the report. Father Garrett will drive us in."

"Us?"

"Yes, Father Elway wants to go along. What with your current situation, he figures you may need some extra help. I'll go too."

Ellen squirmed in her chair. "Oh, no. Please, Mrs. Wick. That's putting everybody out. It isn't necessary. Father Garrett will be there. He's all the help I'll need, and I'm grateful for that. Honestly."

Mrs. Wick walked over to the screen door. "You must know by now that it's going to be impossible to get Father Elway to change his mind."

Ellen breathed a deep sigh of resignation. "What time do I have to be there?"

"We'll leave here in the morning about nine."

Chapter

Twenty-One

ON FRIDAY MORNING, Ellen, Mrs. Wick, and Father Elway rode together into Hicksville with Father Garrett at the wheel of the all-around.

"Couldn't ask for a better day," Father Elway said, ever a cheerful presence.

"Maybe just a better road," Father Garrett said, distinctive in his ability and habit of sorting out the facts of any situation. "Although I believe they're talking about paving it one of these days soon. No one has defined soon."

Ellen sat, silent, in the back seat with Mrs. Wick. As much as she enjoyed the company of the priests, she hadn't gotten over her discomfort about Father Elway feeling he had to come along. There certainly were better things for him to be doing. He surely had to agree that she was better now. No cane. No bruises. No limping. She was pleased that it took barely fifteen minutes to get into town, a good bit shorter than the bus with its multiple stops. If Officer Polly was right, and no shenanigans, she'd be able to sign whatever it was, and they'd be back at the abbey in no time.

Dating back to 1895, the old Hicksville Town Hall and Courthouse that served Oyster Bay was located on a street flanked, as nearly all were, by enormous maples. The venerable, if quaint, two-story clapboard structure, with its gable roof and tall, narrow cupola, had a homey front porch and double-hung windows, the kind of rural charm once befitting the home of the local minister or town doctor.

As the four made their way up the narrow walk, the front door opened, and Officer Polly greeted them with his typical sober demeaner. Ellen felt a shiver as she walked past him into the small, tight vestibule.

"This way," he said, stoic, and led them to a door on the right. He pushed it open ahead of Ellen and stepped aside for her to enter. The cheers were deafening, filled as the room was with people, wall to wall.

Ellen jumped back, astonished. She turned to find Mrs. Wick and the two priests beaming. Thomas stood off to the side, surrounded by the priests from the abbey, the young soldiers, and what appeared to be more than fifty townspeople chanting, "Heer-o. Heer-o."

In disbelief, Ellen threw her hands to her face, embarrassed and speechless. After a few moments, as the crowd quieted down, the Town Supervisor stepped forward holding a plaque, which he presented to Ellen.

"To an amazing and heroic woman who, without a

thought for her own safety, risked her life to save a young child. May God bless you every day of your life."

Ellen's hands trembled as she took the plaque amid the blinding glare of rapid-fire flashbulbs. "Thank you," she said, barely able to get the words out. "I … I don't know what else to say. But thank you from the bottom of my heart." With that, and to further applause, Peter and Louise Crowley stepped forward with young Billy. Their remarks to the room touched Ellen's heart and brought on more cheers.

Afterward, everyone enjoyed lemonade along with a celebratory cake from Englert's. With coaxing and a barrage of stage direction from the photographers, Ellen cut the first slice for the cameras, then stepped away, hoping to remove herself from all the attention. She didn't get far, besieged by appreciative strangers eager to shake her hand, children scampering past, seeking out the cake, reporters with pads and pencils looking for just that detail everyone else had missed, and, finally, after more time than she would ever care to spend in a crowded room, one other person whom Ellen had no idea was even there.

Slow and deliberate, without uttering a word, John Caraballo, in a sport jacket and golf shirt, moved to Ellen's side, put his hand under her elbow, and discreetly led her through the nearest door into the vestibule and out onto the walk, where the two stood facing each other.

She was closer to him than that first day he'd come to the abbey, close enough to see that his eyes were deep gray-green, his chin strong, his expression sympathetic.

"Don't forget this," he said with a canny smile, holding up her plaque. "You really do deserve it, you know."

It took her a moment to respond, taken as she was by his presence and the fact that he had known exactly what she needed—escape. "Thank you," she said. "And not just for carrying my plaque."

"I'd like to take you for a quiet lunch."

She looked about, quickly remembering that she'd come with Father Elway and the others.

"It's all right," Caraballo said. "I already asked. Father Elway agreed you should definitely have a quiet lunch. So, I promised I'd have you back at the abbey before dark."

Ellen laughed. "Is that when your coach turns into a pumpkin?"

"That's when I get back to the city, longing for the next time."

His words nearly took her breath away. She flushed. And with that, John Caraballo offered his arm and led the way to his car.

A hundred years earlier, one easily could have imagined The Rusted Anchor Tavern as the inspiration for Herman Melville's epic Moby Dick, with its sea-worn Cyprus washed white by the salt air and not one angle of its frame resting plumb against the loam and fragmented rock on which it stood. A quiet place it was not, but once inside, Ellen found the truth of John Caraballo's invitation as the thick-beamed interior and low vaulted roof very nearly silenced the great crashing waves of Montauk Point.

Through the windows of the large wooden doors opposite, she could see the tables of a covered patio that faced the ocean. It must have been her expression of surprise and delight that prompted Caraballo to ask, "Outside?"

"Oh, yes. This is wonderful."

They had cruised the wending roads of Riverhead and Amagansett and the Hamptons during their hour's drive from Hicksville, their course taking them past the duck farms, as well as the cabbage and beet fields that perfumed the summer air with an earthy funk.

It was rare for Ellen to travel to Long Island. People from Brooklyn often stuck to the places, even the beaches, easily and not so easily, reached by train—Coney Island, Rockaway, and Palisades on the Hudson. This was a rare treat.

With the car windows rolled down, they had said little. Only the frequent exchange of smiles told of their mutual ease and shared pleasure in the moment. Occasionally, he would point out the window toward something that made them both laugh or nod approval. She had no idea how this came to be, how there was, beside her, this attractive and gracious man with whom she was, all at once, so comfortable. She liked him, and it gave her both a rush and a start.

Chapter

Twenty-Two

"So glad you're here, Major. There's someone I'd like you to meet." Thomas gestured toward Peter Crowley and introduced the two men.

"So good to meet you, Major. My family and I are very impressed by your work with the returning soldiers."

Major O. tapped the side of his face near his eye patch. "Maybe you can imagine how grateful I am for any soldier, man or woman, who not only gets to come home but gets the help and rehab they need." Ever serious, the Major was a model of military efficiency, friendly in a way of his own choosing, distant but gracious in a manner that evoked respect.

The twenty-five-year-old Crowley gave him a slow thumbs up. "I appreciate that, Major. I wasn't able to serve. Wanted to, but I had a touch of tuberculosis as a kid, and that did it for me."

Thomas began walking toward one of the two staircases.

"It's Peter's young son, Billy, who was saved by the woman you probably read about in the papers."

"Yes, I did see that." The Major looked at Crowley. "How is your boy doing … and the woman?"

"Better than anyone might have guessed if you told them what happened. We're all very grateful."

"Ellen, our hero lady, actually lives here at the abbey," Thomas said, "at least for the time being."

"Why am I not surprised?" Major O. said. "Isn't there always something unexpected going on around here?"

Thomas smiled. "Always. Matter of fact, I'm giving Peter a tour of the Lodge. His father-in-law was impressed with what we do here with our soldiers. He suggested Peter come back and take a tour. Our young men are out and about. So, this is as good a time as any. Want to tag along?"

"Thanks, no. I'm meeting a flight at Idlewild this afternoon. A new guy. I'll have him here tomorrow. Just came by today to check things out. I'll see Father Elway and Father Garrett before I go."

Thomas stopped at the bottom of the stairs and turned. "Our present crop has settled in pretty well, Major. They'll be a good welcoming committee for the new arrival when you get back."

Peter Crowley extended his hand. "A pleasure to meet you, Major. God bless you for all that you do."

They turned at the sound of a door opening in the kitchen.

"Ah, that must be our lunch." Thomas looked at the Major.

"Do you have a few minutes to grab a bite? You know Mrs. Wick never disappoints."

"That's an offer I hate to turn down, but I've got to be underway."

As the Major exited the front door of the Lodge, Ellen entered the main dining room carrying a wicker picnic basket. "Chicken sandwiches, with Mrs. Wick's compliments," she called out, cheerful.

Thomas looked at Peter. "What do you say?"

Crowley laughed. "You'll never see me turning down a good lunch."

The two men headed back toward one of the tables.

"Ellen, too bad you just missed the Major. You never got to meet him?"

"No," she said, removing a small container of potato salad. "Maybe next time."

"Looks like there may not be a next time," Thomas said. "He's decided to retire his commission."

Before lunch, Crowley had seen the main floor with its multiple rooms that accommodated a variety of games and interests—everything from ping pong and billiards to Checkers, Monopoly, and Parcheesi, even art supplies and wood burning kits. A separate room was dedicated to rear projection movies and another with floor-to-ceiling bookshelves, a writing desk, and windows that faced the woods.

The second floor housed five bedrooms and two baths along a broad hallway, each bedroom large enough for two to share, the bathrooms tight with modest storage.

"This is quite a place," Crowley said. "I have to believe the soldiers who get to come here are very appreciative of the opportunity."

"They are, but there just aren't enough soldiers. I was telling your father-in-law that it has long been a dream of Father Elway's that we have a lodge able to accommodate many more and, eventually, a retreat center, as well. We certainly have the land for it, just not the resources at this time."

"Well, you can be proud of the important work you've done with those you've helped, a big part of giving them back their lives. That's everything."

"Let me show you the chapel," Thomas said, and with that he picked up the luncheon basket to head back to the main building.

Chapter

Twenty-Three

Mrs. Wick's was a busy little kitchen. Fathers Xavier and Pelletier had stopped by for a nibble and a chat before heading over to the lodge to continue their handiwork. Father Elway checked in for the ball scores before heading over to the chapel to hear confessions, confident that the Yankees had the pennant in the bag. Thomas and Ellen sat alongside each other on the table bench, she peeling potatoes, he shucking what was likely the last of the season's corn crop when, much to everyone's surprise, Father Garrett came pushing through the back screen door with a large catch of fluke and flounder.

Ellen stood as he plopped the brown-paper wrapped bulk on the counter by the sink. "Oh, my goodness. When you go fishing, you mean business."

"You're still new to all this," Thomas said. "But Father Garrett always comes through."

"What's the score?" the priest asked.

"Bronx Bombers up by two in the sixth," Father Elway

said. "I haven't had a chance yet to check on the Dodgers."

Father Garrett turned back around to take the bushel of clams that one of the soldiers handed him through the door. The five young servicemen waited outside, having declined Mrs. Wick's invitation to come in, believing they were too "sea-salt smelly," as one of them put it, but they blew kisses to her through the open window.

The proud and enthusiastic Father Garrett was grateful that the all-around could accommodate himself, the servicemen, and all the fish they could catch. "A tight squeeze but a great time," he said with a laugh in his voice.

"Supper in two hours," Mrs. Wick called out, "but in the meantime, you'll find a light snack and cold beer waiting for you at the lodge."

The group exploded in cheers as Father Garrett headed out the door and back behind the wheel.

"Wonderful young men," Father Elway said. He rose to head for the chapel as Ellen went to the sink to help Mrs. Wick ready the catch for dinner.

"The good news is that Father nearly always cleans the fish on the dock," Thomas said, "so we're all set to go."

Mrs. Wick pushed the flour canister toward Ellen. "We'll start getting them floured."

Thomas stood to come around with the bowl of kernels. "All done with the corn."

Ellen noticed him teeter. Apparently, Mrs. Wick did too.

"You stay right there, young man," she chided playfully. "I'm going to need you to set these rolls out on a tray." Then she traded him the rolls for the corn bowl and followed up with the baking tin.

Ellen admired Mrs. Wick, ever the benevolent observer, for her discretion. She had never mentioned Thomas's apparent difficulties. No one had. A moment or two later, Thomas stood up.

"Well, now that the vets are back, I'd better get back too."

Without any further difficulty, he left the two women to their supper chores. Ellen began to prepare the seasoned flour mixture for the fish and readied the cast iron skillets. She was familiar with the kitchen and accustomed to lending a hand for meal preparation. It had taken her a little while to fully recover from the accident, but here she was, glad to be back helping with a fish fry or a pot roast. There were days when she actually felt as though she were away at camp.

"Mrs. Wick, I have a question," she said. "Do you know anything about a jacket?" She wasn't sure why she asked that question just now—maybe because it had been hanging around somewhere in her thoughts since Kate had mentioned it, and she'd never gotten an answer.

Mrs. Wick stopped what she was doing and said nothing.

"I asked Thomas once, but then we kind of got distracted before he could answer."

"What kind of a jacket?" the woman asked. "I do have a few in my closet. Do you need one? The mornings are going to start getting a little cooler. Who knows, you may want to find your way back to the chapel for early Mass."

"I'm thinking it must be some kind of a special jacket. Kate mentioned it. She said I should ask Thomas, but when I did, like I said, we somehow got sidetracked."

Mrs. Wick continued dredging the fish. "Oh, this fluke is magnificent, Ellen. Look. You can't beat Father Garrett for a fine haul. And now that he's got help from our boys, even better."

"Yes, and I'm dying for a fried fish supper."

"Now, I have a question for you." Mrs. Wick gave her a coy look.

Ellen drew the thick fillets through the flour. "What is it?"

"John Caraballo?"

The very name quickened her heart. "What about him?"

"He's quite a nice gentleman."

"Yes, he is."

"He likes you."

Ellen glanced over Mrs. Wick's shoulder toward the gas range. "I think we should probably start getting the oil ready."

"And … you like him?"

Ellen stopped and rested her flour-covered hands on the counter. For a moment, she said nothing at all. Then she looked at Mrs. Wick. "I do, Mrs. Wick, and I can't imagine how this all happened. I mean, I know it started out because of his gratitude. He's a very caring man. He lost his wife to influenza before the big war. They were very close. He's a family man."

"What is he like to spend time with?"

"He's aware of things. Interested in the people around him, even though he's on the quiet side. Not showy. I like that. I think he likes to help people. He talked briefly about his children, Daniel and Louise. Of course, we met Louise. He likes his son-in-law very much, too, and little Billy is the apple of his eye. I think we could guess that."

Mrs. Wick placed a few of the fillets in the hot oil. "Do you know what he does for a living? He must do well. We've seen that beautiful Cadillac."

"He doesn't talk much about what he does; I just know he works in the jewelry business somewhere in Queens and spends a lot of time in Manhattan."

"That must be interesting work," Mrs. Wick said, turning the fillets carefully in the crackling hot oil.

"He did say he loves his work and that he's been there for many years. I'll learn more about it."

"Well, that's a good sign for a long-term fellow—responsible, dependable."

"He and the Crowleys must do well. They share a home in Munsey Park."

Mrs. Wick turned and looked at Ellen with raised eyebrows. "Ohh, Munsey Park. Very nice."

"He asked me to come for dinner with the family, maybe the weekend after next when I can stay over. It's a six-bedroom house. John made sure he mentioned that, so I'd understand completely that I'd have plenty of room to myself, and no … you know … funny business, as he put it."

"It's a bit of a trip for him going back and forth way out here. And remember, he can always stay over at our guest house any time."

Ellen squeezed her shoulders up in a shrug. "I feel like a schoolgirl, Mrs. Wick. Honestly. He's special. I told him about my situation, all that happened, and how I lost the business, my home. Patrick. He was so sympathetic. I think he has a very tender heart, almost like someone who's suffered a great loss himself. Must have been a terrible thing when his wife died." She hesitated. "Still, I have to admit—I'm a little scared. I don't know where this is going."

"Where do you want it to go?"

Ellen shook her head. "I really like him, but …"

"But what?"

"You know by now that things don't always turn out so well for me in that department."

"How'd you make out today, Peter?" John Caraballo asked his son-in-law. They were having supper in the dining room of their home, a large Tudor located in the wealthy community half an hour from Manhattan. "What do you think?" He took a bite of sirloin steak.

Peter Crowley passed the platter of scalloped potatoes

back to Louise, who spooned a little onto Billy's plate. "You were right, Dad. Absolutely."

"So, you see what I mean? You agree?"

"Considering the relatively compressed space," Peter said, "they're utilizing every foot of it. A lot goes on there. These vets are so fortunate to have a great place to re-adjust, have fun, have some structure away from a rehab facility, do useful work. After what they've been through, it's a really good way to acclimate to a more normal environment before heading home. They are well taken care of."

When they were nearly finished with dinner, a tall, dark-haired woman with a pleasant smile entered the room. "I've come to take Billy for his bath," she said, picking up the boy who reached for her, smiling. "Come on, you little scamp."

"Thank you, Grace," Louise said, "I'll be up in a few minutes to read him his story. And please tell Marguerite that the dinner was delicious. I may not get the chance."

"I will," Grace said. "By the way, Billy spelled a few more little words today."

"I think he's learning fast," Louise said. "Peter and I have been working with him a lot on the alphabet and now his numbers, too."

"Amazing," said John Caraballo. "I'm not sure I learned to read till I was five."

"Times are different, Dad," Peter said. "This is the fifties. There are so many more ways for kids to learn. So many advancements. I bought a set of flashcards the other day. I think they'll make a big difference."

"Modern times, Mr. C." Grace laughed. "I think before long he'll be using that Remington typewriter you've got in your study."

After Grace left the dining room with Billy blowing kisses, Caraballo asked his son-in-law again about the lodge. "So, with all the good that's going on out there, what do you think they need?"

"Let's put it this way—you hit the nail on the head."

John Caraballo looked at his son-in-law, then at his daughter, and back again. "Okay, then." And they moved on to dessert with nods around the table.

Chapter

Twenty-Four

The Boardwalk breeze was chillier than she'd expected. Nights were definitely cooler now. John Caraballo helped Ellen wrap the lightweight black cashmere shawl about her shoulders, then took her hand as they strolled. She could not remember the time a man had last held her hand; the sensation was dazzling. It wasn't just anyone's hand. It was John Caraballo's. She liked that he was at once strong and gentle. That he was kind. She liked his ways. She liked the way he treated people. She liked the way he treated her.

"You okay?"

"I'm fine." She looked at him and took a deep breath. "Such a beautiful night. I'm so glad we came." She had read about it—the fabulous Jones Beach Marine Stadium, open only a year or so, with more than eight thousand seats, part of the enormous oceanside park that also housed an aquacade, Guy Lombardo and his orchestra on stage. They'd started with a light supper at the Boardwalk Café.

"So, I guess this is our first official date," he said.

"What about our afternoon at Montauk?"

"That was a rescue."

She laughed. "Well then, I guess you're right."

He stopped, turned to her, and took both her hands in his. She would always remember the moon's wavy reflection glistening in ripples on the great expanse of ocean behind him. He came closer. "Marry me."

It took more than a moment, stunned as she was, to form her words. "I … how … John … we don't even know each other." Even she didn't believe what she said.

"Is that what you really think?"

"No," she said. And their first kiss lifted her to the stars.

Ellen's room at the abbey was more than a comfortable place to stay. It had become home, a pleasing and most unexpected haven from pending realities. On that night, that night of nights, she turned, fluffed her pillow, turned and fluffed it again, straightened her covers over and over, then turned again and again until she finally got out of bed. She thought of awakening Mrs. Wick but instead went to the window. She couldn't tell how long she looked out at the night where the moon had turned the woodland tree tops into inky silhouettes dancing like the heart within her.

By eight she was dressed and eager to meet up with Father Elway as soon as he came from the chapel after morning

Mass.

"No, I don't think you're crazy," he said. "I've met him. Met his family. I like him. You're not children. I believe you both can make good decisions."

"I had the feeling you might command me to go to my room as if I were some starstruck teenager."

"Do you remember what I said to you that very first night you arrived here with Kate for our community event?"

So, here it was, she thought—wondrous!

He could tell it registered with her.

"But …"

"Yes?"

"But it's all so quick, Father." She looked about as if searching for reason. "From out of nowhere."

"When you came here you were impatient and angry, wearing your despair like a heavy, oversized winter coat. And, now, here you are. What do you make of it?"

"That's just it, Father. I don't know what to make of it, any of it. You know the situation—my faith. Or should I say the lack of it? Why would God bless me when I turned my back on him?"

"You may have turned your back on God, but God never turned his back on you. And he never will because God keeps his promises."

Mrs. Wick entered the room with a cheerful "Good morning" and set a tray of hot coffee, teacakes, and jam on the small inlaid table between their chairs in the library room.

"Thank you, Mrs. Wick," Ellen said.

"Always the best start to the day," Father said. "Nothing better, Mrs. Wick."

"An egg would be better," she said, stiff-backed.

Father Elway feigned a shiver. "I like eggs, Mrs. Wick, as long as I don't have to eat them first thing."

When she had left, the two enjoyed the satisfying early morning refreshments, and then, for the next two hours, undisturbed, they talked.

Chapter

Twenty-Five

THE BAY ROOM at Manhasset Cove was as romantic a place as Ellen could ever have imagined. Dinner tables dressed in white linen with small clusters of orchids floating in crystal amid the glimmer of low light, and unlike Guy Lombardo's concert at Jones Beach, here was Bobby Klein's dance band playing Glenn Miller favorites. Ellen was enchanted. Chateaubriand for two, bananas foster, a dream dinner with a breathtaking view of the Great Neck Peninsula jutting out into Long Island Sound.

"Having a good time?" John asked as they moved around the crowded dance floor to "Moonlight Serenade."

"The best." She had taken the bus to Hicksville earlier in the day, where she found a midnight blue crepe de-chine gown with a sequined neckline. Because she was tall enough, the gown needed no hemming, a perfect fit, and from the look John gave her when he first saw her in it, he appeared to agree. And now, here they were. She loved being in his arms. She loved the smell of his after-shave and the feel of his face against hers. And, especially, she loved the idea of soon becoming Mrs. John Caraballo.

"So, how do you like being at the abbey?" he asked. "It's unusual. I can see it's a very special place."

"I do love it. I'm so glad I've had the chance to stay on a while and work for Father Elway. What about you? Tell me more about your work."

"I will," he said, hesitating. "But first, there's something I need to tell you." His voice had a sober edge to it. "Come with me." He took her hand and walked her to the French doors that opened onto a patio lit with filigreed lanterns and overhung with wisteria. They made their way to a stone bench where Ellen recognized the scent of Lilac and Rose of Sharon.

"I believe I made a mistake," he said.

"What kind of mistake?"

He looked down. "I believe I behaved like a teenager, acting much too impulsively."

His words fell like a hammer. Her mouth went dry as chalk. What was he trying to tell her? She swallowed hard.

"It's just that … you know, Jones Beach … the whole atmosphere that night. It was all so beautiful; you were beautiful. I just got caught up in it. I'm afraid I was much too impetuous, asking you to marry me that way. I'm so sorry, Ellen."

She felt the weight of his words pulling her down into

the misery of all her past years, but she would not let him see her broken heart. She stiffened her back. "I … understand. It all happened so fast. But it's okay, John. It really is." She was surprised that she was even able to say the words because it wasn't okay. Not at all. In that moment, she knew that for the rest of her days it would never be okay. For her, the music had stopped, the stars had tucked themselves away, and the moon shuddered in the night sky.

"I should never have proposed …"

The end of the dream. She didn't need to hear any more.

"…without this," he said, reaching around with something in his hand.

Her gasp was audible. She knew that little box immediately. Every woman did from the glamour shots in all the ads where super-model brides-to-be swooned over its extravagance. Ellen held her breath along with the tiny white satin box with the large embossed letter C scrolled across the top. She looked at him.

"Let me," he said at last, and gently pulled open the tiny gem case.

Ellen drew back, wide-eyed. "Oh, John," she whispered, astonished by the beauty of the one carat emerald set between two smaller diamonds.

He removed the ring and, taking her left hand in his, slipped it onto her finger. "I know a center stone diamond is typical, but an emerald is more precious … like you." He kissed her hand. "Maybe now I've done this thing the way I should have in the first place. I love you, Ellen Castle."

This time, there was no holding back the tears. John drew his handkerchief and blotted her cheek. "Tears of joy, I hope."

"Tears of joy. The greatest joy." There was a catch in her voice. "And, though this is the most beautiful ring I've ever seen, I hope you know I didn't need a ring. All I need is you, John. Now and for the rest of my life."

After a long, slow kiss that rendered the moment even more perfect, he led her back inside, where they danced until the Bay Room had very nearly emptied.

John Caraballo brought Ellen to the abbey door well after midnight. She had invited him to stay at the guest house, but he had to return to the city. Mrs. Wick, who had stayed up waiting for her, waited still, giving them time to linger over their long "good night."

The abbey was as quiet as a kitten's breath. Ellen removed her heels at the door to avoid clacking across the entry at such a late hour to where Mrs. Wick was sitting near the fireplace with her Reader's Digest in her lap. Tony scrambled to his feet and loped toward Ellen, nudging her knees with his square muzzle. "Sweet boy." It struck her with immense pleasure that entering the abbey had come to feel the way it always felt coming home when she was young and her mother was still alive. She drew a deep breath, swooning from all that had happened with John.

As she crossed the room, her hands were concealed in her elbow-length gloves. She extended her left hand to Mrs. Wick, who gave her a puzzled look for only a moment. Then, noticing the bulge, she pulled Ellen down beside her on the sofa and hugged her. Ellen removed the glove, finger by finger, with comical dramatic flair.

"Oh, how beautiful, Ellen," Mrs. Wick said, her words elongated by a joyful rush. "Just gorgeous … and no ordinary engagement ring, I must say."

Ellen opened her gold-beaded evening bag and removed the small white satin box with the embossed C scrolled across the top.

Mrs. Wick grew wide-eyed. "Cara! Oh, my goodness." She giggled. "Either John robbed a bank or he has very good connections."

"Mrs. Wick, John Carabello is Cara."

Mrs. Wick's mouth dropped open just as Father Elway and Father Garrett interrupted the moment, coming through the front door, the blackness of their cleric's clothes underscoring the distressed look on their faces. She clutched Ellen's hand. "Oh, dear, I didn't have a chance to tell you…"

Surprised to see the priests coming in at such a late hour, Ellen got to her feet. "What's wrong?"

"Pray for young Hopper," Father Elway said.

"Joe? Why? What happened?"

"He suffered a kind of breakdown," Father Elway said. "Might be a pretty serious one. We won't know until tomorrow."

"How did it happen?" Ellen asked.

"He started playing catch-me-if-you-can with Thomas in the middle of the night," Father Garrett said, removing his jacket. "It was a blessing that Thomas was able to get to him before he reached the woods. You know Thomas has his own mild challenges."

Father Elway, securing the front door, appeared tired and somber. "Thank God Major O. had not yet moved off the base. We were lucky to get hold of him. He got to the hospital as soon as he could."

"Thomas is with him now, getting him set up in the guest quarters," Father Garrett said. "He'll see what the doctors have to say in the morning when we all go back to the hospital, once they've completed their evaluation."

Ellen sat back down, Tony at her side. "This is terrible. I can't imagine. I've had lunch with him a number of times in the gazebo. We've played Scrabble. He was adjusting so well, I thought."

Father Elway took a seat as Tony sidled over. Father stroked his head. "First one we might be losing in a long, long time," he said, visibly disturbed.

"Such a fine young man," said Mrs. Wick, "such a fine one. And aren't they all? We've come to like them so. They'll likely still have a hard road ahead. Thank God Thomas heard him."

"Yes, yelling in his sleep." Father Garrett adjusted his wire-rimmed glasses. "He's heard him before, the others too on occasion. Restless. Sleepless. Night sweats. Nightmares. Sobbing. But tonight, Thomas heard him crashing out the front door, and got out of bed fast as he could to go after him."

Father Elway pressed his lips together and drew a deep breath. "We've never kidded ourselves—they're going to struggle with their demons for a long time, maybe the rest of their lives. The question is—can they manage the struggle? Joe didn't do so well tonight. He'll need extra prayers. If Joe stays with us, we'll have to get the hospital counselor to start coming out a few days a week instead of just one. But first, we'll have to see how the Major wants to handle it."

Father Garrett sat back and looked up at the ceiling. "These men heard, saw, and felt things that they can never erase from their minds. We know what their injuries were like, but it is hard to imagine what it is like to see your fox hole buddy with part of his face missing, eye sockets smoldering. Or you turn and there's only a head next to you in the fox hole."

Father's graphic words sent a shiver through Ellen. She was struck by such images coming from someone who, himself, had not experienced what he described. No doubt he had heard so many stories from these soldiers over the years that he could easily imagine what they'd experienced."

Mrs. Wick put her head in her hands. "Great Mother of God."

"No matter how cheerful and well-adjusted they appear

during the day," Father Elway said, "night brings it all back to them. You know how it's been here over the years—nearly all of them really are ready to go back home, even though they have often yelled in their sleep. It is unlikely that they will ever be free of those images." Still wearing his jacket, the abbot headed across the room. "Well, we've got Sunday Mass in a few hours. You can be sure we'll offer it for young Hopper." Then, catching himself, he looked at Ellen, managing a weak smile. "And it seems this has all come about on a night that must have brought you great joy, with a beautiful gown to go with it. We passed John's car on the way in. He and his son-in-law are coming by day after tomorrow. He probably mentioned it to you. Do you know what it's about? He wouldn't be specific about the reason they wanted to meet."

"I don't know, Father. He was a little sheepish about it." She held out her hand. "But in any case, we're official now."

"Yes," said Mrs. Wick, "and did you know that John Caraballo is Cara, as in the famous Cara Diamond? Although you'll notice he gave our Ellen the more precious emerald."

Father Garrett gave the ring a look of approval. "Well, my goodness, that is quite a little rock."

"This has, indeed, been a day of many surprises," Father Elway said, "and I'm happy that one of them, at least, is something to celebrate." He walked over to Ellen and put his hand on her shoulder. "Always remember, Ellen—you are the real treasure." He blessed her, then turned to go.

Ellen wished them good night, knowing she would see

them a bit later in the chapel for Mass. It was as if the prayers were building in her—prayers of hope for Joe Hopper, prayers of thanks for John Caraballo, prayers for her dear, blessed abbey family.

Chapter

Twenty-Six

"Mrs. Wick, you make the best eggs. Always have." The Major took another sip of coffee. "Everything good with you, I hope? Grace doing well?"

"Oh, always, Major." The early morning light coming through the windows of the kitchen gleamed off the buttons of his uniform. "Grace and I are blessed to simply keep on." She warmed his coffee with a dash of the hot percolated brew. "And I'm always blessed to see you. You've been such a proud soldier … and friend. I'll miss that once you're off to where you're headed."

"Arizona. And I'll miss you, too, Mrs. W, but I promise to keep in touch. There's a big Army hospital there. I'll be able to continue my involvement with the vets as a civilian, and I'll still be recommending our soldiers for the abbey whenever possible, though they'll have a different escort."

She took a seat next to him at the table. "You haven't

mentioned Ann. I hope … well … you know, the years don't pause for indecision."

"I can't disagree." He looked down at his coffee cup, reticent. "Funny, I've never had any trouble making up my mind when it comes to military affairs."

She could attest to that, remembering how focused and determined he was when he first arrived as a lieutenant. A quiet fighter, Army all the way. "I'll always wish the best for you, Patrick."

"I know, Mrs. W. You've been family to me." He looked up at the clock. "But now, I'd better be getting along to the hospital. I'll hope to see you again soon." He stood and gave Mrs. Wick a hug as Ellen made her way across the main reception room toward the kitchen.

The Major walked to the back door. "I'll just head out this way. I might catch a few of the vets if they're around. I'll see Father Elway and Father Garrett at the hospital."

No sooner had the back door closed than Ellen pushed through the main kitchen door, her arms overflowing with magazines. "Look what one of our kind locals brought to us." She tumbled some of the load onto the end of the table, before clumsily trying to stack the others, as Mrs. Wick finished clearing the Major's breakfast dishes. "All recent issues—McCall's, Life, Look, Ladies Home Journal, Field and Stream …"

"National Geographic, Popular Mechanics. Oh, my goodness," Mrs. Wick said, with a lift in her voice. "Father

Garrett will be so pleased. He'll think it's Christmas." She looked at some of the others. "Ha! Here's one especially for our dear abbot himself, Time Magazine, with Rosemary Clooney on the cover."

"Our little Church community is so thoughtful." Ellen sat as Mrs. Wick placed a cup of coffee in front of her. "Thank you. Any word on Joe Hopper?"

"Not yet. The Major is headed over to the hospital now." She gestured to the back door. "Too bad you just missed him."

"The elusive Major O."

"It would have been nice if you two had met before he left for Arizona."

"Arizona. Hmm. That's a big move. I'm sure everyone will miss him around here, but what about the veterans?"

Mrs. Wick added the Lux Liquid soap to the hot water pouring into the dishpan. "They'll assign someone else to bring the men. But it won't be the same, that's for sure. The Major's been coming for so many years, ever since the day he arrived, same as all the others had, adjusting well to the loss of his eye, wondering what it was going to be like to go through life 'seeing only half the world,' as he put it. But he was strong then, as now."

"Are you saying that he was here in recovery himself?"

"Oh, yes, about two months. And quite determined to get back home—home to the Army. Over the years, he has always remained committed to having more soldiers experience what he and Thomas had here. That's actually when it all started." She placed another rinsed dish in the rack as Ellen got up from the table.

"Do you mean that Thomas was also a wounded veteran?"

"Oh, yes. You've noticed his limp. He has a prosthetic leg." She continued placing dishes in the rack. "He and the Major went through rehab together, then came here."

Ellen picked up a clean cotton towel. "I had no idea. Thomas never mentioned anything about it."

"He's like that. And so is the Major, really. Solid men, both." She emptied the dishpan water into the sink. "And speaking of solid men, your wonderful Mr. Caraballo gave you quite a surprise last evening. Too bad we couldn't give you a proper celebration. Your ring is the loveliest I've ever seen. Cara. Who would ever have known—more greatness in our midst. But quite a humble man, I see."

Ellen stopped and stared out the window over the sink. "Oh, yes, he is that. But I'm still thinking about Thomas. I thought he might have had polio. Honestly, Mrs. Wick, it's hard to fathom it all. And then, yes, this wonderful man in my life … out of nowhere. We're talking about a Christmas wedding. Can you imagine?"

"Oh, dearie, I can imagine. It's the kind of joy that you so fully deserve. I think we'll …"

Some noisy commotion brought Major O. pushing in through the back door. "Good grief," he said, gushing his excited words on a ragged breath. "We were just attacked by a wild bird. I think a cardinal, swooping like a crazy dive bomber. He nearly knocked my cap off. Unbelievable! He wouldn't even let me get through the gazebo door with the others."

Ellen Castle stared, speechless, except for the gasp that accompanied her astonishment. Mrs. Wick turned, seeing only the look on Major Patrick O'Shaughnessy's face, the expression of one stunned by the unimaginable, but, somehow, having nothing at all to do with a bird. Not a word was uttered, yet it was clear to Mrs. Wick that something had just happened, was happening. The moment was so weighted with intensity that she didn't dare speak.

There was no mistaking it. None. Not even with the black eye patch covering part of his face. The Major, of all people. Of all people! Ellen was captured up in the realization like a butterfly pinned behind glass in a picture frame—a still life, not capable of movement.

"Elena?" The name resonated in a powerful whisper, a voice that had lost all of its familiarity, like a distant chord.

Mrs. Wick slipped away from the sink and slowly made her way out the door into the abbey.

"My God." Ellen placed her hand to her mouth. "Patrick." Older now and stronger, more of a presence than the gangly young man she'd pocketed away in that cold and empty little corner of her heart half a lifetime ago.

"I can't believe it. You're the Ellen they've talked about. You're the woman who saved that child. All the times I came here these past weeks, you were here … all along. Right here."

He still had not moved from the door. "Those years I searched for you, never knowing …" He looked away, then back. "How can this be happening?"

Ellen backed up to the bench, holding onto the table to steady herself as she sat, confused and numb. A few of the magazines spilled onto the floor, unnoticed.

"What happened back then? I could never find you," he said.

"My father made sure of that … he made sure." She couldn't even tell if she was making sense; so many thoughts racing, tumbling into a logjam.

"Elena." He reached out and drew her up.

He was stronger now; she could feel the power in his hand. He stepped close and looked at her as if her eyes, her face might reveal a shared suffering.

She touched the side of his face where the thin black band secured the eye patch. "Oh, Patrick."

Their embrace was long and, for her, tearful. "I thought I would never see you again."

He touched the curls that framed her face. "You're as beautiful as I always imagined you would be." Then he kissed her cheek and enveloped her again in his embrace. "I want to know everything. I've prayed for a lifetime that you were well. I prayed grudgingly for your happiness since it was not something I could share." He pulled back and held her at arm's length. "We've got to talk." He looked up at the clock.

"But I have to check on Joe Hopper. I'll come back. I can pick you up later so we can go somewhere and talk. We need to talk."

She hesitated.

"Please," he said, backing out the door.

She nodded her agreement, then sat in stunned silence after he left, turning her engagement ring over and over on her finger.

Chapter

Twenty-Seven

"One of the most extraordinary things I've ever seen." Father Elway tapped his finger against his lip. "Truly."

"This is what I've been talking about, Father—why does God do these things? Just when everything is going along so well, He … He throws a monkey wrench into it. I can't believe it."

It was a moody day, with the gloom of the rainy afternoon filling Father Elway's library study. He turned on another lamp before taking a seat opposite Ellen. "I hardly believe it myself. None of us can. You and Major O. lost to each other for twenty years until this very day, this very place." He looked up at the ceiling. "Oh, if ever we knew the mind of God."

"Patrick is coming back later to pick me up so we can talk."

"Mm." Father Elway rubbed the back of his neck. "Then, of course, I'm wondering about John. You remember, he and his son-in-law are coming over tomorrow. Will you see him before then?"

"I won't be able to—he's at a broker's meeting. People from overseas. He might not even be able to call me tonight."

"And when you do talk? What will you tell him?"

As Ellen struggled for an answer, Mrs. Wick followed Father Garrett in with a tea tray. "I thought you might all need a little something for soothing," she said.

Father Garrett, ever urgent with concern, quickly sat, attentive, but said nothing. Then, they each took the tea that Mrs. Wick served, the clink of spoon on cup the only sound between them. Tony circled the room, stopping near Father Elway, who reached out offering a nibble of Mrs. Wick's tea biscuit. "Good boy."

After a long moment, Ellen looked at Father Garrett. "How is Joe, Father?"

"I just came from the hospital. They think it was a medication issue. Evidently, our young soldier was so confident in his ease here at the abbey that he stopped taking his pills. Thomas always warns them about that, but they sometimes have to learn on their own. This one was a little rough, but it looks like he'll be okay as long as he sticks with his regimen." He sipped his tea. "What about you?"

Ellen took a deep breath. "There's so much happening so fast, Father. I'm still in shock."

Father Elway glanced over his shoulder as a weak spill of sunlight found its way through the stained-glass window behind his desk. "Well, this is nice." He looked at his watch, then back at Ellen. "I'm pretty sure the Major won't be here for another hour or so. Why not join me in the prayer garden."

Hatley's Seafood, a local favorite in the town of Riverhead on the north fork of Long Island, was the first place they passed that seemed suitable for a long, quiet conversation, its empty porch tables evidence of the diminished post-Labor Day crowds. They picked a table along the wooden railing facing the water before realizing how blustery it was, a clear bellwether of autumn's early arrival.

"We can change our minds," Patrick said. "Want to go indoors?"

"Not unless you do. It feels refreshing … for the moment, anyway."

After the waitress took her Coke order and his black coffee preference, they sat for a long moment, taking each other in without speaking. He had a serious demeanor, she could see that, though not unpleasant—maybe a bit intense, different from his ways as a young man. Most of all, she could see the thing that garnered so much admiration and respect—his strength and conviction, together with what she knew of his devotion to the veterans.

"I still can't believe this," he said. "Can you?" He'd worn his civilian clothes, preferring to attract as little attention and comment as possible. Two wars, still so fresh in everyone's mind, often invited interactions between strangers in public—a veteran in uniform eliciting comments of praise and gratitude. She could tell that Patrick would not be comfortable with the attention.

"I was talking with the priests," she said. "They're as stunned by this as we are. Who wouldn't be?"

He removed a pack of Marlboro cigarettes from his shirt pocket, then held it out to her first before removing one for himself. "I remember you never got into the habit." He leaned in, his arms resting on the table. "Tell me about you, Elena … Ellen—something I have to get used to. You know a bit about me now, where I've been all these years. Once I realized that finding you was hopeless, I joined up, and here I am, war wounds and all. But I'm okay, especially now."

"I'm so sorry. I can't imagine what you must have experienced."

"Most people really can't imagine what it's like, and not just because a person loses an eye or a leg, both legs. You step out of reality. You're on another plane. Living to survive, to overcome, enduring every horrific scene, ready to die, ready to kill—Sorry. If you noticed that I can be intense, you've figured me out. I'm known for being too serious, not very friendly. Joy is not my strong suit. I'm working on it. Maybe that's why I've stuck with military life—it's a place where you don't have to be Mr. Personality to get along, even excel. Am I being too cynical?"

"Maybe just a little." They laughed. She understood completely since she could relate so well to that side of life when all seems bleak. "I began to struggle with that myself, Patrick. At some point, it's almost like … I don't know … you get the feeling that you've become some beastly version of yourself. That's exactly where I was when I arrived at the abbey."

Over a lunchtime meal of codfish cakes and potato salad, she told him about the years, how things evolved, her real estate business, her recent financial disaster, and, haltingly, the great sense of loss that she carried through the long, busy years. He was especially surprised by everything she told him about her time at the abbey, including a certain red cardinal.

"Are you kidding? That silly bird?"

"If you can believe it, that silly bird has a name—Solomon. He has a way about him that's hard to explain, but when he shows up, things happen. Unexpected things. Does any of this sound familiar?"

"So, then, it looks like I can actually attest to that, can't I?" he said. "I would never have come back into the kitchen if he hadn't attacked the bunch of us. Not only that, but all the others were able to duck into the gazebo, except me. That bird … excuse me—Solomon … chased me to the kitchen door."

"I'm wondering." She gave him a long look, reticent. "Did you ever … go back to Poughkeepsie?"

He put his head straight back and looked up, the way one does when searching for that certain memory stored in a long-forgotten file. "You can never go back," he said, wistful, "though I often wished we could."

"A day of days, wasn't it?"

"A day of days." There was melancholy in his voice.

That day. They had driven for a few hours from Connecticut, just a little day trip. She remembered his gray trousers, his pale blue shirt, argyle vest. She had worn her blue gingham dress with the narrow, navy-blue belt. They traveled with the top down on his roadster, her hair whipping around in every direction. Lunch at a roadside country diner along the Hudson—meatloaf sandwiches and coleslaw. It was the day he asked her to marry him. The most beautiful of days before it all went wrong with her father, but that's not what they spoke of. It was the joy between them that they'd never forgotten, like a favorite song you'll still know the words to half a century later.

"We had some great times even though, generally speaking, it was the worst of times because of the Depression."

"I remember how I couldn't uncover my eyes the night we went to see King Kong."

The ease with which they could speak to each other so openly, sharing sad memories along with the happy ones, pleased her. It felt so good to laugh together the way they used to. It was wonderful. If he noticed her ring, he never mentioned it. Neither did she.

The sky was low and turbulent, with the sun in and out

the whole time they talked, two hours, maybe more. She had no idea. The waitress checked on them from time to time, refreshing their beverages, unnoticed, and eventually stayed away altogether. What did it matter? This was Patrick, after all.

She asked about his family—his mother, a kind and loving woman who lived in an apron amid the scent of fresh baked cookies and homemade bread, had always been welcoming to her. She would have blessed Ellen's marriage to Patrick. As would his father, a trolley driver, who provided a model of responsibility and decency for his only son. She was sad now to learn that both had passed away.

He told her about his upcoming move to Arizona and the work he expected to continue with war-stricken veterans. At one point, he reached over and put his hand on hers. "No matter what or where, I have never been able to set us aside, at least not for very long." He looked down, embarrassed. "I had a foolish moment right before going overseas when the fighting started—I married a woman I didn't really know very well. A nice woman, but it was all a big mistake, the same mistake a lot of guys make rushing off to war. Misguided as it often is, it's a helpful, reassuring thing to believe you're bound to someone who would wait for you, pray for you, be there when you got back … if you got back." He gestured to his eye. "I got back all right, but she took one look at this, and it was all over. Of course, I wasn't the easiest guy to get along with when I got home. I have to be honest—sometimes I'm still not, but I'm working on it. In any case, I could hardly blame her. I was angry for a long while, although my time at the abbey helped more than anything." He looked off. "I owe everything to Father Garrett. I don't know what I would have done without him or without Thomas, even though his injuries, in some ways, were worse than mine."

"I only just found out about Thomas. I have to say I'm shocked. We've become close, but he never said a word."

"He's like that. But, yes, he lost his leg along with a lot of blood. Very nearly died."

The wind plowed across their table, scattering the napkins and nearly upending the ashtray along with their dessert plates. One of the chairs was blown sideways and took a potted plant with it.

"Wow. We'd better head out," he said, as they quickly made their way through the restaurant, stopping only long enough for him to pay the check. Their waitress had already left for the day. "Be sure she gets this, will you?"

When they were back in the Army sedan, which he would be turning in at the end of the week, she gave him a long and tender look. "Thank you, Patrick. Not just for the lovely lunch. For everything. For telling me things I would never have known." She looked down, rubbing her thumbs. "For remembering … us."

He reached over and touched her hand, and they sat for a while, looking straight ahead. The sky still couldn't make up its mind, gray to blue and back again, clouds rolling in clumps before moving on, coming and going, a sprinkle and a pause, gusts tearing at the trees. It was after five. The dark was coming earlier these days as the year skipped along toward fall. She thought about the passing of time and all its implications, often subtle, like a single day being one minute shorter than the day before it or two decades held together with a ribbon made threadbare, little by little, with the passing of the years.

"I think," she said, at last, "remembering is … about the past, isn't it?"

He didn't answer.

"Isn't it, Patrick?" She touched his arm, the muscled arm of a soldier, mature and heroic, a magnificent man sent to her now, unexpected, as a precious gift for what he offered at long last—freedom.

"Yes," he said, resigned, as she was, to reality, "the past." He turned to look at her as if to be sure she would be all right with what he was about to say. "Elena. There is a woman." He paused, appearing to wait for a response. "A wonderful woman. Her name is Ann." He waited.

Ellen watched him, listening intently, open to whatever he was finding so hard to say.

"I love her. It did take me a while to realize it."

She sensed his struggle.

"We're going to be married," he said. "And one thing I know—this time it's going to last." He kept his eye on her, apprehensive. "I'm sure of it."

When he was through, she reached over, smiling, and hugged him hard. "Oh, thank you, Patrick. Dear Patrick. Thank you."

It was clear that her words were completely unexpected. "You're okay?" he said. "I mean, it's all right?" He was still a boy in the way of tender emotions, hoping for approval or forgiveness. "I mean, you're all right with it?"

"Better than that, Patrick. Better than that." She took a deep breath, the joy bursting within her. "For me, Patrick, his name is John." She pressed her hand with the ring against her heart. "He wants a December wedding, and I can't wait … because I love him more than anything in the world."

Chapter

Twenty-Eight

"Oh, how I wish we could come out and see you," Kate said. "This is all too much."

"You mean you're not going to use the word miracle," Ellen said, "now that I'm finally ready to see things your way?" You would have discovered it a long time ago if, for example, you'd found out about the jacket."

"The jacket. Ohh." It was something that had again slipped Ellen's mind. "I have brought it up to Thomas and Mrs. Wick, but we always get distracted by something. What's it all about?"

"Ask again," was all Kate said. "Matt and I will see you soon as we can. In the meantime, my dear and difficult friend, love that man with everything you've got."

It was an easy thing to do—loving John Caraballo. True, she did have to pause and swallow hard after learning that he was the man behind the extraordinary Cara Diamond brand. Humble as he was, he was nonetheless a man of fabulous means. She knew she would have to be prepared for a different lifestyle; she just wasn't sure how different. As much as he avoided interviews and other publicity, he had already warned her that things about him, about them, could appear in the papers, especially now that they'd become engaged.

She'd been to his home, which he shared with Louise, Peter, and little Billy, and although very smartly appointed with fine furnishings and original artwork, it had a relaxed and intimate feel, not at all lavish. "A new Cadillac every three years," he had told her, "is as showy as I get."

"Not every year or every two years?" she had joked.

"Never even every two-and-a-half," he'd insisted, playful.

Father Elway—and even Father Garrett, whom she had come to like and respect as much as the abbot—had become her confidants. She had finally confessed about seeing the quirky, white-haired man again, and in the very same place, with his crashed-up bicycle, mumbling that things always turn out the way they're supposed to. Well, it seems he might have been right after all.

Father Garrett shrugged. "Maybe he was your guardian angel sent to remind you that God has certain plans for us, no matter what, no matter how long it may take. So, there's no point rushing to the bus or trying to catch the train. Is there?"

"Angels come in all shapes and sizes, all times and places, all means available." Father Elway tapped his lip. "Take Officer Polly, for example."

"Father Elway, really?"

"Well, he made sure there was no way you were going to leave here. Am I right?"

She had to agree, even though she hadn't made any promises about her faith. Still, the chapel had become a special place. She could ponder things there in the silence.

Father Elway eyed the long mailing tube that Peter Crowley carried under his arm. "Well, what have you got there?" he asked as he led the way to his library study.

The young man and his father-in-law had arrived at one—as planned—for the meeting about which the priests still knew nothing. Thomas had also been invited, knowing nothing more than Father Elway and Father Garrett did.

During small talk, they congratulated John Caraballo on his engagement to Ellen, as Mrs. Wick appeared, gracious and perceptive as ever, carrying a tray of coffee and shortbread cookies. She had an uncanny instinct about the tenor of a situation, always knowing when to be cheerful and chatty and when to "serve and retreat," as she called it. She handed John Caraballo the first steaming cup.

"Ah, very nice, Mrs. Wick. Thank you. I didn't have time for a second cup today. This is perfect."

The conversation was light and friendly, curiosity still lingering in the air. "Of course, we're so glad to see you both again." Father Elway said. "You're always welcome here, although you've presented us with quite a teaser, not having any idea what's on your minds."

"How do you feel about surprises, Father?" John asked.

Father tapped his lip. "The good ones can be a lot of fun."

Peter set his coffee cup down. "We think you'll find this a good one." He stood and gestured to the other side of the room. "Do you mind if we go to that large writing table?"

"Not at all."

"You're really doubling down on the intrigue," Father Garrett said with wry amusement, and for the next half hour, the two priests and the seminarian were treated to an astonishing proposal that none of them could ever possibly have imagined.

Chapter
Twenty-Nine

"Yes, Father," said John Caraballo, "I absolutely understand why it sounds unbelievable. But..."

"No 'buts' about it, John," Father Elway said, with the uplift of surprise in his voice. "It is, to say the least, the most ... the most extraordinary thing I've ever heard. This offer of yours ... is ... it's ..."

"Humbling," Father Garrett said.

Father Elway paced a few steps, his fingers laced behind his back. "Among other things, yes, humbling. Very much so."

"Miracles can be that way," Thomas said, studying the blueprints.

"That they can," Father Elway looked again at the large set of detailed drawings sprawled across the writing table. "That they can." He turned to Caraballo. "This will cost you a fortune, John."

"I humbly say, Father, that God has blessed me with great

fortune to share, and it's for a cause that is very dear to my heart." He looked away for an instant. "My son … Daniel … was killed nine years ago at Utah Beach. D-Day."

Father Garrett stopped and turned to him. "Oh, John, we didn't know. I'm so sorry to hear that. What a terrible loss."

"For years, I thought of ways I could honor his gift to our freedom." He smoothed his hand across the top of his head. "I've made donations to veteran funds and bought my share of war bonds, of course, but this … this struck me the moment I toured the lodge with you, Thomas."

Father Elway went back across the room and sat. The others joined him. "Ironic," he said, "how your great cause becomes our great miracle. So very sad, though, to learn this about Daniel."

"And isn't it true," Thomas said, "how we pray for a miracle, and when it comes, we are often so thunderstruck that our immediate reaction is to dismiss or refuse it?"

John Caraballo leaned forward, elbows resting on his knees. "But what you have to realize is that this is my miracle, too—the very thing I've been praying for. And, now, I can only pray that you will not dismiss or refuse it, Father."

"How could I?" The priest fingered the black and silver pectoral cross that he wore around his neck on a long black cord. "This has to be something from God. I know that. I believe it with all my heart. And you," he said, "looking at John and Peter, "you are the angels bearing gifts. And as I say that, I'm even struck by how apropos your names are."

"Well, I wouldn't go that far," John Caraballo said, "but let's talk about how and when this would happen once we had your permission to proceed, of course." He turned and gestured toward the doorway behind him. "Would it be appropriate for us to include Ellen? Would that be okay?"

"Yes, of course," Father Elway said. "I'm sorry I didn't think of it."

Father Garrett rose quickly. "Let me get her."

"Are you serious, John?" Ellen was as stunned as the others had been when they'd first been told of the plans.

"I'm very serious, Ellen. I asked Peter to draw up plans for the expansion of the lodge to accommodate as many as thirty veterans. All new bedrooms, larger kitchen and dining room, two additional sitting or living areas. A large, second fireplace. Two more game and craft rooms, as well as a separate library/reading room. There will also be two small rooms that can double as conference or meeting rooms when a counselor meets with one or more of the men."

Ellen looked again at the blueprints. "I don't know what to say. Peter, these plans are amazing." She turned to the priests. "What do you make of all this?"

"Same as you, Ellen," Father Elway said. "We are still in disbelief. I was beginning to believe that it wouldn't happen in my lifetime."

"I know there are only four veterans remaining at the

moment," John Caraballo said. "I understand Corporal Hopper will be staying. Sorry to hear of the trouble he had, by the way. But if we can hold off having others come for now, maybe you can accommodate the remaining four in the Guest house. Then, with your permission, we can start the remodel and new construction in a couple of weeks, work hard through the fall on all the exterior work, and then spend the winter months doing the interior work. We're keeping in mind, of course, that the lodge will become a more versatile place, considering that the Korean War has ended, and over the next year or two, you'll begin to see the end of the returning vets. You'll find other uses for the space. You might consider that this could easily serve as a smaller version of the larger retreat center to come."

"Makes sense," Thomas said. "It's 1953. Praise God those wars are behind us. Best of all, there doesn't appear to be anything especially threatening on the horizon."

Father Elway gave Thomas a sober look. "We certainly pray that is true, Thomas, but with the Communists always on the move, who knows, and right now Southeast Asia is somewhat of a troublesome question mark."

"We want you to know something else about all this, Father." Peter extended his arm in a slow, sweeping gesture. "We promise you, we will preserve every inch of the rare, vintage architecture, maintaining all those details in the new construction."

John took a sip of coffee. "There's more."

"What more could there possibly be?" Father Garrett chuckled at the thought of it.

"I'm a businessman. I look long-range." He gave them a canny smile. "I know you do too, only in a different way. What I'm talking about is creating a perpetual stream of income to fund not only the lodge but whatever other projects you can imagine. Let's say, for example, a retreat center."

Father Elway rubbed the back of his neck. "I appreciate your thinking, John; I really do. But as challenging an idea as the lodge was, a retreat center is another matter. There is absolutely no funding for it. It's a very different creature."

"Yes, but a creature we can tame, a beautiful creature." Caraballo gestured to his son-in-law. "We don't have any plans yet, but we do have an idea, and we think it's a solid one if you're willing to consider some things you may never have thought about before."

Mrs. Wick came in and politely interrupted with an invitation for the visitors to stay for dinner.

John Caraballo looked at Ellen and the others. "I would love to, if that's all right with everyone?"

"Couldn't think of a better idea," Father Elway said. "Thank you, Mrs. Wick, for thinking of it. And, by the way, both of you are more than welcome to use our Guest house if it will be more convenient for you to spend the night rather than drive back to the city."

"That's a very kind invitation, Father. I'd be happy to. I'm just not sure about you, Peter."

"Under the circumstances," Peter said, "I'm sure Louise will be fine with it. I'll give her a call as soon as we're done here."

"Now," John Caraballo said, "if I may, let me give you an idea of what I've been thinking." He rose, thoughtful, and stood behind his chair, facing the priests. "To get the retreat center you've prayed for all these years, Father, would fifteen acres be too much of a trade? Fifteen out of more than four hundred?"

Father Elway gave John a worrisome look. "You're not talking about selling off our property, I pray, John."

"A piece of it, yes, but not quite in the way you might think."

Father Elway shot a glance at Father Garrett and got to his feet, clearly uncomfortable. "John, I greatly appreciate … more than you know … the plans for the lodge. But I cannot go along with selling our precious abbey land."

Peter Crowley put up his hands in an effort to calm the priest's anxious resistance. "But, honestly, Father, we're not proposing a sell-off … not the typical kind, anyway. We believe you'll again be pleasantly surprised by what we have in mind."

Father Garrett removed his glasses and wiped the lens with his handkerchief, his anxiety clearly rising. "We're still listening."

Father Elway returned to his chair, his face still visibly strained. "What difference could fifteen acres possibly make for a retreat center big enough to accommodate sleeping quarters, a variety of rooms, large and small, events of varying sizes, a small chapel, reception hall, and kitchen, to say nothing of the access road and parking?" He rubbed the back of his neck. "I'm sorry, John, but I just don't see it."

"I'm sure it's a jolting thought, Father," Peter said. "This is where we can really engage Ellen's help."

Ellen straightened up, a surprised look on her face. "Can't imagine how I can contribute anything in this regard."

John turned and looked directly at her. "Ellen, you've got an extensive background in real estate. Maybe you can think of someone, some company, a good one, qualified and trustworthy enough to handle a development project." He turned quickly to Father Elway. "And, Father, believe me, I know the word 'development' must have a terrifying ring to it, but I'm convinced that with the right people in place, you will have your retreat center, along with your wonderful lodge, without sacrificing an inch of this precious property's integrity."

Father Elway rose slow and pensive, his hands clasped behind his back. "I'll need to pray about this, John. I'm convinced you mean well, but I'm going to need a little time and much, much more information and guidance. Especially guidance."

"I promise you'll have it," said Peter.

"But my guidance will come from only one source," Father Elway responded.

Peter looked to his father-in-law, then back to the priest. "Please know. We will not let you down."

Father Elway stood in front of John Caraballo and looked directly at him. "I'm reluctant, John. You can tell that. But let's see what you come up with." He turned and walked slowly to the door, clearly still in thought. "I'll take a walk before dinner. There is much to think about."

Chapter

Thirty

AFTER DARK, THE gazebo took on a chameleon quality—if one were unhappy or dismayed, it was as isolating and lonely as a cell, apart from everyone and everything, the night sounds eliciting torment; if one were happy, it was a joyous refuge where the nocturnal choir of crickets welcomed you into the deep, mysterious beauty.

Ellen and John sat side by side, holding hands in the darkness.

"I was so sorry to learn about Daniel," she whispered. "You never told me."

"It's something I don't usually talk about. In wartime, you're just another father with a broken heart."

She heard him sigh.

"He was everything to me, as Marjorie was. As is Louise. And Peter and Billy." He squeezed her hand. "Now, you. God is generous. Just when we believe memory is all there is, there's more."

The October chill was bracing. They'd come out with light jackets following a wonderful dinner, and now she found she needed the scarf that she almost didn't bring along.

"I like it out here," she said. "To a kid, it might be that special secret hideout." She turned to him, barely able to see him in the darkness. "I like hiding out with you."

He brought his face close to hers. She felt his breath on her cheek before he kissed it.

"Mm," was her only response.

"You said you had something you wanted to talk to me about. Does it have to do with the plans Peter and I presented to Father Elway?"

"No." She drew a deep breath.

"Is everything okay?" He moved in the darkness.

"Everything is fine, John. It's just that something extraordinary happened that none of us here at the abbey ever expected or imagined."

He let go of her hand and moved closer, gently rubbing her arm. "What is it, El?"

"I … met the Major."

"Major O?"

"Yes."

"He's quite a guy. His devotion to these veterans is a wonderful thing."

"All this time that I've been here, John, believe it or not, I had never met him. Then, just like that, he walked in the back door of the kitchen."

"Okay."

She sensed the caution in his voice. "I was in the kitchen with Mrs. Wick. I had come in just after the Major left, but a few minutes later, he came rushing in the back door when the crazy bird that hangs out around the prayer garden kind of … well … attacked some of the vets, including the Major."

"Sounds crazy, all right. Is he all right? Was anyone hurt?"

"No, but when the Major came rushing through the door … that was the first time I'd even seen him. And …"

"And?"

"As it turns out, John, the Major … is Patrick."

"Patrick?"

"Patrick from twenty years ago, John. My Patrick."

"That Patrick. How is that possible?"

"I know. None of us could believe it. We still can't."

"Except, of course, that it was him. Is him," John said. "Quite a shock. I can imagine." Before she could say anything, he went on. "So, what is it like to see someone … who meant so much … after all those years? Someone so important in your life?"

"Once we realized who each of us was, we … we spoke very briefly, then decided we needed to talk. So, when he got back from seeing Joe Hopper in the hospital, we went to lunch."

"I see."

"I want you to know everything, John, and to make sure you understand. We drove out to a restaurant where it looked like we could speak in private. He told me about his life, and I told him about mine. He was married once. It didn't work out."

"So, he's … still single."

"He's engaged to be married. And I was glad to hear it, John." She pulled herself closer to him in the dark, taking hold of his arm, leaning into him. "Because I wouldn't have wanted him to think there was any chance for us. Any chance at all. I was relieved to know that he had someone in his life, the way I do."

"That's all pretty unbelievable, isn't it?"

"There's more."

"I'm amazed that there could be."

"You wouldn't be if you had any idea what this means to me, John, … the closure … the half a lifetime of wondering, done now, finally, without disappointment, sadness, or regret. Over."

"So, no lingering feelings for him?"

"None whatever. My feelings belong to someone else, John. Deep and sure. The dearest man in the world."

She could hear him getting up out of his chair. In the darkness, he reached down and drew her up into his arms, and there, in the chilly nocturnal sweetness, he warmed her in his embrace, and they kissed with all the passion and conviction of that very first time their lips had met.

Chapter

Thirty-One

ANGIOLO'S IN WANTAGH was every bit the elegant, intimate Italian restaurant Kate had described and recommended. It was, in fact, the place of Kate's first date with Matt Reagan, an appealing locale with deep red walls and a dark beamed ceiling, white tablecloths, and pewter lanterns. The aroma of garlic and pasta and pizza permeated the room with the fireplace adding even more to the welcoming ambiance. But this was no romantic occasion; this was going to be all business.

Lenny Feinman reached out and shook Ellen's hand. "It was good to hear from you, Ellen. Thanks for calling." Although they had never met in person, they had been in touch a number of times over the recent weeks while he handled the closing on her brownstone.

Ellen introduced Lenny to John and Peter. "You have no idea how grateful I am to this man for helping me with the sale of my house. Truly grateful."

They were shown to a table off to the side—perfect, Ellen thought, for such an important luncheon meeting. After a bit of small talk, they placed their orders for drinks and an appetizer, while continuing to look over the extensive menu of entrees for which this thirty-year-old four-star restaurant was highly reputed.

John Caraballo regarded Lenny amiably across an inviting antipasti platter of genoa salami, sharp provolone cheese, and large cerignola olives. "Like me, you're a little far from home, Lenny, but Ellen tells me you're interested in expanding your real estate company out this way."

"Definitely. It's not only a beautiful area, but as a business, we'd be foolish not to at least consider being part of the growing migration from Brooklyn."

"That sounds like a pretty smart thing to do," Peter said, filling a small plate.

Over baked pasta, Caesar salad, and a bottle of superb Tinta Negra wine, recommended by the owner himself, Tony Angiolo, who had come to their table and greeted them like family, they fell briefly into small talk before Ellen went on to explain a little about the abbey and their need for a trustworthy partner to join in a very special project. She could tell Lenny was absorbed in what she told him. He had a kind look about him, a face to match what she remembered from all their phone conversations, especially his sympathetic encouragement the first time they spoke not long after she'd arrived at the abbey. She couldn't help sensing that his was a benevolent energy, not at all the aggressive personality she'd often encountered over the years—men with great self-regard and feigned interest in their clients before revealing their shallow attentiveness. She was pleased, and she could tell that John and Peter were as well.

Lenny set his glass of club soda on the table. "What can I do to help?"

"From everything that Ellen has told us about you," John said, "we have a feeling that you and your partner might well be the ones we're looking for to join us in an unusual venture."

"Tell me more."

John rested his arms on the table. "First and foremost, we must protect the integrity of the abbey at all cost. Agreed?"

"Agreed," Lenny said.

"We'll give you a tour of the property, a bit more than four hundred secluded acres, a good portion of which is woodland. What many people, including local residents, don't realize is that one end of this amazing property is that virgin woodland strip that forms over a one-hundred-and-fifty-yard border along Old Country Road."

Lenny pulled back, wide-eyed. "Roadside? Are you kidding? That's gold."

"You bet it is," John said. "That frontage is priceless. There's no doubt that within the next five to seven years, as the population continues its upward trend, that road will be a major four-lane thoroughfare."

"The way we look at it," Peter said, "why not make the most

of it at a time when we can be at the forefront of development while serving the abbey's very noble and useful cause."

Lenny looked at Peter. "I believe you're right. I really do. Stu and I have already researched the trends in Nassau County. The migration is remarkable. Many Brooklyn neighborhoods are changing. People want to move away. As that trend continues, and I keep telling my partner this, you'll see more housing developments out here, nothing high-priced, mostly middle income, a thousand square feet. Levitt has already started, and he's doing very well—heated floors, double-sided fireplaces."

"Good." John continued. "We want to propose to the abbot, Father Elway, that we take just fifteen acres of that border—that's all we need—to build a housing development of about twenty-five homes.

"Such a development," Peter added, "would be easily accessed with a road coming off Old Country Road but would not utilize the frontage."

"That's curious," Lenny said. "Why not feature the houses up front?"

John took a sip of wine and put his glass down. "Privacy, for one thing, And we propose to utilize the frontage for a line of individual, high-use, high-interest stores, not a strip mall, but a cluster of quaint shops with unique charm. Ten acres for the housing, five acres for the shops, including ample parking."

"A pharmacy and hardware store," Peter said.

"An Italian or Jewish deli, I hope," said Lenny with a hopeful grin.

"I don't think we'll need a milk, butter, and eggs kind of place," Ellen added. "There's a popular dairy barn right up the road." She looked from one to the other. "Maybe a beauty parlor?"

"Definitely a bank as the anchor store," John added.

"And," Ellen gave Lenny a wink, "if that location suits you and Stu, why not your realty office?"

Lenny gave an approving look around the table. "I like the sound of this. Where exactly do Stu and I figure into it? Doesn't sound like it's all about us opening up an office."

"Not at all." John sat back in his chair. "We want to offer you the opportunity to buy it and build it. The whole thing." He gave a nod to Peter. "We've got the architect, so you won't need to worry about the plans. We'll work together on that."

Lenny rested his hand on top of his head. "Whoa!" He looked around the table. "That's big."

John smiled. "Big good or big too much?"

"Oh, definitely big good, but how would it work? Just a direct purchase? I have a feeling that's only the beginning."

"Smart," Peter laughed. "Yes, we have to control the planning; there would be certain critical stipulations."

"And you'll see that everyone will benefit," John said. He hesitated, collecting his thoughts. "Our main goal is to build a retreat center for the abbey. This will cost a lot of money, as you can imagine. So, we figure that part is about three to four years away. Your purchase of this prime property is the start, and we have to be honest, the abbey's not giving it away—you'll pay top dollar. That's what will fund the major portion of the construction of the center. But we just can't consider the construction alone. There has to be revenue of some kind to operate the center ongoing, even though many of the church organizations, and others, who will book a retreat event there will pay a fee. Still, there are many operating expenditures, as you can imagine."

Lenny, thoughtful, took a sip of club soda. "How will that part affect my end of it?"

"We propose that the abbey collect a one-time, small percentage of the purchase price of every house you sell, and, secondly, a small percentage of the monthly rent, into perpetuity, from those seven retailers that will occupy the frontage. We'll hash out the numbers to come up with a percentage that's amenable to all. And you can trust that you and your partner will do very well."

"Wow." Lenny sat back. "What a concept."

The table fell silent.

Ellen had sat, admiring and grateful, watching John Caraballo, the smart, charismatic businessman, the man who built his Cara Diamond brand into the most highly desirable and respected name on the lips of every bride-to-be in the country. She was happy that he didn't do business with a dagger in his teeth. She was proud that he was so ardent and committed to this project when none of this was for his profit. She was content to have finally seen the full picture of the man she would spend the rest of her life with.

Chapter

Thirty-Two

ALTHOUGH THE GAZEBO had been her great delight almost from the start, the chapel was now Ellen's favorite place on the entire property, a comforting and uplifting blend of the sacred and the serene. Early each morning, even before the priests arrived for Mass, she draped her paisley kerchief around her head, fastened it in a loose knot under her chin, and slipped into the last pew, committed to the silence and solace that now enriched her spirit.

Father Pelletier was always the next to arrive, quiet and reverent, to set the altar cloth and light the semi-circle of votives that fragranced the chapel with the honey scent of the beeswax candles. She enjoyed watching him, knowing that, for him, this was a joyful act of devotion. The others soon followed. She would hear their low chant as they approached in unison along the colonnade. Not long after, the local people who attended daily Mass trickled in, often filling the chapel. More than once, in overflow, they had stood along the back and down the far wall, where the narrow aisle sloped toward the altar. She was getting to know them, often taking time after Mass to chat with them—Mrs. Di Melo, Agnes Finnerty, the Lombardi's, to name a few. She looked forward to the occasional feast day when all were invited to enjoy Mrs. Wick's coffee and teacakes with the priests in the abbey reception room. On the night that John and Peter stayed over in the Guest house, they had joined her for Mass and, afterward, John surprised her by asking if this was the church where she would like to have their wedding.

"Oh, yes, John, yes, if that's okay."

"A perfect place," he said, "to marry the perfect woman."

"But there must be so many people you'll want to invite. They won't all fit here."

"I know a lot of people, El. I'm a businessman. But I keep my private life very close to home and family. There won't be nearly as many as you might think."

Afterward, he and Peter stayed for breakfast in the downstairs kitchen and were as taken with the old-world ambiance as she had been that very first time Thomas brought her there. She was beginning to realize how many things there were about the abbey that she was excited to share with people.

One morning, Thomas chose to sit with her at the back of the chapel. He had also arrived before the others but quietly chanted along with them as they started filing in. She was enormously pleased by this and had made a private vow that, when the time came for his ordination in a few short months, she would hope to be the first to meet Father Thomas in the confessional.

"Thank you so much for sitting with me," she said to him after Mass.

"I'm happy, as we all are, that you're coming to Mass again. What a blessing."

She thought so too, but had to wonder if she was just caught up in the joy of her love for John. Still, she intended to recapture the sense of the divine, if it were possible for her. If it were to happen, she believed it would surely be ignited here in the midst of these amazing holy people.

"Thomas, there's something I'd like to talk to you about." It had crossed her mind that he might be offended if she brought up his injuries, but she would trust his forgiving nature. "I've learned that you were severely wounded in the war … in Europe." She paused, looking for his reaction, which was simply a short nod of the head as confirmation. She could only guess it would be all right to continue. "I had no idea. I had noticed that there was … that you had some difficulty, but I assumed that maybe it was … you know … something you were born with. Or even … Polio."

"I've had people ask me about it over the years," he said, appearing unfazed. "Some thought the same thing." He gave a wry laugh. "I'm still not sure which would have been worse."

"I can't imagine, Thomas." After they sat silent for a moment, she asked. "So, you and the Major … you and

Patrick … were together? In the same unit?"

"Different units. We'd never met. It was odd the way it happened. After days of scrambling around, hunkering down in the mud for strategic positions during the endless firefights, I somehow ended up behind a hillside berm about twenty feet from the Major's foxhole, though I didn't know it at the time. I didn't know him or any of his platoon. Grenades were exploding all around us, along with gunfire, shrapnel pouring in on our positions. I was pretty sure I wouldn't get out alive. Patrick later told me that he was pretty sure he wouldn't either, especially after the hit that took out his eye."

Ellen shivered visibly at the thought while the two sat there, quiet again, watching Father Pelletier snuff the votives and remove the altar linens.

"Sorry I got so graphic," he said. "I should know better."

"Sometimes, I think more of us need to hear about it. Truth is, after learning what these veterans like Joe and Eugene and the others went through, I felt awful. But then learning that you suffered the way they did. Oh, Thomas." She touched his arm. "I'm so sorry."

"It's okay." He looked away before turning back to her. "Imagine how it has been for me, as a person who's devoted his life to God … imagine how great my sorrow has been knowing what you lost all these many years. Believe me, Ellen, my loss pales in comparison. I would rather have lost my life than my faith."

His words shocked her. They might even have offended

her if there weren't such great truth in what he said. She'd been living amongst these generous, kind, and accommodating priests, all the time more curious or concerned about their opinion of her without ever considering how they must have carried a great fear for her very soul. She looked into Thomas's eyes and, for the first time, saw a depth of wisdom that had eluded her. She recognized some of John in him, something behind the eyes, beyond mere seeing—serious but kind, connected without having to assert himself. He was more laconic than the others, likely a trait that served him well with the veterans—listening without commenting, saying much without speaking. When Thomas spoke, she paid attention. She pressed her lips together. "I have to admit that all of these … miracles … are convincing me that I have underestimated God."

He leaned forward, his arms resting on his knees, his fingers linked. "Why would you think a woman such as yourself, or nearly anyone for that matter, required a miracle to find true love, to find kindness and generosity, peace and beauty in the world? We don't always need to seek miracles, Ellen, when we're in touch with the concept of God's blessings, even when they may not be the particular blessings we're looking for, longing for. Everything that God has created is, in itself, a miracle."

He was right, of course; she could see it. This was Thomas, always showing her more than she knew for herself. She had always enjoyed their time together. She had admired him from the start but never more so than right now, knowing of his wartime experience, his survival, his brilliance, his calling.

"How did you deal with it all? Were you like Joe Hopper and the others?"

"Sometimes worse. It was the hardest thing I ever went through in my life. A dark and harrowing time." He spoke haltingly, as one searches, stalling at what one's memory settles upon. "There were days … I have to be honest … even though I prayed hard, I didn't want to live, but I just kept on. I never gave up on God because I believed, and still do, that he'd never give up on me. Still, I questioned. I struggled. I had days filled with grave doubts, days when I was so angry that I wrestled my beliefs to the ground. I once threw my Bible across the room so hard that it bounced off the wall and broke a lamp. That's when Father Garrett rushed in. He actually held me as I sobbed. His great faith was our cornerstone." He looked about. "And so, little by little … more like, very little by very little … the fog lifted, the smoke began to clear. Then, I began to wonder what God had saved me for. What purpose? Major O. … Patrick … and I talked about it a lot, asking the same question. Never once in my life had I considered becoming a priest. Ultimately, each of us found our own path."

"Thank God," she said, words that had not come from her mouth in … how long? She couldn't tell, and although they surprised her, she knew they were the right words, the only words. "You were so young."

"I was in my late twenties, not as young as some. I was an athlete who got through college on an athletic scholarship. I became a physical education teacher and a coach, the work I loved. The work I had planned to dedicate my life to."

"I didn't know." She had always steered clear of asking about his life, cautious, not wanting to appear to probe because of his physical condition. She'd had no idea.

"While I was recovering in the hospital in Virginia, my father passed away. It was sudden. A heart attack. He was only fifty. My mother had died when I was six. My father was closer to me than anyone in the world. He'd been an athlete himself. His death crushed me. I started going downhill fast. Coincidentally, so did Patrick. He and I were in the same hospital. His wife came to see him, and after her visit, she immediately filed for divorce. So, we were both in rough shape, in more ways than one. That's when Father Garrett came for a visit and, afterwards, arranged to take us back here with him."

"What suffering our military endure."

Tony whimpered, having become impatient waiting in the colonnade just outside the door of the chapel, as he did most mornings. Thomas went to the doorway. "Go to Mrs. Wick," he said in a low voice. "She has a cookie for you. A cookie. Go on now. Good boy." As Tony turned and loped toward the main house, Thomas returned and sat back down.

"You know," Ellen said, "over the years, I often wondered

what my life was all about. What was my purpose? I still don't know really. Loving John, marrying him. I couldn't ask for anything more. Is that purpose enough? I won't become a mother; that time is past. I suppose I can continue to help here at the abbey when possible. Community. Excited as I am looking forward to these next chapters of my life with the most wonderful man in the world, I still have to wonder what God may want of me." She gestured toward the altar. "But I do feel I'm now on the right track."

After a few moments sitting there in silence, Thomas put his hand on Ellen's. "There is only one thing I pray for you right now."

She turned to him, his eyes seeking something in hers. She would tell him anything.

"I pray that you will not be a fair-weather faithful— pleased with the Lord as long as …"

"As long as I get what makes me happy?"

They sat a while longer in the quiet, looking straight ahead, almost meditative, before she stood to leave. "I'm curious. How did you and Patrick know Father Garrett? Where did you meet him? It sounds as if you knew him before you even came to the abbey."

"That's right. This whole vets program didn't even exist."

"But I thought … I just assumed …" She tilted her head. "Okay, now I'm confused. How on earth did Father Garrett from Spiritu, of all places, find both of you in a Virginia hospital? How did you know each other?"

Thomas took Ellen's arm. "Come with me."

She followed him down the side aisle through a wooden plank door at the left of the altar into a room with deep amber-textured walls and racks filled with colored chasubles. Rustic plank shelves like the ones in Mrs. Wick's downstairs kitchen held an assortment of gold and silver chalices of differing sizes and styles, along with a number of ciboria, the gold and silver cup-like receptacles used to save or serve the Eucharist for Holy Communion.

"Oh, Thomas," she said, her voice a whisper.

"This is the Sacristy." He stepped back for her to explore the room.

"I've always wanted to go into a Sacristy. When I was a young girl in Catholic School, a few of us peeked inside after Mass, but the nuns chased us." She turned to him with a sly grin. "The nuns always chased us; we were never in the right place." They laughed.

"There's something else I want you to see."

She followed him to another door, past the shelves and one of the long racks of chasubles, where he reached up and removed a small, deep blue velvet pouch. He loosened the gold cord and removed a heavy, ornate brass skeleton key, which he turned in the keyhole until he heard the click. Then, he pushed open the door.

Chapter

Thirty-Three

ELLEN FOLLOWED THOMAS like a child invited to her first party. "What is this place?"

"We call it the Far Room."

Similar to the Sacristy in style and structure, the room was filled with items of varying types she couldn't identify, many in gold and silver frames on the walls, while boxes and chests, small and large, rustic and ornate, were set about on tables and shelves. A number of pieces were stored in glass enclosures—an elaborate brocade cape, a pair of ancient-looking sandals, and something like a shawl made of exquisite lace, among others.

Ellen stood still as a statue, her eyes alone exploring the objects with curiosity and delight. "What is this place, Thomas?"

"This is where we keep very special things, including a few relics and an item or two connected to miraculous events."

Whenever Ellen heard the word "relic," she recalled

stories she'd read over the years about the catacombs under the Vatican, in her mind's eye a creepy, cavernous facility for storing bodies of the long-ago dead. This was very different. "Where did these items come from? Who did they belong to?"

"Some belong to saints, the brocade cape was worn by Pope Leo, The Great, from the four hundreds, that white glove belonged to Padre Pio who has the stigmata—the wounds of Christ—on his hands."

She walked over to the case with the glass door that held the ornate lace. "This is so beautiful. I've never seen anything like it. Where did it come from?"

"This is our most recent addition just this year. I'm sure you've heard about the girl in Brooklyn, maybe not far from where you lived, the one who had the miraculous experiences that started with the gift of a shawl for her Confirmation." He pointed to the case. "That's the shawl."

"Oh, my goodness, yes. Margaret … something."

"Margaret Ferry. She and her family were concerned about the safety of the shawl. They asked us please to keep it safe. We have to keep it locked up because, believe it or not, it is known to travel when loose."

"I didn't know if that was true."

"Oh, it's true, all right." Thomas walked over to a small cabinet on the wall, where part of a man's uniform was displayed on a hanger behind a glass door. "Not long ago, you asked me about a jacket. Remember?"

"Yes." Ellen stepped closer. "Is that it?"

"That's it," he said, opening the door. He removed the hanger and held the jacket up for Ellen to look at.

"It looks like some kind of uniform jacket. It's covered in holes." She turned to Thomas. "Are these bullet holes?"

"That they are."

"Then, this person died in battle."

He put his fingers through the holes. "You would think so, wouldn't you."

"How could someone survive that? Did you know who it belonged to?"

"It belonged to an Army Chaplain positioned behind enemy lines. A very brave man. He happened to be the one who pulled Patrick to safety."

"I can't believe it."

"Dragged him across a field under heavy fire. Then, he came back for me. He saved both our lives."

"That's unbelievable. He died saving both of you."

"No," Thomas said. "Not one of those bullets touched him."

Ellen looked closer, examining the holes along with the inside of the jacket. "How could that be?"

"Because this is what a great miracle looks like."

She fell silent for a moment, still holding on to the jacket. "I can't imagine, but here it is."

She turned to Thomas. "Did you ever see this Chaplain again? Do you know what happened to him?"

"I do," he said. "As a matter of fact, so do you."

She gave him a puzzled look. "How could I possibly know an army chaplain?"

This uniform jacket belonged to Chaplain John Garrett—Father Garrett."

Ellen stepped back, mouth agape. After a moment, she slowly handed him the jacket, then left the room, back into the Sacristy where there was a chair for her to sit. Thomas placed the jacket in its glass case and locked the door to the Far Room. Then, he returned the key to its velvet pouch on the shelf. "Quite a shock, isn't it," he said.

"Father Garrett," she said, dazed. "Who could have imagined?" She reached out and took hold of Thomas's sleeve. "Thomas, you know how very much I care for Father Garrett. But do you know what I thought when I first met him? I'm ashamed." She hesitated. "When he stopped by my bungalow one morning out of graciousness and concern, with a newspaper, asking how I was doing, inviting me to come talk to any of you if I ever needed to." She looked up at him. "You know what I thought? I thought—what real use are these priests in their sheltered little world, untouched by reality? That's what I thought."

Thomas took her arm. "Come on," he said. "Let's go find Mrs. Wick. She'll have some breakfast for us."

Chapter

Thirty-Four

NOVEMBER BROUGHT THE deep chill of autumn, and with it, the first snowfall that transformed the abbey grounds into a sublime winter-scape reminiscent of Currier and Ives, temporarily halting construction at the lodge. But by Thanksgiving week, the roar and rumble of heavy equipment again echoed through the woods, chasing the birds, shaking loose the pine cones, and filling the air with the scent of diesel to accompany the constant pounding of hammers. Only a smattering of tall oaks and broad-canopied maples had to be removed—something that the priests kept close watch over—making way for the grading to be done and the footers to be set. Now, the trucks routinely made their way up the new rough and rutted drive to deliver the stone, studs, and concrete, along with timbers for the struts and trusses that would give form to the long, sloping roofline that would match the original.

Matt Reagan, Kate's husband, who was also the general

contractor, had been on the job each day, all through the day, overseeing the plans with Peter Crowley, as well as supervising the subcontractors. His close relationship with Father Elway over many years accounted in part for his commitment. He'd also gotten to know John Caraballo, and to Ellen's delight, both were becoming good friends.

For weeks, the place was a sightseer's dream, attracting the priests, one at a time or in clusters, each with his brownie camera at the ready. Father Pelletier, who long enjoyed filming nature, even produced a Kodak movie camera along with a Philips recording device to capture the full effect. His idea was to create a kind of documentary that could be archived.

As was the way of things at the abbey, Mrs. Wick continued to satisfy everyone with her biscuits and breakfasts, now with the generous added accommodation of sandwiches for the work crew's lunch, while Father Elway came and went, as usual, for this and that. The season had yielded its best pumpkin harvest ever, some specimens as heavy as thirty pounds, the profits from which enticed Father Garrett to take one of the churchgoers up on the opportunity to purchase a used Ford pick-up truck in excellent condition. "The boys would have loved this," he said more than once, but the boys were all gone back home now, even Corporal Joe Hopper, for whom things had finally leveled out.

This was the time when Thomas would have returned to his administrative duties, but Father Elway appointed him to work with Matt Reagan and the others as one of the overseers of the lodge construction, which meant that Ellen would continue with the office work, at least until the wedding.

She and John planned to live in his Munsey Park home until their house was built in the spring. They had decided to reside in Hicksville with its somewhat easy commute to the city for John and its close proximity to the abbey, where they would remain part of the Church community and help out wherever needed.

By now, Ellen had visited John's two elegant and famous Cara Diamond showrooms, the one in midtown and the other just across from the Metropolitan Museum of Art, learning more each time about his work. She had met the people closest to him, outside of his family—Leon, his long-time closest friend and business partner, as well as the other trusted employees, including Ida, one of the first he'd ever hired, long past her general usefulness for the daily tasks at hand, but someone John felt the need to remain loyal to and keep in his employ.

"She's a quirky one," Ellen had said, with affection, after meeting the tiny, fast-talking woman, now in her early eighties.

"Ah, yes," was all John said in reply.

And there was still more.

To everyone's surprise, even himself, Father Elway wholeheartedly agreed to the plans for development of the precious fifteen acres along the Old Country Road frontage. He enjoyed meeting Lenny Feinman and Stu Wasserman, looking forward to a lasting and blessed relationship.

"What a time this is," he said more than once. "A wondrous time. Who would have thought it?"

One week before the December wedding, Father Garrett drove Ellen to Jeanette's Bridal Shop in Hicksville to pick up the outfit she chose to be married in—an ivory linen suit with ivory embroidery on the collar and cuffs.

"I have to say, Father, that I'm disappointed we're not taking the pick-up truck. I always wanted to ride in a pick-up truck."

"Another time," he said. "Not when I'm transporting our favorite bride-to-be with her wedding dress."

Father Garrett always had a bit of a quirky streak, more of a dry humor than Father Elway, who was far more likely to laugh out loud at things. She gave him a long look, lean but solid behind the wheel, dressed in his black clergyman's clothing. "You know, this probably isn't the right time to bring it up, but I've thought so many times about what you did, Father … on that battlefield. Knowing what I know about you and your … your quiet spirit. I can't imagine. And, then, to have nothing happen to you. How was that possible?"

Without hesitating, he said, "We have to trust that God will give us what we need for the trials we face, for whatever we can do, for whatever must be done."

"I'm beginning to believe that must be so, Father.

Otherwise, how do we survive anything in this life? How do we ever rise above to find joy and peace again?"

"All set?" he asked when she got back in the car outside Jeanette's.

"All set," she said, having laid the suit flat on the back seat. "I'm so happy, Father. Thank you so much for driving me. Sometimes, this all still seems so unreal. I'm so happy, so grateful."

That night, a tractor-trailer truck with a sleepy driver at the wheel drifted into oncoming traffic on Northern Boulevard in Manhasset, Long Island. Amid the scream of sirens, the driver of the truck, Henry Milligan, 36, from Bryn Mawr, Pennsylvania, was transported to North Shore University Hospital, where he later died of his injuries. The driver of the other vehicle, identified as John Caraballo, 51, of Munsey Park, founder of the famous Cara jewelry brand, was pronounced dead at the scene.

After

Chapter

Thirty-Five

June, 1957 - The Adirondacks

"I LIKE THE good part—the part that it's your birthday. Happy Birthday, Ellen. Not at all happy about the other part—where you've decided to leave for the summer."

"If I weren't truly needed back home, Irene, I would have loved to stay while the school is on break." She looked at the other faces around the teacher's lounge—Josephine and Clara, Noreen, Adeline, Hope, Adrian, Henry, and Harris. "I wish you all a wonderful summer. And thank you again for making my birthday special."

Such seemed to be the way in these rural parts—a small town with a tight, caring community, sometimes a bit tighter than Ellen felt comfortable with. She was, at once, gratified by the sentiments and eager to be done explaining the reasons for her departure, with no more than the limited details she wished to share—they had no idea that the home she spoke of was a monastery. Neither did they know about … anything. But now, having put off Father Elway far too long, she couldn't bring herself to disappoint him again. This time, she wasn't sure whether there had been real urgency in his letter or whether that was a little something she had added on her own.

When most of the others had left the room, Professor Edwins set down his paper plate with its half-eaten slice of Ellen's coconut birthday cake. "I think you know my feelings on the matter." He reached out to take her hand, but she turned away.

"I think I'd better help tidy up this room, or I may not be welcomed back," she said, feigning a laugh.

Edwins stepped closer. "Ellen, please."

With his tweed jackets and traditional manners, the esteemed Professor of Natural Studies, Harris Edwins, was a man Ellen very much respected, a tall, scholarly gentleman with not unpleasant angular features. She had enjoyed his friendship and believed she had managed to discourage his polite advances.

"Harris." She didn't turn to look at him. "I am not a free woman. I've told you. And that's all I can say about it."

"But it makes no sense. It has never made sense. You're not married. You're not engaged. And you know how well we've always gotten along since you came here. It's nearly four years now."

She turned and took hold of his arm as if wanting to

shake him into understanding what she could not bring herself to fully explain. "Harris, you are a wonderful person. Truly. And you've been such a good friend."

"That's all?"

"That's all it is, and that's all it's ever been or ever can be. If I gave you any other impression, forgive me."

He held her gaze and, after a long moment, dropped his eyes in resignation and left the room.

Oh, Lord. Lord. Why is it all so hard? I'm trying to do the right thing here. Father Elway needs me. Let me go in peace.

Four years earlier, in the very month when her happy little world toppled off its axis, she left her abbey family and traveled by train out of Penn Station to the farthest point the train would go, then took a bus until she reached a little town near Saranac Lake that appeared inviting, and had a small private college in need of an administrative counselor. She couldn't even recall the details of her hiring or imagine her thinking at the time, for that matter, but she applied and got the job. Someone later hinted that it was her "big city experience" that had done the trick. Apparently, it made no difference which kind of big city experience a person had.

From then on, she forced herself to tolerate things until she ended up liking the people, the job, and the quaint little town of Willery. It helped that she was able to once again tuck certain pieces of her past into a tiny corner of her heart.

She enjoyed the students who occupied so much of her time and attention on a daily basis, not all of them young.

Many were first-timers in their thirties and forties, some even older, looking to learn things that might serve them in a different line of work due to the major economic and cultural change that had devastated the workforce.

Ellen had never known that as far back as the late 1800s, before antibiotics, Saranac Lake had been famous for the healing powers and cures that the fresh mountain air afforded. People young and old, the ordinary and the famous, stayed in the many sanitoriums in the area for weeks, months, and in many cases, even years, Robert Lewis Stevenson and Mark Twain among them. There were even luxury sanitoriums for the wealthy. But now in the 1950s, with fewer deaths and fewer patients because of advances in medicine, a shattering decision was made to close down all those treatment facilities, putting more people out of work than the area had ever seen.

"You think that's bad," Adeline said over lunch one day. "You never heard about the Big Blowdown, the strongest storm you could imagine. One of those hundred-year kinds. In only one day, a single day, if you can possibly believe it, hundreds of thousands of acres of timber were damaged or destroyed, including the great spruce forests that this whole area was known for."

"How awful. I never heard anything about it."

"Oh, yes." Adeline went on. "Complete shutdown of roads, along with the famous trails that run through the National Park here. It's the biggest park in the country, you know. People come just for the trails and ski slopes, and many of those never recovered. They just had to be abandoned. A tragic mess. Telephone lines, homes and businesses, fire observation towers. You name it—gone or badly damaged. Right now, nearly five years later, there are still crews out there working on the woods?"

As shocked as Ellen was, she also felt a sting of doubt about whether this was a place to settle, even if temporarily. "But it's so beautiful here. How would I ever have known all this? I don't see any of it."

"It's that kind of a place. The fortitude of its God-given nature with a capital N, replenishing itself. It's a living thing, after all. Grows in green and lush and hides a lot."

"Was Mrs. Starr one of those affected?" Wonderful, hopeful Adelaide "Birdie" Starr, who graduated the year before at the age of seventy-six with a degree in biology, now in an entry-level position at the local hospital as a greeter of sorts in a blue smock, eager to share with patients and visitors alike as much as she deemed appropriate about the various parts of the human body.

"She sure was. She and her husband, Owen, had one of the biggest Christmas tree farms in the state, in the whole northeast, really. Lost everything, including Owen. Heart attack. Poor man. It was all just too much. How do you like the pineapple Jello salad?"

Not long after arriving in town, Ellen rented a beautifully renovated and furnished, turn-of-the-century carriage house with a short, peaked roof over the front porch entry. Located on a quiet, rural street, as most were in the Adirondacks, the house had a large eat-in kitchen with a long, vintage walnut work table, a living room with a wood-burning stove, and a second-floor bedroom and bath. She felt blessed to have found such a wonderful little place, part of an estate parceled off by the heirs. There was a small yard in front and a modest garden in back, where the sprawling canopy of a single maple afforded her enough shade to quench the relatively short-lived summer heat. The rent was just as wonderful—thirty dollars a month. Such a place in Brooklyn would have cost at least forty-five dollars, sixty, for sure, in Manhattan.

One downside—she'd had to leave her beloved Tony behind. As much as she missed him, her comings and goings would have been too uncertain to provide the best home for her sweet boy, to say nothing of the lost affections of his entire abbey family, a wise decision, as it turned out.

At the school, she worked weekdays from nine to five and spent many of her evenings painting glass Christmas tree ornaments, which she enjoyed selling at the local market on Saturday mornings. Ellen had never done anything like that before, especially since she had not been one for hobbies in general and crafts in particular. But she met a talented and generous woman who was just friendly enough without being overbearing, who taught her how to create these little treasures.

"Your work is coming along nicely," the woman had told her as the weeks passed. Vernice was her name, a sweet and quietly energetic neighbor of fifty who had since died of lung cancer. Toward the end, Vernice, whose name came from her two grandmothers, Veronica and Bernice, gave all of her supplies to Ellen, exacting only the promise to keep trying. And try she did, with no small amount of success. With just enough talent to perfect the simplest of designs, she created enough to satisfy the weekend shoppers and bring in extra income. Mostly, she could lose herself in the task, and losing herself was of prime importance.

Then, Vernice taught Ellen something that brought her even more enjoyment and eventually took over as her main pastime—bread-baking. Ellen found great pleasure and relaxation working with the soft, pliable mounds of yeast dough. Something in the scent and the texture and the meditative aspects of the kneading allowed her to get lost in the task.

Perhaps her only mistake, as she saw it, was making friends with Harris Edwins. Ellen had been so accustomed to spending time with Thomas, and Father Elway, and Father Garrett, and the others at the abbey that, in a way, it never occurred to her that Harris was no priest. They had eaten lunch together in the cafeteria many times, gone to a Christmas concert once, and interacted on a daily basis about school things. He was a friend and a co-worker. Anything more than that was out of the question … for all time. Her heart was not open for business.

Whatever real peace and comfort she had experienced

in these years had certainly come not only from her painting and baking past-times and neighborly school friendships at the college but also from getting to know Father Curry, Pastor at the Church of the Most Precious Blood just outside town. She had become acquainted with him by way of their short chats after Mass and later enjoyed bringing him homemade yeast rolls and rye bread with caraway seeds, which she had learned were his favorites. Still, she kept her distance for fear that she might ultimately be obliged to share … too much. There were a few occasions, however, when she and others had engaged him in a pleasant chat about Church matters over tea or coffee in his parish office. Sometimes, she half expected, or perhaps merely wished, that dear Mrs. Wick would come through the door carrying her tray. She had been so lonely for the very place that she had not been able to bring herself to return to. Still, now and always, she would put Father Elway's desires before her own, and he needed her now.

A few months after arriving at the school, she purchased a Nash Rambler. Once fitted with snow tires and chains, it was all she needed to deal with the wintry mountain roads. She would now rely on it to take her back to the last place on earth she wished to go.

Chapter

Thirty-Six

TIME HEALS ALL wounds. Whoever said that could not possibly have ever been terribly wounded. It is not about time, after all, but what we choose to do with it. Ellen knew she was about to find out whether she had used her time well or merely spent it.

As she traveled south, she wished she could recognize the saving grace of this trip. Summer should have been it—the most reliable weather for traveling, windows rolled down, the endless verdant scenery of upstate New York, easy-breezy on the wending roads. But that wasn't it. Fall would have been no better; winter the worst, even though she loved the long, cold Adirondack months. Perhaps it was the isolation. Still, here she was headed back to her Long Island destination to see the people she cared most about in the world, but the closer she got, the greater the pain.

The entire trip was only a long day's drive, but she wasn't interested in rushing it, and although the reception was sketchy in the mountains, she was never more grateful that she'd paid the extra money to buy a car with a radio—the likes of Buddy Holly, Sam Cooke, and Fats Domino made for good travel companions. She was even pleased to see that the price of gasoline got cheaper the farther she moved from the mountains—twenty-five cents a gallon instead of the thirty-three she'd paid in Saranac Lake before leaving home.

After stopping overnight at a respectable-looking roadside motel with a clean, comfortable room and an attached eatery that served a homestyle meatloaf dinner and creamy scrambled eggs for breakfast, she started out early the next morning. It had been several years since she ventured this far from her home. Three summers prior, when Kate took the train up from New York City to visit, they meandered here and there by car, enjoying the nearby sights. It was Kate's first time in the Adirondacks, and she enjoyed every minute. She had since given birth to a boy named Paul.

Designed for Sunday pleasure drivers before the shift in population required more direct roads for commuting, Long Island's Northern State Parkway curved interminably through the wooded scenery of Nassau and Suffolk Counties. Ellen was impatient now, eager to arrive as best she could and put all expectations to rest.

Just as always, it was Mrs. Wick who answered the heavy plank door, her usual jubilant greeting restrained by tears and a long, doting embrace.

"How are you, Mrs. Wick?" Ellen said with an affectionate stroke of the woman's face. She had hardly aged a day.

"Better now. Much, much better."

Ellen's first glance at the reception room gave her a shiver of remembrance. She turned away quickly. "Is Father Elway here? Father Garrett?"

"They're hearing confessions, but they'll be in soon. Let's take some of your things up to your room."

Your room. The words were nostalgic and painful—going back was going to be an impossible thing to do. Impossible.

"Here she is now. Here she is." Father Elway's voice was a tonic as he crossed the room, making his way toward her, hands extended. "Oh, what a sight you are, what a blessing."

She took his hands in hers. "Father Elway, I'm so happy to see you." He still had a youthful grip, but he was grayer now, the light in his eyes just a bit dimmer. She could see that this years' long project had left its mark on his age perhaps, but not on his grace.

Father Garrett came in energetically through the front door carrying what amounted to an armful of roses and baby's breath. "You said not to make a fuss about your birthday." He handed her the bouquet. "These are 'welcome home' flowers." He seemed to have not changed at all.

Following Father Elway's lead, they joined hands, and with that, he offered a prayer of gratitude.

Through the afternoon, Ellen made sure she caught up with the other priests, who were as eager to see her. There were three new clerics, Father Dixon, who'd transferred from a monastery in Minnesota, Father Bergman from Oregon, and Father Maximillian from a parish in New Mexico, all of them needed now with the expansion of the lodge, and the increase in the number of veterans, along with the more abundant and complex paperwork and bills, especially since both she and Thomas were no longer there. She appreciated that they quickly joined in the small talk along with a good laugh or two.

"So glad to see you back, Ellen," Father Pelletier said. "It's been a very long few years."

She already knew about Thomas; Father Elway had written her that, following his ordination, Father Thomas had moved on to his first assignment, a parish church in South Dakota. He and Ellen had exchanged a few letters over the years but eventually stopped writing. He was one that she had dearly missed, and it saddened her that she might never see him again.

After a quiet early dinner with only a few, as Ellen had requested, Father Elway rose from the table. "Let's go see our boy," he said in that whisper of his. He led the way out to the prayer garden, where Ellen placed a rose from the bouquet Father Garrett had given her on the grave of her beloved Tony. "He had become a little sluggish," the priest said, "and so unlike himself, staying longer and longer each day in his favorite spot near my desk. Then, one afternoon, with the warm winter sun streaming in, he just went to sleep. He was a good boy."

Too many changes and too many things exactly the same. She wasn't sure which was harder. In the morning, Father would take her over to see the lodge expansion and then to the Old Country Road development, two heralded additions. He also mentioned a surprise, which she was not sure she was up for.

That night, in her comfortable, familiar bed, she was even too exhausted to toss and turn. Burdened by memory and sentiment, her tired mind refused to give in until her last woeful thought floated off with the sad and urgent realization that she must leave and never return.

In the morning, they let her sleep in. It was nearly ten-thirty before she opened her eyes. She couldn't remember when she had slept so late but knew she had needed it. Within the hour, she was downstairs in Mrs. Wick's kitchen, enjoying a cup of coffee with Father Garrett, who, in his typical summer mode, was all about the Yankees and the Dodgers. After catching her up on the baseball standings, he put down the sports page. "You had to have missed Mrs. Wick's eggs," he said.

"Always. And a lot more, Father. Her biscuits, for one."

"That'll teach you to wander off." He still had that low-key way about him, homey but sharp, serious looking, but always that glint of humor or wryness. How could she ever make sense of his bullet-riddled jacket in the Far Room? But then heroism was not required to make sense, neither were miracles.

"Mrs. Wick, you still make the best coffee, but I'll have to skip breakfast. I don't have much of an appetite this morning."

"That must be why you've lost a good bit of weight," the woman said. "I'm going to have to work on fattening you up at least a little over these next few weeks."

If Ellen was sure of one thing, it was that there was no way she could stay that long. Her affection for them had never wavered, nor had her love for this place. She would always remember the best of it, but the rest of it weighed so heavily on her heart that she truly needed to move on and stay away, even though she knew the disappointment it would bring to all, herself included. She would have to tell them after dinner.

Chapter

Thirty-Seven

"Well, what do you think?"

"Oh, Father, it's wonderful. I couldn't imagine how they would ever match the original."

They were standing outside the low-beamed main entry of the expanded lodge, Father Elway with his hands behind his back, satisfied. "That's what happens when you have the right people doing the work." He nudged her shoulder with his. "We were blessed, Ellen. We were."

"We have much to thank Peter Crowley for," Father Garrett said. "He and Louise will be coming for dinner in a few days. They're bringing Billy. That boy has grown, and a sweet one he is. We thought it might be nice to see them."

"Yes, of course," she said, gripped by uneasiness. "Have you had any veterans come through yet?"

"Two small groups from the Vietnam fighting." Father Elway rubbed the back of his neck. "People aren't paying too much attention to that miserable little conflict, but it's there, and I have a terrible feeling it's not going to end very well, very soon, or stay very small."

After touring the new construction with Father Elway, Father Garrett picked them up in the all-around.

"Father, I can't believe you're still driving this car."

"Why wouldn't I? It runs, and it's roomy. What more do I need?"

"What about your pick-up truck?"

"I have it," was all he said and drove them around to the new road that led to "Abbey Gardens" with its curving little tree-lined streets of houses.

"It's like a storybook village," she said, scanning the surroundings where, here and there, a man was mowing his lawn, a woman was pushing a baby stroller on the sidewalk. "It's hard to believe that it's actually here, finished, up and running."

"As we said, good design and good people to carry it out."

"I never imagined all this could fit on fifteen acres."

Father Garrett raised a finger in the air. "Only ten, remember. Let's go look at the other five." He continued along the curve that exited onto Old Country Road, then made a quick right turn into a parking lot that ran along a stretch of quaint little attached stores beneath a sign that read "Abbey Garden Shoppes."

Ellen exited the all-around and stood speechless, taking in what she could only recall as a plan, an idea, a vision.

"You'd have to agree, wouldn't you," Father Garrett said, "that we've made the most of our time and effort. Yes?"

She turned to Father Elway. "But your letters only said things were progressing slowly. Why didn't you tell me?"

"We wanted it to be a fine surprise."

"It has been four years, after all." Father Garrett said.

They strolled along a sidewalk constructed of pavers, and stopped at each entrance—the hardware store, and pharmacy, the hair salon, and deli café with fanciful arched doors and windows, the names of each shoppe written in gold calligraphy.

"I can't get over it," she said. "This really is a dream come to life."

They stopped in front of the "Abbey Bake Shoppe," where they could see Father Xavier with his back to the window, placing loaves of bread on a shelf.

"Does Father Xavier work here now?"

"A few of the priests contribute, but a lovely family owns it." Father Elway tapped on the window, and Father Xavier turned with a cheerful wave.

Father Garrett pointed to the names painted on the door window, Roseanna and Louis Corporini. You'll be happy to know they used to have a bakery in Brooklyn. Might have been right around your neck of the woods. Park Slope, I think. Is that near you? You'll have to ask them when we come back."

They spent the next hour looking at the shoppes, including the one marked Church Realty, hoping to see Lenny Feinman or Stu Wasserman, but they were both out.

"They've been busy men," Father Garrett said.

Father Elway laughed. "At first, we didn't even know what the name of their real estate company was, but how absolutely appropriate—Church Realty. Who knew?"

"Probably more of God's sense of humor," Father Garrett said. "And we've been blessed by their good work, helping to pull all of this together." Then, he turned to Father Elway with a sheepish grin. "Where to now?"

"Let's take the next turn." And they drove off, making a right that took them back onto abbey property and another new road.

Ellen was curious. "Where does this go? There was never a road here. What's it for?"

A few hundred yards in, there it was, something that Ellen would never have dreamed possible. They stopped the car and stepped out to look at a broad, two-story building similar in architecture to the abbey and lodge. It was clear that the building was nearly complete but still in need of landscaping, among other finishing touches.

Father Elway took Ellen's hand. "Dear Ellen, may I present The Daniel Caraballo Retreat Center. We thought that might be the name John would have chosen."

Ellen stared in silence for a long moment, fighting to

contain the tears. "Yes," she said. "I believe that's exactly what John would have wanted."

She could not stay. She could not have dinner with the Crowleys. As gratifying as the day had been, she knew she couldn't handle more. Everyone meant well, but to see everything she had seen, knowing that John's kindness, his vision, his great generosity, the memory of his son had been at the heart of it all … the pain was exquisite. Still, Father Elway had said he needed her.

"Ellen, I want you to stay and run the retreat center."

This was not at all what she expected when she sat down with him in his library study the next day. The warmth and beauty of the sun streaking brilliantly across the room was just as she had remembered, but her thoughts were chaos.

"You can't be serious, Father."

"Never more so."

"But I don't know how to do something like that, and I don't even live here anymore."

"I can't think of anyone more capable of doing the job. You know us, you know the abbey and what we are all about, the spirit of this place. That's what we want for the retreat center—someone who senses the heart and soul of it. You can do this, Ellen."

"Father, this just isn't possible for me."

He looked at her in silence for a long moment, then walked to the bookshelves, his finger pressed to his lips, thoughtful. "A priest can be a fool, you know. I had no idea how hard yesterday would be for you. I thought that seeing John's vision come to life would somehow override your grief. And, of course, in my mind, I was sure you'd delight in running the retreat center." He walked back and sat, leaning in towards her. "I'm so sorry, Ellen."

She couldn't answer. In that moment, she was so moved by his vulnerability that she found herself unable to tell him she was leaving the next morning. He was showing more of his age after all, that playful glint in his eye fading now, likely not just because of the passing of years but the pressure of this enormous project. She stood.

"Still," he said. "I wish you would give this prayerful consideration. I've always believed this place had special meaning for you on so many levels."

She walked with him to the library entrance, then stopped. "You have to know what a great honor it is that you would consider me for something that is so special to you, Father. Thank you." She looked up and drew a deep breath. "You made this place home to me, where I found a family, where I found purpose and meaning, acceptance at the lowest point in my life." She swept the room with her hand. "This is where I mended the past, and where I found true love. Where I found God again. But right now, Father … and it breaks my heart to say this … I don't believe I'm strong enough to stay and do what you ask. I'm just not."

Early the next morning, she sat in the last pew in the chapel before Mass. Like the rerun of a favorite movie, she watched Father Pelletier set the altar cloths and light the scented beeswax votives. She remembered sitting there with Thomas and wondered about him, as she always did. She remembered how Tony would sit by the chapel door waiting for her. Patrick came to mind. Was he a happily married man? She hoped so. And little Billy? He would be about seven now. And Kate. What would her best friend think now that Ellen would not even stay long enough to see baby Paul? Would Ellen ever have such a close and trusted friend again? She had new friends in Willery, but was it the same? Could it ever be? She had held back too much of herself to build such a bond. She thought about Mrs. Wick and all the dear priests. She knew that when she left this time, she would never see any of them again. But even as she sat there before Mass trying to pray, she believed that life had already made the choice for her.

Chapter

Thirty-Eight

THE WEATHER WAS wicked the next morning when she set out for the trip back to Willery. It had stormed all night and, at daybreak, had not let up. Unlike her trip down, she was planning to go straight through without an overnight stop. With the visibility as poor as it was, she would have to take it slow and stop a lot earlier if she had to, choosing not to chance the conditions on the winding mountain roads. But first, she knew it would take forever to navigate the morning rush hour and get through the city, all the way up through Westchester in the pouring rain, cross the George Washington Bridge, the traffic being more stop than go, then on to the Bronx River Parkway before she reached the Taconic, where traffic tended to ease up, but likely would not be the case if this downpour continued. After that, well over a hundred miles before reaching her Saranac Lake exit.

She had left before breakfast, before seeing Mrs. Wick in another tearful parting, before morning Mass, before having to face Father Elway and Father Garrett one last time. She knew there would be broken hearts, none more broken than her own. She had tried. "Oh, Lord."

By early afternoon, with still more than sixty-five miles to go, Ellen had to get off the road. The weather had not been merciful, and the stress of watching out for every patch and puddle while sheets of rain lashed her windshield had worn her nerves to a frazzle, on top of which she had not slept well at the abbey.

She was relieved to come across a tidy-looking gas station café. There was no need for a fill-up, but a cheese sandwich and a bowl of soup were all the temptation she needed to settle into the comfort of a booth. It occurred to her that after eating her lunch, she might take a nap in her car. She had never been this way—weak, worrisome, and exhausted—but she wasn't going to argue the situation or deny it. She had prayed about it and, for now, would accept that she needed to take it easy until she got back to Willery, back to the reasonable comfort of her little made-up life.

"Scottish Potato Soup or Salmon Chowder?" the waitress asked.

"Scottish Potato, please, and a grilled cheese sandwich."

She had trouble keeping her eyes open, and when the hot soup arrived, she could barely lift the spoon to her mouth. Her head dipped and jerked back.

"Your scarf looks damp. That can't be good," the waitress said. "Let me have it; I'll dry it by the stove." She was a hearty-looking woman with strong, plain features, perhaps the face of a person quickly liked and trusted.

"That's very nice of you," Ellen said, exhaustion underscoring her words, and pulled the scarf from around her neck and shoulders.

In exchange, the woman handed her a small, clean white tablecloth that she'd unfolded. "Here, I warmed this for you. Just drape it around."

"Oh, that feels so good," Ellen said. "I didn't realize how cold I was from the dampness. You really are too kind."

"Never heard of any such thing as too kind." the woman said without changing expression.

Deadpan all the way but wonderful, Ellen thought. She remembered a line from a play called "A Streetcar Named Desire," which she and Kate had seen on Broadway just before it closed a few years back—"I have always relied on the kindness of strangers." Ellen had surely benefitted once again from the kindness of someone she didn't know.

The woman returned with Ellen's cheese sandwich. "You're not planning to drive after this, I hope." It was more a command than a question.

"I don't know why I'm so tired. I hadn't planned to stop anywhere for the night." She looked out the window. The rain had slowed to a heavy drizzle. "It's not even night. But I don't know of any place."

"Now, look," the woman said. "My daughter, Libby, is going to take you about seventy yards from here—my sister's bed and breakfast. Leave your car right where it is. It'll be safe. My husband runs the gas station. Nobody messes with him. Libby will drive you over, so you don't get wet. And besides, you're not in any condition to be walkin' seventy yards. I'll let Pearl know you need a room. You'll be fine. And you get right into bed. Don't care if it's afternoon or midnight. Tired is tired. Pearl's got good eats and hot coffee when you're ready for it. Meantime, I'll wrap your sandwich to take with you."

Ellen would barely remember meeting Pearl or getting into bed in the cozy room with the white crisscross curtains, but at four the next morning, she opened her eyes for the first time in twelve hours, wearing the fresh, white cotton nightgown Pearl had given her to sleep in. With her neck stiff as a wedge from not moving all night, she sat on the edge of the bed to get her head about her, then picked up her wrapped sandwich and staggered to the chair, unable to contain her appetite. About ten minutes later, there was a light tap on the door. "Who is it?"

"It's only me—Pearl. I have hot coffee."

The sound of that was more than music to her ears; it was an entire symphony. "Oh, thank you so much. Thank you," she said again when Pearl entered with a tray covered in a blue and white plaid cloth and an enticing assortment of toast, muffins, and jams, along with a pot of the dark, aromatic brew that enlivened all of Ellen's senses. "How did you know I was up?" She looked again at the clock. "And what are you doing up at this hour?"

"It's what we do. I've been checking on you." Pearl set the tray on the wide cushioned ottoman in front of the upholstered armchair. "Now, you take your time and relax. It's way too early for you to even be thinking about getting back on the road. Where you headed, anyway?"

"Willery. Up by Saranac Lake."

"I know it well. The great blowdown. Vacation?"

"No, I live there." It still seemed such a strange thing to say—she lived there. But was it home? Was she there yet? Where was this place that she was finally meant to call home, truly home? No tease, no doubt, no gut-wrenching circumstance to again snatch it away, snatch her away? For now, it was the place known for the great blowdown. Could there possibly be a more appropriate name?

"When you're ready, I'll be happy to fix you some eggs and waffles. Bacon? Whatever you like. My sister says don't worry; she still has your scarf. Later on, I'll give Libby a call to drive you back over. For now, just go easy on the day. You've got plenty of time." Then, with a wink, she closed the door behind her.

Maybe the truest home is the one given to you by the kindness of people, the ordinary, natural loving hearts that make us a home wherever we go. "Thank you, Lord," she said as she sat back in the comfortable, over-stuffed chair with her cup of hot coffee. "Thank you."

Still, she had more than a ripple of guilt about fleeing the abbey. Father Elway had made his plea for her to stay and run the retreat center. It was so important to him. But she couldn't. She just couldn't. Now, as she sat comfy in a chair, having been rescued once again by the most hospitable of people she'd never even met, she wondered—couldn't she? Couldn't she really? Couldn't she set aside the despair that Father Elway said had once hung about her like a heavy, oversized winter coat? Couldn't she be the one offering the kindness instead of drawing a circle around her life and not allowing anyone to enter? Birdie Starr came to mind. What did she do at seventy-six when she lost everything, even her husband? She went to college and continued to delight those around her with her joyous spirit.

It was after eight before she decided to get moving. She had dispelled her troublesome thoughts by sitting with her feet up, listening to the radio and flipping through the fall issue of Redbook Magazine, aware only that there was no place in the world she needed to be. School was out for the summer. She had gone back to the abbey as Father had requested, and now here she was, out of obligations. Once back in Willery, she would lose herself again in her bread-baking. She would paint Christmas ornaments to sell at the Saturday morning market. She had prayed about things, and if there was any answer at all, it confirmed that she had grown accustomed to being a loner. And yet, she wasn't always sure if those were the Lord's answers or her own.

There was another tap on the door. Libby. "I just wanted you to know that I'll be happy to drive you back to the café whenever you're ready. No trouble. Oh, and my dad put air in your tires and cleaned up your windshield."

Chapter

Thirty-Nine

AFTER MUCH THANKS and the offering of tips no one would accept, Ellen was back on the road, rested, well-fed, and cared for. The sky was clear, she had a fresh change of clothes, and the air felt good. What more could she ask, except the easing of her thoughts? The farther she traveled from the abbey, the greater her guilt. She knew Father Elway would understand why she left, why she had to leave. But was it right? Was he less in need of her help because of his understanding?

She turned on the radio. Stan Musial had set a new National League consecutive-game streak. Father Garrett would be happy to hear that, even though Musial was not a Dodger. She changed the station. Jimmy Dorsey's "So Rare." She hummed along. Then, after her restless fingers changed station after station, she turned off the radio and prayed. Father Elway said he always needed guidance. But she wasn't fooling herself—she wasn't asking for guidance;

she'd already made up her mind. She was asking for relief, maybe forgiveness, certainly mercy.

A sudden clunk and the car began to buck, then evened out to a steady grinding sound. Half terrified, she wondered where and how she would get help. Without any idea where the next exit was, she pulled over onto a wide shoulder and stepped out of the car. There was no point lifting the hood—car engines were a mystery to her. She looked about. How would she get to a telephone? At least it was daylight, and the weather was clear. After about ten minutes, a car pulled over in front of hers, and a man in a business suit and fedora stepped out, offered to take a look, then shook his head.

"I can't tell what's going on. You're going to need a mechanic. The next exit is about seven miles along. I'll get off and call the police. I would suggest just staying in your car until help arrives. You're safely off the road."

She thanked him profusely, and as he walked away, she called after him. "I wonder. Do you happen to know of that gas station café about ten miles back?"

"Rooney's. Oh, yeah."

"I was just there. Do you suppose you could call them? I believe Mr. Rooney has a tow truck."

"Sure. Gus. He's a good guy."

"Let me get my purse from the car so I can pay for the calls."

He waved her off. "No, no. I'm happy to see what I can do."

She got back in the car and waited.

"Well, now, we've got something going on," Gus said, hunched over the front of the engine in his blue-striped overalls. "Can't say what. I will have to tow her. I will have to put her up on the lift." He gestured to the cab of his truck. "You get in. Let me get her set, and we'll be on our way." He took off his cap and scratched his head. "But here's the thing—I've got a big ole Pontiac on that lift. Fella's waiting on it. I got to finish her up first. It's gonna end up being later than you might care to get back on the road. You're looking at another overnight."

It was now nearly three hours from the time she'd set out, and here she was back. Mrs. Rooney, Doretta, she'd learned, greeted her in the café. "I don't know where it is you're headed, but someone sure don't want you to get there. Coffee or Coke?"

"Coke, please, Doretta. My mouth is dry as sawdust."

"If you're hungry, look over the menu. Brisket's our best. Gus smokes it himself out back."

"Then I'll have it. I'm starving."

This time, after eating, she walked over to Pearl's Sleep Tight Bed and Breakfast, happy to get the same room as the night before. Libby walked over with her, carrying Ellen's little overnight case, chatty about this and that. A sweet and generous girl, Ellen thought and, like the others, would not accept a tip.

A few hours later, the phone rang in Ellen's room. Gus.

"Well, Miss Castle, let me start out by saying, minimal damage. Small repair. I've got the part on hand. You'll be all set to go in the morning."

"Wonderful. Thank you, Gus, but what on earth caused it?"

"Well, it's kind of odd and a bit of a sad thing. Something I've not seen before. A little bird somehow got pulled into the engine. Just a little bird. That's all it took."

Ellen swallowed. "A bird? Do you know what kind, Gus? Could you tell?"

"Oh, yes, plain as could be. A little red bird. You know, the cardinal kind. A little red cardinal."

Ellen plopped down on the side of the bed. "Is he? He's…"

"Oh, yes. Done for, poor thing. First time I ever saw it."

She had always said she didn't believe in signs, but this, this was … had to be … a sign. And what greater sign did she need than for Solomon—crazy, precious little Solomon—to sacrifice his life.

The next morning, she was on the road again, heading back—hurrying back—to Willery. She had to be careful that her new-found zeal did not override her sensibilities, especially behind the wheel. She seemed to cover the sixty or so miles in no time, and even before going to her house, she went by the college. There was something she had to set straight. She stopped by the front desk.

"Miss Castle. How nice to see you. Didn't expect you back, not till September, anyway."

"Nice to see you, Flora. Is Professor Edwins in class?"

"Just finished his nine o'clock."

Ellen found him in the teacher's lounge. "Harris."

He turned. "Ellen? What happened? Is everything all right?" He walked over to her with a worrisome look.

"Everything is fine, Harris. But I need to talk to you. Do you have a minute?"

"For you, always. Come to my office," he said, leading the way. "What's going on?" He closed the door behind them.

"Harris, I owe you an apology and an explanation."

"For what? I don't understand."

"You are such a nice person. You've been a friend to me. I should have realized you might have wanted more, but I've been … I don't know … full of my own grief and selfishness."

"Grief? I don't know what you're talking about. Did something happen?"

"Yes, Harris. The worst thing that ever happened to me in my life. That's why I came here from Long Island, where I was living and working in a monastery."

"A monastery? Were you a nun? Is that why you aren't free?"

"No. I was there temporarily, but I was preparing to be married."

"Oh." He took a step back. "I didn't know."

"Of course, you didn't because I never tell anyone anything, even people close to me. You would think I'd learn."

"But you didn't marry?"

"He died. In a car accident. Actually, a truck. A week before the wedding." She sat as still and silent as he did, unable to fathom how she got the words out without sobbing. The amazing thing was that she didn't feel like sobbing.

Harris ran his fingers through his hair, the look of disbelief lingering.

"This is the first time that I've told anyone since moving here. The first time I've even mentioned it or thought of mentioning it. I should have told you, Harris. I'm so sorry. I still love him. I don't believe I will ever stop. Can you understand and forgive me for not being open with you? For not being at all sensitive about what your feelings might be? I'm so sorry."

He got to his feet and took her hand, and when she rose, he put his arms around her. "This is only the hug of a friend who will always hope to remain your friend, Ellen. I cannot imagine your loss and pain. You are a strong and admirable woman for whom I have the greatest respect." He backed away. "I sense that you are leaving and not planning to return. Am I right?"

She nodded.

"Would you like me to share with the others what you just shared with me?"

"Yes, please, Harris, and thank you." She reached to kiss

his cheek. "I will never forget you."

The next day she called the abbey twice, but no one answered. She did manage to reach her landlord, however, who refused to levy any penalty for breaching her lease. And the day after that, she set out with her Rambler packed to the hilt, with only one stop to make. Before leaving, she tried the abbey again. Still no answer. She could imagine how busy everyone was, especially with the final work being done on the retreat center. She felt exhilarated by the idea of surprising Father Elway.

After about an hour's drive, Ellen entered Rooney's café and found Doretta busy servicing two booths. Libby came from the back carrying a tray of food and saw her at once. "Miss Castle. You're back." Her excitement caught Doretta's attention.

"Well, I'll be." She handed two food orders to Libby, chasing her to the back. "Everything okay with you? Not more car trouble, I hope."

"Everything is just fine, Doretta. I'm headed back to Long Island—to stay—but I wanted to stop to thank you again. I have something for you, for Libby and Pearl, too. Can I borrow Libby when she's got a minute?"

"Okay."

After the girl came out from the back and served the plates she carried, Ellen led the way to her car, where she reached in and removed two large cardboard boxes. Ellen and Libby each carried one back inside and brought them to an empty table at the rear of the restaurant.

"What on earth?" Doretta remarked, rubbing her pencil against the side of her face.

"Go ahead, open them up."

Doretta and Libby carefully pulled open the box flaps and unfolded the tissue paper. "Christmas ornaments," Libby said. "Mama, look. Look at how beautiful."

"I can see that." She turned to Ellen. "What are these for?"

"They're for you and Libby. And Pearl, too, if you wouldn't mind letting her pick some for herself. I'm sorry that I don't have anything for Gus."

"But where did these come from?" Libby asked.

"I made them. They're all hand-painted. A wonderful woman taught me. I guess she was just about as kind and generous as all of you have been. So, I wanted you to have them."

"Go get your aunt Pearl," Doretta said to Libby. "Go on."

"Will you thank your sister for me, Doretta? And will you accept my sincerest thanks? I'll always remember your great hospitality and kindness."

"There was no thanks needed, Miss Castle. But you certainly have our thanks. You'll make our Christmas look extra special this year and a good many after that." She put her hand to her mouth. "Oh, and before I forget … go see Gus. He's got something I know you'll be interested in hearing."

Ellen and Doretta said their goodbyes one more time before Ellen made her way out the door and walked the short distance to Gus's garage.

"Hey," he said, excited, when he saw Ellen. "I didn't think I'd see you again, and I'm so glad you're here because there's yet another odd thing I want to tell you about. Something I can show you."

Ellen couldn't imagine. She hoped he wasn't about to tell her that he'd forgotten to put some important little part back into her engine. "Is it something I should worry about?"

"Oh, nothing like that." He looked straight into her eyes, pointing his finger in her direction. "You know that little cardinal bird I removed from your engine?"

"Yes," she said with fearful exaggeration.

"Well, you know, when I took that little guy out … you know, out of the engine … he was a bit … well … mangled, as you could guess. And, after all, he was a living thing, not like a piece of trash or something. So, I decided to bury him. Took that little body around back and put him in a hole no deeper than a teacup."

"That was sweet, Gus. Very sweet."

"Well, wait. Here's the part. I went around back the next day. You know that's where I smoke the brisket. I have a smokehouse. And what do I see? Right on top of that little teacup hole? A rose." He noticed Ellen's expression. "Yes, an actual rose where no rose was planted. A red rose. A single red rose. Just one. Big as life. Overnight. Just like that—from that little bird's grave. Durndest thing I ever saw. Come see for yourself. I'll show you."

Ellen accompanied Gus around back of the garage, and there it was—a single red rose growing straight up out of the little mound of fresh-packed earth.

"Now, just what can you make of it?" Gus asked, having no idea how many times she had asked the very same thing.

Chapter

Ellen rode along, windows rolled down, music playing on the radio, remembering a movie she had seen in which the hero had a special type of portable telephone in a little carrying case that he took with him wherever he went. He could even hook it up in his car and make calls with it while driving. She wished there really were such a thing—she'd call Father Elway right now and tell him she was almost there. Maybe she was just reading too much Dick Tracy.

She was shocked when it was not Mrs. Wick but Thomas who opened the front door of the abbey. "Thomas … Father Thomas. Oh, my goodness. What a wonderful surprise. I'm so happy to see you. I didn't know you were coming."

"Very happy to see you, too, Ellen."

She knew instantly that something was wrong. "What is it, Father?"

"It's Father Elway. He's had a heart attack. Collapsed in the prayer garden. I came as soon as Mrs. Wick called."

"Oh, Lord, no. Please. No. Where is he? Is he …?"

"He's in the hospital. It's touch and go. Mrs. Wick and Father Garrett are there with him now."

"Father, I've got to see him. Please, can you take me? I need someone to show me how to get there, but my car is packed."

"I've got Confessions starting in a few minutes. I'll get Father Pelletier to take you in the pick-up truck." He managed a thin smile. "I'm late saying this, Ellen, but it is very good to see you again. I'm so glad you're here."

"This is my fault," Ellen insisted when she arrived at the hospital. "It's all my fault,"

"You mustn't think that way," Father Garrett said. "The whole project was just too much for him."

"But that's the problem, Father—he needed me, and I turned my back on him for my own selfish reasons."

Mrs. Wick put her arm around Ellen's shoulder as they sat in the hospital waiting room. "Father is right, Ellen. You had nothing at all to do with this. Believe that, as you should."

They saw the doctor coming down the hospital corridor and stood quickly as he approached.

"I can see how anxious you all look," the doctor said. "You can relax. Father Elway is doing much better. I expect he'll be here for about a week, so we can keep an eye on him, do more tests as needed. He'll get good care. No need to worry. He's out of danger."

The very word "danger" sent shivers through Ellen. "Can we see him, doctor? Can we go in?"

"Not all at once. No more than two at a time. He may go in and out of wakefulness. He's pretty well medicated. That may cause him to say things that don't make sense. That's all right. Don't worry about it. Most of all, don't stay too long or talk too much. He may not even know you're here or remember that you came."

"Thank you, Doctor Patel." Mrs. Wick turned to Ellen. "Why don't you and Father Garrett go in."

"He's in a special coronary care room, just down the hall," the doctor said. "Room 202. There's a nurse's station there if you need help."

Ellen and Father Garrett hurried along, then entered the room quietly. It was a shared room with an elderly man resting in the next bed. Ellen put her hand to her mouth to stifle tears at the sight of her beloved priest and friend lying there so lifeless, surrounded by lines and tubes and a liquid drip, along with a cardiac monitor ticking off his heartbeats.

She looked at Father Garrett. "Could I please have just a private moment or two, Father?"

Father Garrett nodded and closed the door softly behind him on the way out.

Ellen moved to the bedside chair and sat. Oh, Lord. Lord. "Father," she whispered, "I am so sorry I let you down. So very sorry. How selfish I have been." She leaned over, cupping her head in her hand. "I'm not here because you got sick. I was coming back. I am back. I'm here, Father. I'm here to help you in any way that I can." She reached into her purse and removed a handkerchief to dab her eyes. "So, you've got to get better. Please, Lord, make him better." She touched the bed and turned to go.

"Oh, he's a good one," came the whispered words from the man in the next bed. "You family?"

"Yes," she answered without thinking. "On both counts."

The days that followed were all about the wait—waiting for updates from Dr. Patel, waiting for word that he was better, waiting to hear that he might be able to return home to the abbey. But the updates did not offer the news they hoped for. Status quo. More tests. Continued medication. The priests offered an extra Mass each day. Many more of the local people came to the abbey to attend Mass and pray.

Dr. Patel had cautioned them to discourage visitors other than those from the abbey, although flowers arrived daily, enough to fill every flat surface in Room 202. Mrs. Wick made sure she invited the other patient in the room, Henry Boitano, to share the flowers, placing some, with his permission, on his side table and across his window ledge.

"I never saw a sick priest," Mr. Boitano said more than once, seemingly surprised that a clergyman ever got sick or needed hospital treatment. Or maybe it was that he couldn't imagine ever sharing a room with a priest. "I thought about becoming a priest once, but then I met my wife. I mean, she wasn't my wife yet, but once I met her, that was it. And I did make sure I told God how sorry I was. And I have to tell you, I actually have felt much better with a priest in the room with me, especially this one, for some reason." One day, the man asked Father Garrett to hear his confession, and, of course, Father accommodated. And one day, he told them that he heard Father Elway say something. "I could be wrong, but I thought he was asking someone … I don't know … a Mrs. Witt … something like that, I think … to bring a tea tray. Of all things. Does that make sense?"

"Oh, that makes perfect sense, Mr. Boitano," said Ellen, offering Mrs. Wick her biggest smile. "Maybe …?"

By then, they had met Mrs. Boitano, Edie. "You've done a world of good for Henry," she told Ellen and the others in private. "We very nearly lost him. But … and don't let him know I told you … he talks to Father Elway every night before going to sleep. He spoke about his faith and his life, which has not been an easy one. He doesn't ever speak about his life. I'm his third wife, you know. He lost the first one in childbirth along with the twins she was delivering. His second wife died of polio complications in her early forties. They had a boy, Russell, but he's still missing in action and presumed dead in Korea. Henry was actually considering going into the priesthood himself before we met. So, you can imagine what a blessing this has been, at least for Henry, if not for Father Elway.

"I have a feeling," Father Garrett said, "that Father Elway was, in some way, fully present and blessed to hear your husband share his story."

Henry Boitano was released the next day. And two days later, Father Elway was sitting up in bed. With Dr. Patel's permission and Ellen's help, Mrs. Wick brought a tea tray that included Father's favorite powdery tea biscuits, enough to share with the floor nurses and with the doctor as well.

Chapter

Forty-One

Two weeks later, Ellen joined Father Elway and Father Garrett in Mrs. Wick's kitchen after Mass. Father had been back home a week, good as new, according to Doctor Patel.

"Father, I … I want to make sure you know—I didn't come home because I heard you were sick."

"I know."

"I'm so glad they told you."

"They didn't tell me. You did. In the hospital. I heard you."

"But how …?"

"I heard all sorts of things here and there. I'm not clear what they all were. It was just this kind of … I guess you'd call it … radiance. God was in it, I'm sure. I couldn't speak, and it wasn't as though I'd actually heard the voice of God, but I know that, somehow, we were communicating."

Father Garrett spooned a dollop of Mrs. Wick's raspberry jam onto his plate. "Very interesting, Leo. I've read about it—reports of the oddest things, mostly spiritual, that people experience, even in a coma."

"I do believe I was praying, but there were no words, just a sense of things, all moving about in a kind of glow."

Mrs. Wick went to Father Elway's side, her hand on her hip. "Glow or not, Father, I'm going to have to insist that you finish your plate. Doctor Patel says it's a must."

"But only the eggs and toast, Mrs. Wick. I promise to do better at lunchtime with a small sandwich and a glass of milk."

"Now that you're back and settling in," Ellen said. "I have a bit of news. "I was talking with Matt Reagan yesterday about the finishing pieces for the retreat center, and …" She could tell Father Elway was somewhere else. "Father?"

"I can't put my finger on it," Father Elway said, distracted, searching.

"What about?" Father Garrett said.

"I'm not sure, John. Something about a boy. It's vague."

Father Garrett put down his coffee cup to offer his full attention. "Do you know who the boy is, Leo?"

"Billy Crowley, maybe?" Ellen said. "Or what about Mrs. Kelsey's son, Charles, the boy she brings to Mass in a wheelchair."

Father Elway looked off, eyes narrowed. "No. No one I could see, but I had the feeling it was not someone I knew. And yet, I was asking and asking about him. I must have been asking God to help him, whoever he is."

"Did you get an answer?" Mrs. Wick asked.

"Yes, I did. The boy is fine. He will get what he wants, what he has prayed for. I'm sure of it. I distinctly remember it was a boy, a boy who will go home." He looked around at their faces. "What on earth was going on in my head?" He chuckled. "You all think I'm still a little sideways. I know."

"No, not really," Ellen said. "But you did have a lot of medication."

"That's right," he said, slapping both hands on his knees. So, let's make no more of it. He turned to Ellen. "So, what was Matt Reagan's good news?"

"He believes the center will be completed a week early. Louise Crowley did a rendering of it for an ad that ran two months ago in a few Church publications and in the more general meeting publications as well. I already have three requests for late fall bookings. We might be on our way, Father."

"Doesn't get any better than that," Father Garrett said. "Praise God."

"I can't imagine you'd had time to see it," Father Elway said to Ellen, "but there's a little house backing up to the line of trees the other side of the retreat center. Peter Crowley had suggested we build it in case we ever needed to house a manager or caretaker or such. You can have that house, Ellen. Fix it up however you like."

"What a lovely offer, Father. Thank you." She looked about the table. "Actually, I was wondering." She hesitated. "Might it be possible for me to keep my rooms upstairs, next to Mrs. Wick's?"

Father rubbed the back of his neck. "Well, if you're sure that's what you want …"

"I'm sure, Father."

"Then, of course, the answer is yes. And …"

The kitchen door swung open, and everyone looked up to see Father Pelletier with an urgent expression. "So sorry to bother."

"No bother, Harman. Is everything all right?"

"Father, there's a man on the phone. He's so frantic, I could hardly make out exactly what he wants, except that he must speak with you."

"Oh, dear," Father Elway said.

Father Garrett got to his feet as well. "I'll come too."

"Do you have any idea who the man is?"

"It was hard to make out. Something like Bowton, Boitan."

Father Elway stopped. "Good Lord, that's it. That's the boy. Boitano. In my dreams, at the hospital. Boitano."

Ellen stood, excited. "He was in the next bed, but he was discharged before you even woke up. You never met him or saw him."

They hurried out. "I have a feeling he did," Father Garrett said, following close behind.

Moments later, Father Elway picked up the phone on his desk. "Mr. Boitano?"

"Yes. Yes. Is this the priest who was in the bed next to me? Father Elry?"

"Yes, Mr. Boitano. I'm Father Elway."

"I don't know how to explain this, but I believe in my heart you made this happen. My son. My son is coming home. They found him. He was being cared for in a small village in South Korea. He has amnesia, but he's alive, and they say he will recover over time. I know you did this, Father. I spoke to you every single night. I prayed with you and for you. Praise God. Praise God!"

A few days later, Mrs. Wick asked Ellen to take Father Elway his lunch. She found him sitting on the low stone wall that surrounded the prayer garden. His appetite had improved and so had his color. It was good to see him taking a respite from the heat of these late June days, reading his breviary in the shade of the huge garden maple.

"You've been a busy bee," he said as she set the tray beside him on the wall. "Sit with me."

"I'm happy to see you out here. You've been a busy bee, too."

"Well," he said, taking a sip from the glass of cold milk. "I'm happy to say it's good busy. As with bees, things are getting pollinated. The shoppes are doing well, the new priests—new to you, anyway—are accomplishing a lot with our latest group of soldiers. Wonderful work. Wonderful blessings. And how many event requests do you have? Quite a few more, isn't it?"

Father Elway didn't miss much. "We're up to eight," she said, "and the good news is that they are not all for the holidays but spaced nicely into the new year. So, we're not having any drop-off once the Christmas season ends."

"Nice."

"It was also nice seeing Father Thomas, wasn't it?"

"Oh, yes," he said. "One of the nicest things of all. Too bad he's so far away."

They sat for a while—he, enjoying his cheese sandwich; she, enjoying the silence between them that both had long grown comfortable with.

"Father, there's something I have to tell you."

"You sound dire. I'm just getting my appetite back. I hope you're not going to spoil it." They laughed.

"Sorry. It's about Solomon."

"What now?"

"Something happened to him."

"Oh, that," Father Elway said, dismissive.

"Well, it was pretty terrible. And how did you find out?"

"Find out? That a cat found his way in here and chased that bird all around the garden?" He put his napkin to his mouth. "I laughed my head off. That crazy bird went plunk right into the birdbath. You know that clipped wing of his sometimes fails him. But that's what he gets for dive-bombing me the day before."

Ellen listened, wide-eyed. "When exactly did this happen, Father?"

"Yesterday."

"Oh," was all she could say.

Chapter

Forty-Two

As Ellen settled back into the only place that truly felt like home now, she was discovering the many pleasures of visiting the Abbey Shoppes. The salon made it easy and convenient to get hair and nails done when needed. She enjoyed having an occasional lunch with Mrs. Wick at the Deli-Café with its wonderful Italian hero sandwiches, even more so when Mrs. Wick's sister, Grace, came along, or Lenny Feinman when he and Stu Wasserman were not out developing their now not-so-little Long Island empire.

But the bakery was her treasure. Father Xavier had sampled one of the bread recipes that Vernice had taught her and insisted they feature it. "We'll call it 'Adirondack Bread,'" he suggested, and it became a best-seller. "Here, try this," he said to her and Grace one day, handing each a roll in the shape of a crusty, golden knot of buttery goodness with a hint of black pepper.

"Wow! Delicious," they both agreed.

"We put them out yesterday for the first time," Father proudly said. "Went through the entire batch in one hour."

"One hour. Hmm," Ellen said with a wry smile. "I know exactly what to call these—'Blowdown Rolls.'"

"That's a unique name. Catchy. I like it. 'Blowdown Rolls' it is."

Because the retreat center was still in its start-up phase, Ellen had a long lead-time for events, which made it possible for her to enjoy everything from the bread-baking itself to seeing the delighted faces of the customers returning for more.

Grace had come on part-time, finding as much pleasure at the bakery as Ellen did, and many of the same people who came to Mass at the abbey were now regulars, along with the residents of Abbey Gardens and the Hicksville community at large. There was only one person who had never come around, and it gave Ellen an idea, one that she never imagined she would actually entertain.

One day, she packed up a neat little basket containing the now famous Adirondack bread, along with half a dozen Blowdown Rolls and half a dozen of Mrs. Wick's tantalizing blueberry muffins. Then she got in her little Rambler and headed out.

When she arrived at her destination, she found the door wide open. She had never been there before and hesitated before entering. "Is he in?"

With a dip of his head to the left, the man in uniform directed her to the back office, where she found Officer Polly at his desk.

"Good morning," she said, having to speak above the whir of the oscillating fan.

The officer looked up, then dropped back, tossing his pen onto his desk.

"I hope I'm not interrupting an important report or something," she said. Somehow, his sullen look didn't disturb her.

"I think I can spare a minute for this unexpected visit," he said politely enough.

"I have something for you."

He gave her a side glance, noticing the basket but said nothing.

"We have a bakery now, along with other shoppes."

"That, I know," he said. "Quite a little thing they put together, subdivision and all."

"And a retreat center," she added. "We're already booking events."

He curled his lip, as close to a smile as she imagined he was possibly able to manage. "Something I never would have guessed," he said. "You and those two real estate gentlemen must have a lot of pull with Father Elway and Father Garrett." He paused, looking away for a moment. "It's no wonder a fella has a heart attack. He's all right, though, I understand. Tell him I asked."

"I will," she said, wondering where the question was.

"You realize, of course, that for the Hicksville Police Department, all this means is more crime potential—alarms going off, burglary, break-ins, bounced checks, home invasions, purse-snatching, arson, grease fires, electrical fires, vandalism, fraud, accidents like trip and fall, parking lot fender-benders, traffic snarls …"

"I brought muffins." Gingerly, she rested the basket on the edge of his desk. "You like bread? Here's bread for you to enjoy. See, you don't even have to visit the crime scene."

He kept her in his gaze and raised an eyebrow without cracking a smile. Tough audience, she thought, but he did lean forward to glimpse the basket's contents.

"Why did you bring all this?"

"You like it? We make it." She let go of the basket and backed into the doorway. "Besides, you're too important around here, Officer Polly, to miss out on something so good. I hope you have a lovely day." She turned to leave.

"I know about the bird," he said abruptly.

She slowly turned back around.

"I had a first-hand experience with him."

"Ohhh."

"Oh, is right." Then, he picked up his pen and continued with his reports.

As she headed toward the front door of the station house, she heard him call out, "Tell Father Xavier I'll bring Catherine by."

Outside, Ellen looked up, closed her eyes, and breathed in the summer afternoon. Glorious, she thought. A wonder to behold.

The End

About the Author

Mary Flynn is an award-winning author of fiction and poetry, as well as a celebrated speaker. A highly diverse writer, Mary has medaled in nearly all of her genres. Her powerful debut novel, "Margaret Ferry," won a gold medal in fiction, a silver medal in religion, and a silver medal in Christian writing. Her Disney leadership book is also a silver medal winner, while her novella for middle-grade readers took gold at The Royal Palm Literary Awards. Mary is working on her fourth novel, a cozy murder mystery.

A former full-time staff writer for Hallmark Cards, Mary's observational humor has appeared in the *Sunday New York Times*, *Newsday* and other dailies and magazines. One of her award-winning short stories appears in the esteemed The *Saturday Evening Post's Anthology of Great Fiction*. She was a winner in the *Writer's Digest* poetry competition. She is also a writing coach, conducting writer's studios across Central Florida.

During her nearly fifteen years as an international conference speaker for Disney Institute, the second most recognized training brand in the world, Mary appeared before almost three-quarters-of-a-million people, often sharing a conference platform with names such as Malcolm Gladwell and Tony Robbins. She is also an on-air radio host for Salem Media, and loves entertaining audiences with her fun and informative "Confessions of a Hallmark Greeting Card Writer."

Mary's books are available online and through bookstores, as well as through her website.

Be sure to visit Mary at »
www.MaryFlynnWrites.com

www.ingramcontent.com/pod-product-compliance
Lightning Source LLC
Chambersburg PA
CBHW021223310726
48971CB00006B/1666